America
the
Beautiful

America the Beautiful

Moon Unit Zappa

review

For my mother, Gail, and
trees everywhere

The man pulling radishes pointed the way with a radish.

— Issa

PART ONE

Bliss

ONE

Pre-Sent

'Hooray for Hollywood.'

— Author unknown

'Yes,' I heard myself say when the total stranger asked me to coffee, 'well, er, – um, I'm, uh, I mean, I didn't think; uh . . . well, why not?' is what actually came out, but in my head it sounded a lot like just plain yes.

OK, so no, he's not exactly a *total* stranger; I mean, he has served me hot beverages on a number of occasions, so no, it's not like we've never talked; I mean, no one's denying we swapped pleasantries here and there, in between refills of French roast coffee with just a hint of cinnamon (his touch, in spite of his management's disapproval), so it's probably fine. I liked his defiance and said so. He liked that I brought my own cobalt-blue mug from home and lobbied for free refills. (Thanks to me, the chalkboard sign with the thumbs-up now says, 'Refills free if you save a tree!') And once I watched him give someone change entirely in ones. So big deal, I said yes.

At least that explains why I am sitting here across from the King's Road Café, in my little '89 Silver Audi with the sunroof open, parked at the corner of Beverly and King's Road directly in front of a trendy furniture store and a two-hour meter at 10.01 a.m. on a crisp, windyish day, exactly fifty-nine minutes before

Otto is due to arrive. It also half-way explains why I am being forced to watch a pear-shaped bald man check his reflection in the window while he wrestles his wind-blown comb-over back in place and looks longingly at a black and maple futon. What it does not explain is why I agreed to meet Otto so early in the day, when anyone with any claim to know me will tell you I am in no way a morning person.

I once broke up with a man for continually trying to wake me in the early a.m. to have all-hour intercourse. His name was Angie. He was diurnal. He taught me that word. It means he was the devil and woke with the rising demon sun. One morning, he woke me with a massive pre-dawn erection, I sat up, rested my elbows on Angie's cat-fur-encrusted futon and faced this cross-legged man with the Egyptian-style beaded goatee and said, 'I am the daughter of an artist; I thought you understood that the day begins around eleven *at the earliest*, but really, in a perfect universe, commences no earlier than one, you jackass.' I was trying to be nice. Disciplined Ben understood this, toy-obsessed Ed did too, even collegiate Liam did in his own redneck way, but not Angie. He just looked away and covered his sunrise lap with a pillow. Behind him the sky had begun to take on an annoyingly yellowish hue. I held my hand up to block out its enthusiastic urgings. Angie's back began to tremble. I softened then and placed my wayward hand on his knee. 'You could be a male model or an adorable underweight baby in an incubator, and if you woke me I would still give you a Cuban necktie for disturbing my sleep.' Angie still wouldn't look at me, only absent-mindedly tugged at a hand-painted bead he got in Sedona that accidentally hung sideways in his beard near the eraser-sized mole at the base of his neck. As soon as I heard the garbage trucks I called it quits.

I shift a little in my cracked leather seat and adjust my visor to the morning sun. My God, do I think this coffee encounter with Otto might amount to sex?

I check one of the many clocks in the window of the trendy shop, next to the day-glo hammock; an orange one reads: 10.04. I watch a skinny lady with muscular legs jog past me in her

4

royal-blue satin windbreaker that says 'Jazz' in rhinestones. Of course, none of this explains why I am here an hour *earlier* than I need to be. I tell myself, Relax, Mer, you know you just like to get a feel for a place, to tune in to the frequency of a spot . . . Hell, you like getting a good parking space. Just breathe.

What kind of a name is Otto, anyway? Odd-o is more like it, with all that talk about history and physics and light noticing itself being observed. When I asked him what he liked to do for fun he said he enjoys reading, ping-pong, and creating an internal double of himself energetically, ('yunno, to let off steam'). He does make the most perfect head of foam I've ever seen. 'Low-fat is the key. Non-fat is bullshit. But then, haven't the sages been telling us "the middle path" all along? Moderation, chum.' All this, before handing me his number written in black ink from a disposable fountain pen on the inside of a custom-made matchbook with the first amendment typed inside the flap.

I hold my hand to my stomach. Surely he understands romance is out of the question, since we are meeting during business hours. I think I might be sick. I look at myself in my rear-view to see if I look sick. Instead I find a stray eyebrow hair I can't pluck or pull, so I lick my finger and smooth it back in place. Relax, Mer, I tell myself again. This time I say it like my Scottish yoga teacher, 'ReeeeLOXshh', which makes me always want to say 'bagel and cream cheese' in my best Sean Connery right afterwards.

Over the last year and a half, since the Jasper Husch Incident, I have come to realize that I am a nervous person, especially when I am subjected to my first, official, dare I say it, 'date' in over nine months. A year ago I would not even have noticed this guy, looks, foam skills, and all. Six months ago his kindness didn't even *register*.

I hate that word, date. It makes everything sound tough and chewy. Date. Like all the sweetness and moisture of life has been sucked from your bones and, well, in a way it has, if you are forced to get back out there and . . . *date*. Why couldn't it be called a cloud or a pudding? Something bouncy and hopeful. I'm going on my first pudding in over nine months since the Jasper Husch Incident. That sounds a lot better. Funny. Like a Nancy Drew novel with accompanying illustration of the shadow of a man fleeing down an endless spiral staircase along with a small, incriminating pool of pudding. I smiled. Otto is so nice.

I was wearing a pale blue calf-length rayon dress with little white-painted moons along the hem, an orange shawl and pink platform shoes that fine Wednesday. He was standing behind the counter of my favourite Mom and Pop Koffee Haus like he always did, this time wearing a pair of too-short navy-blue vintage cords, brown suspenders and a Rainbow Brite T-shirt.

'Otto Guthrie,' he said, extending his arm, which I accidentally shook at the wrist.

'Nice to meet you,' I said, awkwardly pumping away, 'I mean officially, for real.' When I released his arm he backed away slightly. I watched him massage the wrist back to life with his spare hand. That's when I noticed how nice his hands were. Are. I mean, really noticed. That's probably the main reason why I didn't just turn and run screaming out of the building. That's when he said, 'Hey, what's your name, anyway?'

I froze then, and fixed my eyes on a ball of tinfoil hanging from a thin red piece of twine Scotchtaped to the ceiling. It was one among many; a local artist's tribute to clouds, displayed in a row above loose tea stored neatly in glass jars. I gripped my cup too tightly, and we both watched coffee tumble over the shiny, lacquered rim. He reached for a yellow-and-white-striped rag and filled it with ice, while I blew my hand and watched the skin redden, highlighting the little white raised scar at the base of my knuckles. The rag was cold and smelled like coffee and lemon-scented furniture polish, and dripped, making dark grey circles on the cement floor.

'America. America Throne.' America Thrown was more like it. I scanned his eyes for any recognition of my famous name and the famous dead father that went with it: B. Throne, painter, writer, Renaissance man, dead of a heart attack at age fifty; but *nada*.

'America Throne,' he repeated, swirling it around in his mouth like a fine wine. 'Hippie parents?' he said, after a small eternity. I decided he was either clueless, had a good poker face or didn't care.

6

'Yeah, I guess,' I said. It was either that or blurt out my entire defining history complete with the death of my infant sister, and those last few minutes with my father, the only other man I loved best in the world besides Jasper, who had broken my heart so completely. But I didn't. Why? Because I've had *therapy*.

Then he said, 'Hey, can I take you out sometime? I know you like coffee.' I said 'Great,' meaning awful, and he said, 'How's about Friday?' and then a blushing silence passed between us and then he said, 'America Throne, huh,' and I said, 'Yup' while swinging my arms and pressing my lips together like I was about to get a bassoon lesson. Which brings me to here; me, parked in my little car, playing the scene over and over again in my mind's eye, while I case the joint like a shitty private eye, exactly fifty-six minutes before the rest of my entire life begins.

Across the street I watch a waiter in black jeans roll down the awning to give the pine tables and chairs and its few customers some shade. In a little while the place will be crowded and assaulted by full sun.

I check my mirror again, this time to see if I'm still cute, then tug on the little Saint Christopher that hangs on the rear-view from a pale blue ribbon. My mother gave it to me a long time ago. She had been travelling through Europe with my father on a second honeymoon – well actually a first, considering they had been married for close to sixteen years without a first honeymoon. She went into one of those little churches in France or Spain or Italy, someplace in the middle of nowhere, and lit some candles. Outside they sold trinkets and mementoes in little kiosks. She wrote me a postcard and told me about it. I still have the card, The Blessed Virgin with a flaming sacred heart. Apparently it had been blessed by the Pope to protect you from the dangers of travel. I was about to get my driver's licence. My parents wanted to make sure I was safe, even though they were raised Catholic and forbade me to go to church. She got my dad to sign it too. 'Bugs and Fishes', it said, meaning hugs and kisses, 'Mom and Dad'. I guess when it came right down to it, religion aside, none of us could resist the beautiful little icons and their tender sentiments.

10.05. In less than sixty minutes, if he's on time, Otto'll arrive and take his seat at the King's Road Café. After a while we will get into a deep conversation, and swap family horror stories. The old me would have told it all with a humorous, detached irony, in between mouthfuls of a stale, poorly made scone. I would have broken down and told him about the birth of my stillborn baby sister Shiva Plum when I was nearly three and leapt right into how my mother would not even begin to smile again until the birth of my brother Spoonie, 'the miracle baby', two years later. I would have launched into my jealousy of the wunderkind with the golden curls and longer eyelashes than my own; the one who restored laughter to our house but who stole all the attention. I might have told him about dropping out of school early because we moved so much, and about the financial rollercoaster we endured as a family but how we saved money by staying behind while my father travelled first class to exotic places. I would have told him how my father's worldwide fame and respect seemed incongruous with my anger about his notorious but covert affairs, and about my mother's bouts of depression as a result. This would naturally lead me to expound on how difficult it is to be hippie royalty *and* find your own identity — which would have lead me to confess to being a late bloomer. Then, without warning, I would have stopped stirring the sugar in the bottom of my too-bitter espresso and described seeing my father dead of a brain aneurysm in the arms of a woman who was not my mother. Otto might have looked down thoughtfully and said, 'I wish I could take your pain away', or something slightly more vague and altogether fatherly, like, 'There, there, everything's going to be all right', or, like Jasper, he might have freaked out and left without any explanation, leaving me to pay for his half-eaten sandwich.

I dig my pinkie finger into a perfect little doggie hole where Tulie has scratched and dug her little doggie nails into the passenger seat. My mother always says, 'One day you will like all the damage that little dog has done because when she is gone, they will be sweet reminders of creature comfort.'

10.07. I reach into the bottom of my purse in search of a stray

Chicklet. Anything to *do* or *chew* to settle my stomach and its building nausea. What if Otto is my future husband and I don't even know it! Or worse, what if he *isn't* my husband? What if he's just a ship passing in the night, a stranger, a fling or something awful in between? Would I even be able to tell? Is everything just a choice? A choice to be made based on the collected data from several, awful, cosmic science experiments gone bad? What if I have to go on a hundred, no, three hundred more puddings before ending up *alone*? They say if you haven't found someone by the time you graduate high school you will be in a kind of loveless inferno until you are in your forties and *have* to settle. No soulmate for you, America Throne. Bad America, bad.

What if my husband-to-be is a bum? I mean, he makes coffee for a living and talks philosophy and politics with customers while getting his master's degree . . . Or so he says. Master's degree in what? He could be crazy! He could be getting a master's degree in Crazy.

I close my eyes, count to five on the inhale, count to five on the exhale. 'I am a river and those are just mind thoughts calmly rushing by.' Stop it, Mer, just stop. But I don't.

What if he drives a jalopy? What if he takes the *bus*? Who cares about cars and stuff like that? That kind of thing only matters if you're going to have kids. And, really, it doesn't apply at all given that our generation has to bear the weight of society's ills; I mean it is *way* harder getting started up, and staying that way, than it ever was.

Jesus, what if he's a murderer! What if I am on stake-out and he's a murderer! I shouldn't be here to see this. Drive away quick, Mer! I have never wished for hand cream more in my life.

I count to five again, relax relax relax, it's just your fear talking. I pound my breastbone lightly, calm calm calm, only love lives here. Then I reach for my cellphone. Maybe there's still time to catch him.

Where would he be driving from? Jesus, I don't even have his number! What kind of a responsible person leaves the house without the ability to cancel everything at a moment's notice? Drive away, Mer!

Suddenly a young couple in black rushes towards me, jaywalking against speeding traffic, spilling coffee-to-go. They pile into a big blue convertible parked in front of me. I watch as they are both wearing sunglasses as big as globes. I hope Otto doesn't wear sunglasses. I hate people who wear sunglasses; they embarrass me almost as much as small foreign cars. Jesus, what if he drives a *Porsche!*

I feel my palms go all sweaty. I reach for the key in the ignition. That's when I see him walk in. Walk in! This is *so* my life. What kind of loser shows up for a date an hour early?

I scrunch down a little lower in my seat, hoping he hasn't seen me. He's wearing jeans and boots and a bandanna around his head. No sunglasses. He looks handsome. A little too handsome. I watch him signal to someone inside, and then choose a table outside in the sun. I watch him sit down, hit his knee on the underside of the table, stand up, pull his chair back, hit the customer's chair behind him, apologize, sit back down, slide forward and bump the underside of the table with his legs again.

I think, drive away Mer, but I don't, because he has a rose in his hand. A big, fat, orangey-pink straight-from-somebody's-real-garden type of rose.

TWO

Bugs and Fishes

'You forgot to carry the zero.'
— Built to Spill

In the dream someone hands me a bouquet of roses. I am Miss America, and I am being crowned. I am in an opera house with red velvet curtains. I am on a stage in a dress made of clown noses. One of the judges, dressed like a courtroom judge in a long black robe, hands me the flowers. People in the audience are laughing and applauding. They are all dressed like nurses, including Jasper. My brother Spoonie and my mother are there, too. As I turn to wave to them, I see Jasper sneaking out through a side entrance. For some reason I know he has given me a fatal disease and he wants us to die from it. Separately. My heartbeat quickens and I run towards the exit after him. Just then the bundle in my arms turns into a squirming baby. I look down and find it's a girl. I know it is my dead sister come back to life. I am so happy to see her that I lean in to kiss her, but she starts to turn blue. I watch her turn blue and die in my arms with her eyes wide open. I look around for help, but there is no one there. That's when I realize night has fallen and I am in a forest dense with spiny trees and fog, and that I am utterly lost. I start to cry and when my tears fall they turn to rose petals. Now I am in an industrial kitchen decorating the baby's coffin with icing instead of paint. I write 'Bugs and fishes' in pink along the edge where the hinges are. Just then the baby's eyes blink open and her mouth forms a perfect 'O' as if she will speak. 'Don't be afraid,' she coos in a croney old voice.

I woke up on my back, sweaty and frightened, hands clenched at my chest gripping a handful of nightgown. I heard an owl in the giant pine tree outside my window. I fixed my eyes on the white-painted beams along the ceiling overhead and listened to the sound of my pounding heart. I caught my breath: oh yeah, our new place.

It was our third night together there. In the morning Jasper would fly back up to San Francisco, finish one last illustration job for yet another Internet billionaire, pack up his painting studio, cats, clothes and furniture, along with everything else he owned, and hand the keys to his Specific Whites apartment over to his deadbeat friend Benny in exchange for help loading up the rented moving truck. Then, Jasper would drive back down to make Los Angeles, and me, home once and for all.

I turned my head to make sure Jasper was still by my side. Lying next to me, beatific in deep REM was the best boyfriend in the world. His long eyelashes looked like feather dusters set against those milky-white eyelids. One of his perfect hands cradled his perfect hairless cheek while the other perfect hand lay pressed between his perfect thighs. Jasper always amazed me with his ability to sleep on the very edge of any bed without falling off.

I rolled on to my side and inched my way towards him. I curled my legs under my nightgown, stretching the white cotton so that it pulled tight at my lower back and hips. It felt a bit like a hug. I listened to Jasper's breathing, watched his lungs fill his upper back, watched his freckly shoulders rise and fall in the moonlight. I heard the owl screech again. I sucked on a strand of long, loose hair that I had twisted around my index finger, and scooted a little closer to Jasper.

Why couldn't I have a good dream, like those recurring ones where I'm a long-distance runner? I love those dreams because they mean endurance. They are better than flying dreams to me. Sometimes I cross a finish line. Sometimes Jasper is there to greet me. Sometimes my father is there in a pair of skin-tight snakeskin pants, when he was at his happiest. Something about an even, measured pace and knowing I have the stamina in body, mind and spirit to continue going and going for ever and ever.

I made my body into a crescent to match Jasper's shape, curled my flesh and bones into his, two cosy spoons. 'Baby, I had a bad dream,' I said, nuzzling my way into Jasper's ear.

'Err,' he groaned. 'Try to fall back to sleep.'

'Baby, I can't,' I whispered into his night-smelling shoulders. I had to exhale the other way because Jasper hated it when I would breathe on his naked back. Not me. He could breathe his stink breath directly into my nose and it would still smell like honey kisses . . . 'Baby? Are you still sleeping?'

'Go get a drink of water,' he groaned, 'that always works in the movies.' Jasper amazed me, he could be dead asleep and he would still manage to say something clever.

I got up and pulled my favourite brown and grey stripy wool sweater from its bedpost resting-place and wrestled it over my head. My long brown hair hung in loose braids against the warmth of the wool sweater, silky-smooth against scritchy-scratchy. I aimed for the kitchen, bare feet against hardwood floors through an obstacle course of half-unpacked boxes. I kept my fingers extended, trying to get a feel for the new space in the dark. I could hear Tulie making licking noises in her crate. That made me feel safe. Maybe she thought it was time to get up because she had heard me clomping around.

In the kitchen, leaning against the door frame, I fumbled around the wall for the light switch. It still smelled like paint, pale pink walls with red trim.

I turned on the Jesus nightlight I had found at a junk store on Vermont, and examined the necessities I had managed to liberate in the dark from a box I had labelled 'Essential Living': my kettle, a strainer, an I Heart SF mug that Jasper bought me as a gag one afternoon while we played tourists down at the wharf, and a lone camomile tea bag. My plan was to wait for the water to boil and then remove it from the heat before the whistle blew.

I love tea; I love the ritual of making tea. The alchemy of water and tea leaves, heat and a love-worn teapot passed on from one generation to another, and so on. As I waited for the water to boil I imagined big ships since the beginning of time carrying important cargo, spices and teas from exotic places just so I could drink it a million miles away. I sat on an ice-blue rag rug from Ikea, hugged my knees to my chin and listened to the gas pilot as it glowed and hissed.

Our third night together in our new place, I thought proudly. Even in the dark, I could see that the house had already begun to come together.

We, well I, had managed to find the place for a mere twenty-five hundred dollars through a friend of my mother's. A steal compared to my last place, which was a 'guest cottage', an eighth of the size for almost two thousand dollars a month.

The house itself was an old, rustic wooden one-bedroom nestled in the canyon. It used to be one of several getaway cabins for movie stars back in the twenties and thirties. Even though we were only fifteen minutes from Hollywood, the broker with the chipped, fill-in nails told me that in the olden days it took forty-five minutes to get there via trolley, past orange groves and ranch houses. The roads weren't even paved. This was considered going to the mountains! Nothing but miles of dirt back then. Now the place our own canyon store and dry-cleaner's! In less than an hour I had put down the deposit, plus first and last, signed the lease, got the keys, organized a moving truck and called Jasper.

I didn't mind paying for it all up front myself because in the first place I was the one who found it and I wanted to secure it, and in the second place I had the money saved up anyway so I figured he could always pay next month's, and square the rest with me when he collected on an up-coming art show. After that it would be fifty-fifty. I mean we were in this for keeps so, no big. So, Jasper flew down for a quickie visit, gave the final thumbs up and helped me paint a thing or three. I glanced at the iris-covered flame beneath the kettle and stuck the end of the braid in my mouth.

It would be weird not to have Jasper's magical spot in San

Francisco as a refuge any more. We weren't planning on making the move to live together this fast, having only been together a year and half, but this place was too good to pass up. I admit I pushed Jasper a tad. Even though it was only a one-bedroom, I assured him there was plenty of charm here to make up for the space we would be missing, and as soon as he saw it he agreed. Plus he would be closer to the better galleries and the people with *real* money to buy his art. Besides, we had a genuine wood-burning fireplace place now, and we were planning to convert the garage into Jasper's painting studio, since having a 'public transport only' boyfriend meant we only needed one parking spot.

I thought, my God, soon we will probably be married! Isn't that what comes after living together? I wouldn't mind being married to a painter, like my mother; at least I knew the ropes: the creative highs and lows, the pouting, the thieving gallery owners, the pretentious buyers, the awe over Jasper's art. Next comes children and buying a house together! Or maybe it's the other way around, buying a house, *then* children. I imagined our children, a boy and a girl each with his long limbs and caffeine-free groundedness and maybe my hair and aesthetic.

Tulie let out a little yawn. I looked over at the brightly coloured orange and magenta Mexican blanket that covered Tulie's crate in its spot, next to the ice-blue kitchen table, near the breakfast nook Jasper and I painted periwinkle. The kettle began to hiss so I reached my hand up to turn off the gas, catching it before it cried out in agony.

I watched the steam rise up to meet my new ceiling as I poured. The solo tea bag bobbed up and down until it finally surrendered, releasing its essence. Then I sat back down again, this time crosslegged, and pulled the lacy edge of my nightgown over my knees and thought about how good Jasper's Star Wars action figures were going to look lining the cabinets of our new kitchen.

I held the cup in my hands to warm them, felt the steam drift up and wash over my nose and eyelids and forehead; leaving a fine dew in the baby-fine hairs that framed my face. I ran the flat of my hand over my cheeks and neck. I liked how my features, though individually kind of funny, formed a pleasing incongruity when arranged all together. Jasper claimed that I most resemble Princess Leia. Sometimes he said Bjork or Alanis. That's because I usually like to keep my hair coiled up about my ears like fuzzy wintery muffs, or hissing cobras lying in wait, depending on my mood and the company. The smell of night-blooming jasmine wafted its way in a little screen window. I traced a lone chickenpox scar with my finger and thought, it will be light out soon.

I sipped the scented yellow water, leaned my back against my newly painted built-in kitchen cabinets and just listened.

I looked up at my God wall, a portable altar on framed corkboard in the breakfast nook. In the dark I could just make out the postcards and magazine tear-outs I had collected over the years. Images of lovers, pioneers, poets, post-war survivors on street corners, at the beach, poised on a crescent moon, or in elaborate costume. A Valentine I had painted and stickered with little gold stars myself when I was seven. Chrissie Hynde, her face daring you to do or not to do something, arms crossed, bare-chested, wearing a g-string that seductively crept out from a pair of black leather trousers. Emma Thompson in a suit of armour, fist clenched against her protective metal breastplate. The Dalai Lama's hands holding prayer beads. Images of birds and crosses and tree-lined roads and sacred hearts and girls with folded palms.

One postcard was by far my favourite, and depicts an old classroom, circa 1880, the names of children written in thoughtful cursive on an old school blackboard, names like Sam and Harry and Jane and Mary Swope. Maybe I liked it because people always make such a big deal about me being named America. I took a sip of my tea. It was starting to get cold.

I heard the birds then, trying to coax the sun up. I decided then and there that I liked that house and our new life together there. I didn't even care that I looked like an ad for coffee sitting there by myself grinning dopily, save the slats of sunlight on my face. On and on they chattered, our new birds. Our new sounds. Our new home, I thought happily.

★ ★ ★

16

I climbed back into bed. Once safely under the covers, I wriggled out of my sweater, and let it fall to the floor. Jasper exhaled deeply. I curled in close to him, pressed my hands together in prayer. I thanked God I was me, America Throne, the broke, stressed-out, struggling-to-get-her-career-together owner of Tallulah, the all-black, all-gas French bulldog, best friend to one Sadie McGuire, daughter of Camilla and the famous dead-before-his-time genius painter Boris Throne, sister to the deceased Shiva Plum and the very much alive, bursting with hormones and musical talent Spoon 'Spoonie' Throne, sorrows and all; blessings to us and the lives we touched. And of course, oh Lord, an extra-special thank-you for Jasper Husch and his constellation-covered shoulders. Sweet, poetic, lanky Jasper Husch with his art and his downright global awareness. Jasper was my proof that life was good and worth living. What is it about being so truly loved that makes you feel invincible to the outside world?

'Baby?' I whispered, poking my head out from under the covers to check if he was sleeping.

'Hmn?'

'Goodnight.' I kissed his back.

'Go back to sleep, Guava,' he said before rolling over and away from me on to his perfect, hairless belly. I loved when he called me by my pet name. He pushed some of the covers back and let a leg dangle out, and let out another nostrilly sigh. I rolled on to my back and closed my eyes. Then I heard what sounded like a cat being eaten alive by a notorious-in-this-area-for-such-behaviour owl or coyote. I opened my eyes and turned on my side, inching my way closer to Jasper.

'Jas?'

'What?'

'I can't sleep.'

'Think of something good,' he said before turning on his side and disappearing into his little corner of the universe. Yes, think about something good. I scooted towards him a little more, faced his back and smoothed my nightgown over my knees. You are something good, Jasper Husch, I'll think about you for a while.

On our first date, he took me to see the giant sequoias and

instead of kissing me, we lay on our backs and pressed the crowns of our heads together under a canopy of trees that went straight up into toothpick points in the sky. I felt so happy to be so small, so insignificant. We were insignificant together.

I stared at his starry shoulders now, a smallish Milky Way of freckles. I found Cassiopeia, the Big Dipper, the North Star. 'You are true north,' I whispered as my fingers lightly tickled their way up the nape of his neck to his latest Art Boy hairdo. I gently tugged on one of his white, matted dreads, feeling the brittle clump between my thumb and index finger.

Suddenly I am five and my father is unsuccessfully attempting to untangle 'rats'-nests' which have taken over the back of my fine, honey-spun hair because my mother is still too grief-stricken to get out of bed. My daddy is in charge of me. I have just gotten out of the bath. He wraps a fluffy purple bath towel around me. He plops me to face the mirror in the pink-tiled bathroom. Armed with a black plastic comb, he sprays some baby-smelling oil into the hair pile he will inevitably cut to expedite things instead of unfastening every strand, one at a time.

I felt Jasper twitch beside me, exhale long and deep. His mouth was open. I wanted to say I love you and hear him say it back, but he was already long gone. Inwardly I said it anyway. Then I turned over, curled into a ball and, pressed my spine against Jasper's. I thought about that little dead baby from my dream. I thought about its little blue face and what it said about not being afraid.

'Afraid of what?' I wondered before falling into a dreamless sleep.

THREE

Collect Call from Zeus

'Freeze, don't move. You've been chosen as an extra in the
movie adaptation of the screenplay to your life.'

— Pavement

At 7.10 in the morning I woke to probing fingers attempting to
harden my nipples. And, even though Jasper and I were unbelievably
in love, it made me mad for, like, eight reasons. For one thing, I
didn't like the way he poked at them. It made me feel like a pet-store
kitten with an eye infection being poked at by someone who had no
intention of buying me. I didn't appreciate being woken from a
sound slumber just to be poked at like that. For another thing, he
totally could have let me sleep for at least forty-five more minutes
before driving him to the airport in rush-hour traffic because, upon
waking in the full light of day, I realized I don't want to be the
national spokesperson for crotch cream. Caress me, massage me, lick
me but for God's sake don't poke.

I mean, it's not like he didn't know I hadn't slept all that well the
night before. Didn't he understand we would be officially living
together in less than a week, and could have all the sex we wanted
when it was convenient for me? Jasper *knew* I didn't like morning
sex. I was certain I had told Jasper about Angie, during the same
conversation that he had confessed to dumping one girl for her
squirting orgasms.

19

And, even though getting up sooner meant we could start our new life together sooner, who wakes someone with a trust fund at seven a.m.? Especially to have sex. Especially when I wore a nightgown and big granny-style undies to bed. Especially when I was seven to twelve pounds overweight about the fact that I was almost thirty and still sponged off my family and was forced to audition for a yeast infection ointment radio spot to earn my keep.

I knew that at twenty-nine I was, by Los Angeles' terms, a failure, no doubt the result of the pressure associated with being the daughter of a critically acclaimed and much celebrated, certifiable 'genius'. Of course my mother, who believed herself to be a sainted patron of the arts, dubbed me 'a late bloomer', swore up and down it didn't bother her to wait for me to make my fortune. It made me feel mad and glad at the same time to be a poverty level trust funder, collecting two thousand dollars a month while I figured it all out, yet unable to do little more than pay my rent and bills but barely. I kept meaning to learn how to manage money and cut back, but then there was the house, first, last and deposit, not to mention the moving in together. The furniture, paint supplies and of course groceries for the moving in together ... it adds up, living together.

Didn't my almost live-in boyfriend understand I needed every last ounce of rest on the astral to figure out what I should be *doing* with myself? That the sleep he was poking into probably contained vital information which would inform the rest of my natural earthly life as to my actual PURPOSE? My God, did he think I WANTED to be the spokesperson for itchy tweeters? On top of everything, I had to pee like a racehorse!

So, even though I was in no mood whatsoever, I let him continue his advances. You do that when you're in love ... and my back-up plan was that the alarm clock would be going off any minute, putting a definite finish to the a.m. frolicking since Jasper couldn't miss his flight if he was to make his fancy magazine deadline. (This was before Jasper had a fancy computer to e-mail all his illustration jobs, when he was still on a first-name basis with the whole of Federal Express such that once I saw them wait ten whole minutes while Jasper fastidiously finished taping up an urgent parcel containing a portrait of a dental surgeon for a magazine dedicated solely to diseases of the gums.)

While he poked at my nipples like a handyman testing a new doorbell, I checked my glands both fearing and hoping for a sore throat. Normal. Too bad. I feared my job interview that morning for two reasons. One because it was a national ad for a crotch cream and two because I wouldn't be getting another cheque from my trust for another three weeks. With only two hundred dollars to my name I kind of *needed* the voice-over job. Jasper always said it was better to do something and make some money than to do nothing and make none. But what did he know about the struggle for career identity? He'd known he wanted to be a painter since before he was Da Vinci in another lifetime. And, just like my father, he didn't care if he made five dollars or five hundred dollars so long as he was doing what he loved. I guessed I should be grateful subsisting on a monthly, albeit meagre, 'allowance'.

Jasper rolled over on top of me, spreading my legs open with his legs. I reached my hand into the drawer of our little, yellow bedside table and felt around for my diaphragm and a disposable, single-serving of sperm killer. Jasper removed the wrapper of the applicator tube and squirted some gel into the little rubber cap I held in my hand, then I pinched it in half and inserted it. It was so cold it made my stomach muscles tighten. Then he tossed the applicator aside, pulled my arms above my head, lifted up my nightgown, parted my underwear to one side, and missing, pressed his giant, early-morning erection into my belly which was bad because by now I *really* had to pee.

On the second pass my face reddened, not from passion but from extreme concentration. I could tell he was in down-and-dirty passion mode by the way he moved. Up and down, down and up. He moved his hips in slow, grinding circles with speedy jerks pressing into me on the upstrokes. Ow. Ow.

While he kissed my neck, I turned my head to check the clock. It was only 7.17. The alarm wouldn't go off until 8.00! I panicked. Jasper bit my ear. If my chequebook, the Burbank airport and my bladder weren't breathing down my neck, I might be into all this.

Think Mer, think. Aha! To put an end to my escalating urinary situation I playfully pushed him off me and seductively licked my way past his belly button to his best feature. In this ass-up position I felt some relief. Sucking on him and tasting myself I discovered I was somewhat pasty. I found this a bit ironic considering my job potential. I looked at the clock. Seven-nineteen.

Suddenly, he pulled me up by my armpits and positioned me on top of him. My eyes began to water. I checked the clock: 7.21. At 7.23 accelerated jerky thrusts kicked in. At 7.24 the two of us twisted and contorted our bodies in various positions, him in passion, me entirely in search of comfort. I checked the clock: 7.25. Damn! If I were underwater I'd be dead by now. Moaning and low groans and grunts kicked in at 7.27.

Then, at 7.29, he pulled my legs up and over my head rather suddenly, lurched forward and came, screaming, 'I don't want to have a baby!' That's when I accidentally kicked him.

'Ow! Christ, Mer!' he said, rubbing his jaw.

'I'm sorry,' I said, wriggling out from under him. 'Let me get you a cool towel.' I ran to the bathroom, turned on the cold water to drown out the sound, and relieved myself. After almost a year and a half I was still too shy to discuss bodily functions with Jasper, let alone let Jasper hearing me pee. I thought, perhaps being inundated with erotic art had managed to raise a prude.

'Are you bringing the towel or what?' I pretended not to hear. 'You aren't fooling me in there, you know.' Over my porcelain din I could hear Jasper clomping around. I heard the zipping of a suitcase. I pulled up my undies and turned off the water.

In the bedroom I caught Jasper piling clothes into a small, brown, tattered suitcase. He had already climbed back into his faded navy-blue boxers that had lain crumpled in the corner only a few minutes earlier. I snuck up and hugged him from behind. 'Why are you packing?' I said, passing my hand seductively over his deflated crotch.

'Because I'm gonna need some of this stuff this week,' he said, pulling away. He made his way over to the chair in the corner where his grey T-shirt and brown cords lay and slipped them on.

'Just leave all that stuff here.'

'I'm gonna need a suitcase, Mer.'

'Yeah, but why are you taking your clothes?'

'Because I'm gonna be up there for at least a week. Besides, you know these are my favourite things.'

'At least a week? You said a few days at the most.'

'Yeah, well, I got an extension on that job.'

'You didn't tell me that.'

'I'm telling you now.'

'Why can't you just come down earlier and do it all here?'

'Because it's easier just to use everything while it's still set up. Plus the cats have a vet's appointment they can't miss on Tuesday.'

'Oh,' I said trying not to sound disappointed.

I watched Jasper hop on one leg now while he pulled up a green and purple argyle sock. Then he put on his grey runners, and, standing, stuffed his hands in his pockets to make sure they lay flat against his thighs. Fine, I thought, as he walked past me to zip up his suitcase, I don't need this, not today. Today I needed all of my positive energy to save the orphanage called my bank account and our new life.

I took a speedy shower and slathered vanilla-and-sandalwood-scented lotion on my legs. Towel-less I dripped my way back into the bedroom, where I retrieved a few items from an open box. I slipped into a loose, flowing magenta and pale green, floor-length, patterned skirt embroidered with tiny mirrors, a black spaghetti-strap baby tee, an olive cardigan and my black suede Boston-style Birkenstocks. I quickly checked my reflection in the mirror. Indian hippie chic. While I brushed my teeth I let Tallulah potty potty potty on our steep, ivy-covered hillside.

'Good girl, good Tulie,' I said, validating her good behaviour in a new setting.

'Off off *off!*' I called out as I watched her chase a squirrel between three fruit-bearing avocado trees. Just then I heard our Ganesha alarm clock belt out its droning *Om Namah Shivaya*.

'Jasper?' I called, but he didn't respond, so I went in the

bedroom, whacked the white plastic elephant on the head, grabbed my hand-woven purse, walked outside, and locked the front door. Jasper was waiting for me in the car.

The drive to the airport was a stressful race against the clock in commuter traffic heading north; leaving with more than enough time didn't look like it would even make a dent. My car eked along behind a car so in need of a smog check I couldn't tell you its make or model. Somehow I managed to get over into the turning lane and make a right on Riverside. I picked up some time speeding along the four-lane surface road.

I looked at Jasper, reached my hand over to give his spindly fingers a squeeze. Jasper hadn't said much since we left the house, just stared out the window and watched scenery whizz by. Past foliage, trees and shrubbery in a hundred varieties, from olives to oranges, from Kelly green to greenish-grey. Past double-decker mini-malls, shops boasting pizza and felafel and frozen yoghurt, yoga and hot tubs. Past a *piñata* shop with a paper R2D2 and C3PO. I thought about my ex-boyfriend Ed, and how ironic it was that here Jasper was, going home to fetch his Star Wars action figures, and how adorable I thought Jasper was for that, and how good they were going to look lining the kitchen cabinet tops, whereas with Ed I had found it pathetic. Maybe it's because Jasper's were still sealed in their plastic packages and were treated like saleable collectors' items rather than actual toys, whereas Ed had an in-body need still to do things like race miniature cars and make prank phone calls. It never could have worked with Ed. Mainly because his name was Ed. It just didn't sound right with America. Ed and America. Ed and America Schwartz. Plus sex with Ed always brought out his Catholic guilt, even though he was a Jew. I despised his wadded-up masturbation tissues and speedy trips to the shower after tender lovemaking instead of good solid cuddling post, like Jasper provided. Jasper liked toys but he was a man.

'I'm gonna miss my flight.'

'You'll be fine.' I stepped on the accelerator, sped to a light turning from yellow to red. I unconsciously popped in an old mixed tape Jasper made for me when we first met. He looked at me, then looked away.

'Can you believe it?' I said.

'What?'

'Us living together. I am so excited!' I hopped in my seat a little to prove it. Jasper made a sour face that made me wonder if I bounced too much. 'In just a few days it will officially be you and me against the world!' This time no hopping.

Jasper looked at his feet, uncrossed them, then crossed them the opposite way. 'Yeah,' he said, rolling down his window. His attention seemed to be on the little beige tract houses with the brown lawns all in a row. They looked like a slightly dressed-up shanty town.

Traffic moved slowly even once we arrived at the tiny valley airport. I didn't have time to wait at the gate with him like I usually did, since I had to get from Burbank to Culver City fifteen minutes ago. I caught myself hoping the session would run over, then felt disgusted with myself all over again.

As I pulled up to the small white zone, I kissed Jasper more on his ear than his cheek as he turned towards the seat lever to pull the chair forward to get his suitcase out of the back.

'Oops,' I said.

'Sorry,' he said, rubbing the eye closest to the wet ear. Then I watched him wrestle the suitcase past the automatic seat belt. Even in a hurry, he moved so slowly it could make a person go strawberry-flavoured batty. He pulled his ticket out of his purple hemp shoulder bag.

'Baby, I gotta go,' I forcibly cooed. He shot me a sideways look and continued to gather his belongings at his own meticulous pace.

'Sorry about this morning,' I said, watching an airport police-man signal for me to get moving. 'I'm just really stressed right now.'

'I know,' he said, and we stared hard at each other for the briefest of seconds.

'I love you, Guava,' I said, gearing up to merge left.

'Me too,' he said, closing the door. I pulled out and looked back. He looked like a dishevelled punk-rock college professor standing there in the white zone. I waved like a maniac, staring back at him in my rear-view, but he had already turned and begun to walk inside. Just then Eddie Vedder got cut off in the middle of singing, 'Don't call me daughter . . .', letting me know side two of Jasper's tape had completed itself, so I ejected it, and turned on the radio in time to hear some lady morning DJ say that a massive forest fire in Bali had wiped out a batch of patchouli trees. Good riddance, I thought. I hated the smell of patchouli.

Careening over Beverly Glen Canyon at daredevil speeds, taking it all the way to Washington Boulevard, I still managed to get to my appointment fifty minutes late, but the gods took pity on me for being so taxed that they gave me a parking space right out front. My stomach growled.

I flew up the stairs two at a time to suite 207 because the elevator wasn't working, and apologized to an angry, black-haired smoker, who I nicknamed Captain Issues because she berated me for being late. 'It's a national, you know.'

She bade me follow her down a dingy corridor with beige carpeting and ushered me into an all-beige room with a ratty-looking couch, a mic stand and a music stand with the pitiful copy highlighted in orange.

'Are you ready?' I had not even had time to put my purse down and she already had her headphones over her ears and her finger on the record button.

'Uh, yeah, I guess so.' I dropped my bag on the floor.

'Slate your name.'

I leaned into the mic. 'America Throne.'

She threw her headphones back, 'Please don't lean in,' and returned them to her ears. Her hair looked even greasier in all that fluorescent light. 'Slate your name again and begin.'

I cleared my throat. 'America Throne.'

'Take one.' She nodded.

I began, 'Did you ever feel so uncomfortable you could cry? Down there, I mean? Now try new doctor-recommended Itch Begone and say goodbye to that embarrassing odour and discomfort!'

'OK, let's try that again, this time stress "down there" a little more and really nail the beat between "new" and "doctor-recommended". Try to sound sexy and have fun. Take two.'

When I did it the second time all she said was, 'We'll let you know.'

Outside I was assaulted by chirping birds and daylight galore. It was so bright I had to squint. My stomach growled again. I was starving. Now what? I held my hand up to shield my eyes and looked around. The Greazy Spoon looked somewhat inviting with its neon 'breakfast served all day' sign.

I sat down at a table with a blue and white chequerboard tablecloth and fake plastic flowers. The place smelled like burned bacon and burned coffee. An erasable sandwich board described their daily special: potato deluxe – health-baked with all the fixins', which I ordered from a woman named Shawanda with four-inch-long brick-red nails with a diamond stud on one index finger and a tiny portraiture of Jesus' face in the centre of the other.

What arrived a few minutes later was a small, microwaved potato, split down the centre and drenched with margarine. On the side, parboiled, frozen, stir-fry vegetables and a side of healthy plain non-fat yoghurt instead of sour cream, and some freeze-dried chives.

I thought about my father. When he left Russia as a boy of twenty, before he changed our name from Tronov to Throne, sneaking through to Italy via Yugoslavia, he had never seen so much food. When he got to the Land of Sauces he was amazed when he encountered four different kinds of sour cream! When he finally got to America, he saw twenty different kinds and thought, poor Italy! He came over here and never looked back. It's one of the few stories I know about his traumatic childhood. I never met my grandparents on his side. He said they died a long time ago but, when anybody asked, my mother always made a face at him that made me think he might have been lying. I wanted to send the potato back, but I happened to see a homeless man outside digging through a wastebasket to retrieve what appeared to be bagel remnants.

I signalled to Shawanda for my check and knocked on the window, hoping to catch the bum's attention. In five minutes you'll have a jackpot! But Shawanda blew our big chance at getting into heaven because she was too busy learning how to use their new, but unnecessary for the business they ran, computer system, and Sir Hefty Bags moved on. She was still busy adding the tax when I saw a well-dressed, very determined David Schwimmer-type enter the restaurant to ask if they needed any servers. 'No,' was her reply, but maybe he could leave a résumé, which the guy promised to do, even though we all knew he wouldn't. He caught me watching him so I smiled, but he just looked down and kept walking. He looked sad. Fuck him, I needed a job too.

As I drove home I thought about that guy from the restaurant and how he left, probably thinking he was rejected, and would never know he was the one who was spared while I sat there and took the real beating by eating there of my own free will. Then I thought about Jasper. In a week he'd head down and make his very last drive down the five, unless of course we were visiting friends or what have you. I felt invigorated. Going home to unpack boxes had suddenly begun to sound like a vacation.

'Any messages?' I said to Tallulah as I made my way to the answering machine on the floor with no blinking red light, that I could see quite clearly from the front door. I leaned in closer, wiped a bit of dust off the speaker part. 'Right-e-o.'

I slipped off my shoes and made my way to the bedroom to make the bed. Tulie followed me and licked my foot. I flopped down into the unmade heap. Tulie whimpered. 'Up!' I said, giving her permission to cuddle with me. The smell of Jasper on my sheets had made me generous. I held them to my nose.

I remembered the first time I had visited Jasper, the first time we made love. It was in his bed. I remember how shocked I was to meet someone who did not wash his sheets for weeks at a time.

Shocked that I agreed to sex with such a one. Not only agreed to, but actually craved. I remembered how the faded purple-flannel sheets felt from weeks of neglect, how my mind resisted but then softened to falling deeper into him, weeks of him, showered and un, dreaming, sweating, crying, breathing, masturbating, lying still. I remembered feeling creepy at first, then like an animal, like my most human natural self, and this made me fall utterly in love with him. Because he had stretched a part of me beyond my previous capacity and perception of myself. He had surprised me, and no one does that. Then I thought about how good his orange, leather chair would look in the living room and whether or not we should buy a porcelain or metal toothbrush holder and if it should be installed on the wall or if it was better to use a glass and rest it on the edge of the standing sink, or maybe we could mount one of Jasper's old paintbrush tins instead or maybe it would make a better vase, and if it was better that his drafting table face toward or away from the neighbour. Time to finish unpacking, I thought, but first a cup of tea.

I stood up, stretched, spotted the plastic wrapper from our stilted escapade, picked it up and tossed it in the waste basket. 'Tea, Miss Tulie?' I said as I headed for the kitchen. Tulie trailed behind me, waddled to her little bed to watch the show. That's when I heard the fax machine go off. My first fax in my new house!

As I moved toward the library slash breakfast nook slash my office and the dusty machine I inherited from my mother before the estate went all computers, I thought, maybe it's an appointment sheet for another voice over audition, or perhaps I booked the crotch-cream job and my agent is sending over directions to the recording studio, or maybe it's a flyer for some jobfair or workshop to help me figure out what I want to do with the rest of my life. Or a love letter from Jasper!

I smiled as I watched the ancient machine chug out its insta-message, and froze.

If this were a movie, the camera would zoom through the darkness of a night sky, past the Hollywood sign set against the backdrop of purple mountains majesty, past twinkling city lights below, past telephone wires and treetops, jacaranda, cypress, oak, past eucalyptus, cactus, magnolia, maple, elm, palm, and into the open window of a quaint, one-bedroom house nestled in the hills.

There'd be a slow pan around the living room revealing a brown-leather couch strewn with pillows in brightly patterned fabrics and a comfortably cluttered kitchen table in the corner that could easily double for a desk. Past a single gardenia in a little blue shot glass from Italy, past a handmade pear-scented candle, past an old tea tin full of pens and coloured pencils and a sleeping dog with shiny, ebony fur on a gingham and fleece bed near the floor heater. The camera would pause briefly at the fax machine resting on a white, wooden bookshelf while the sound of a tea kettle screamed ominously in the background. Foreshadowing? Yes.

Then the camera would travel down a hallway towards a girl with long, brown hair whose face we don't see. We would follow her to the kitchen from the heart down. The heart. That's very important. You wouldn't notice how small her breasts are at first because she'd be wearing her favourite cotton nightie, the one that makes her think of blue sky and fluffy white clouds.

The camera would follow her hands now as they turned off the gas stove. Her hands, because, if this were a movie, especially, say, a French one, you'd already be won over by her hands. Why? An extreme close-up would reveal short nails, a little white scar on her left index finger and a sole beauty mark near the centre knuckle of her right hand. Hell, you'd fall in love with her on the spot.

The camera would be seeing her hands move, clutching the handle of the tea kettle, removing it from the fire, turning off the gas burner while the kettle's crying begins to die; the hands that once made the boy weep just to look at them, the hands the boy said looked like something right out of a Flemish painting. You'd notice the care and grace with which she'd scoop loose Earl Grey tea from its chocolate-brown tin into her favourite grandmother's sterling-silver teapot. You'd think, I hope nothing bad happens to this person because she makes things from scratch.

As the steam continued to rise, the camera would pan up and

you'd see her face. The face the boy once claimed to love even though 'sometimes things just don't work out', according to the fax. But she doesn't know that, not yet.

If this was a movie she'd make her way into the office sipping her tea in the big porcelain china cup with the red and white flowers and matching saucer, half-and-half and two sugars, and we'd notice a page in the fax machine tray.

Now the camera would stay on her face as she crossed to *it* and began to read it. There'd be an insert of the tea's milky steam spiralling and evaporating into nothingness. Then a shot of her eyes darting across the page, then of the fax in her shaking hand, only you'd hear the boy's narration, his deep voice resonating directly from his wide, flat hip bones:

America, I found this in a book of channelled information and it says things better than I ever could: 'Souls come together not to remain together but to grow and move on. Loss is natural, like the setting sun or the falling leaves, and always leads to new beginnings. Detachment is a hard lesson to learn. Even animals cling together in their little nests because they are afraid. O Earth Human, do not be afraid of death. For there is no separation though it appears to be so on the physical. In reality, it is more akin to simply having entered another room.' Please don't call me. I have entered another room. Love always, Jasper Husch.

We would hold on a close-up of the girl's face and then, in slow motion, the cup and its contents would fall to the floor and the sound of the girl's heartbeat would be louder than thunder. The camera would be above her now, pulling back, back, back, as though the perspective belonged to her soul having left her body. And the camera would hold on the girl, head tilted back in a silent, anguished scream, arms outstretched like Jesus. Blackout!

FOUR

A Few Minutes Later

'Baby's got blue skies up ahead. But in this, I'm a rain cloud.
You know she likes a dry kind of love.'

– U2

But this was not a movie, it was real life and I was pissed.

'Hello?'

'I got your fax.'

'Oh. Good.'

'Is this some kind of a joke? Because I said I was sorry about the whole sex thing. You know I am stressed about money right now . . .'

'Look, I don't want to get into this with you on the phone. It's not about yesterday. It's about . . . Sometimes things just end. Sometimes people just don't get along—'

'But we *do* get along!'

'No we don't. I'm sorry, but we don't. Maybe in a few years . . .'

'In a few years? What are you talking about? Jasper? Are you still there? Fine, then I'm coming up there.'

'Mer, don't.'

'Then you come back here.'

'If I come down there, this thing will just drag on and on.'

'This thing! This *thing*? Do you think it was easy for me to make closet space for you? Jasper?'

33

'It's over, Mer. I gotta go.'

'It's about the cats, isn't it? You are mad that I don't pet your cats enough.'

'It's not about the cats.'

'Then what is it?'

'Just calm down.'

'Answer me! Please? The least you could do is say all this to my face.'

'It's the living together, it's the fighting . . .'

'That's it? That's what you're afraid of? The fighting? So what, big deal, we have dumb fights. That's all part of loving someone. I hate it too, but so what? No big, you're worth it. We're worth it. Jasper? Guava? Why won't you answer me?'

'Look, I'm just not ready. You are and I'm not. We have gone as far as we can go. I'm not ready.'

'Baby, please, let's just try it. Pleeeease!'

'It's over.'

'Then why do I have a pile of your stuff in our new house? Jasper? Jasper? Talk to me! Jasper? I love you!'

'Please don't call me. I gotta go.' He hung up.

My knees buckled. I let the phone drop out of my hand as I slid down the wall. Tulie came over and started licking my face, but I pushed her away. Chocolate. I needed chocolate.

FIVE

San Quentin

'Twist. Twist.'

— Korn

I put a big pile of it on the 7-Eleven counter with my credit card with the hand that wasn't collecting snot on its sleeve: a Snickers, a Mounds, a Chocodile, a Cadbury fruit and nut bar, four Chunk Bars, a Skor and ten miniature Reese's Peanut Butter Cups. I read somewhere once that chocolate has some of the same chemical effects on the body as love.

'Hello, my fire-end, hello my fire-end,' chirped the man in the turban with the long woolly beard behind the counter. He meant friend, but it sounded more like Fire End. 'Why are you crying, prettygirlyou? No tears, my fire-end, no tears. Five-dollar minimum on credit card, my fire-end,' he said, cheerfully ignoring my overwhelming sorrow, just like Jasper.

'What?' I said, staring at the Irish cream logo on the cappuccino machine. I knew it didn't taste like it looked.

'Five-dollar minimum on credit card.' I looked back at him. He pointed to a hand-made sign, black magic-marker on taped-up yellow legal-pad paper turned sideways, to prove it.

'Fine, forty dollars' worth,' I said, slamming a fistful of Milky Ways on the counter.

'What?'

'Charge me forty. Forty dollars' worth,' I said, maniacally piling more and more candy on the counter: Clark, Mars, Peanut and regular M & Ms, a bag of Hershey's Kisses, Hostess Cupcakes, anything with chocolate in it, and then a Charleston Chew, for variety. 'Voila!' I said, like a top athlete completing a high-bar dismount while he punched in the numbers.

'That's only thirty-seven eighteen.'

'What,' I said, leaning in to get a better look at him. I stared hard at how his moustache seemed to come directly out of his nose. It made me wipe my own nose on my sleeve.

'It is true, thirty-seven eighteen, my fire-end,' he said merrily, smiling. He was a despicable contrast to me and my chocolate dilemma. 'See, my fire-end?' He pointed to the digital numbers in the tiny window display on top of the machine. 'See? Three. Seven. One. Eight.'

I added two bags of chocolate-covered mini-donuts. He chuckled. 'That won't do it.'

I added another fistful of Reese's Peanut Butter Cups.

'Nope,' he said gleefully, brown teeth appearing under his nosestache.

'Look,' I said, planting both hands firmly on the counter, 'if it wouldn't be too much trouble, could you just ring up what's here.' I slid my credit card a little closer to his stubby fingers.

'So, no forty.' His eyebrows came to a woolly point.

I stared at him. 'No, just ring up what's here.'

He matched my stare, then turned. 'OK. It is your life.' He punched some numbers on a little machine that looked like a futuristic calculator, slid my card through a narrow slot along the side, then handed it over for me to sign my cyber-signature.

'Any relation?' he said, beginning to smile again.

'What?'

'To the famous important painterwriter?'

'What?' I said again, in utter disbelief.

'Any relation?'

'Yeah, I'm the daughter.'

'Oh, my goodness, oh, my goodness. I don't belief it. I don't belief it.' He looked like a duck in a shooting gallery, running like that from the inside of the hot-dog station to the edge of the magazine rack. 'Why didn't you say? I am a painterwriter too! I am a poet because of your father. He was genius! Genius from heaven above.' He pointed towards heaven above. I noticed a lightbulb needed changing.

He reached forward, gesturing wildly. 'I mean, his was political and sexual and gratuitous and sub-tle and personal and deep and sad and transcendent and var-nar-ball honest and aesthetically pleasing and hard to stomach and, and . . .' He acted every emotion out while he continued counting out my father's attributes on his foreign little fingers. This is like a reverse stick-up, I thought as I backed up, arms raised in surrender. Please sir, leave me alone, I pleaded with my eyes.

He put his hand over his heart. 'The daughter of Boris Throne. I don't belief it.' Then he leaned his elbow on the counter. 'Yunno, I saw him read his short story, *Kent's Tiny Pony*, in Carnegie Mullen at Pittsburgh, Pennsylvania. Sorry, in, at, at, in. Sorry, I am nervous. He was . . .' he became solemn for a moment, almost presidential, then finally managed '*original*.' For a moment he was speechless. We shared a suffocating moment of silence and before I could ask for my goodies and scram, the dams burst. He was crying. Wailing, really. 'There will never be another one like him.' I'm the sad one, I thought venomously, not you.

Then, as mysteriously as it began, so the crying stopped. He touched a finger on to the corner of his eye, wiped his moustache three times and said, 'Hey, what is the brother working on? The brother does music, right? I read about the son named Spoon.' This was all a bit too much.

'He just . . . well . . . uh . . .'

'How 'bout your-self? I read somewhere that you were doing some acting?'

'Uh, yeah, voice-overs actually, because I like my privacy.' I stressed the word privacy, hoping he would catch on.

'How's that going?'

'Terrific. I mean, look at me.'

'Yeah,' he said, holding his belly mirthfully, 'I guess it pays the bills, huh?' He pointed to my forty-dollar chocolate allowance spilling across the counter, then leaned in conspiratorially, 'What was it like? Growing up with Boris Throne for a father? That must have been a trip.' He took a hit off an invisible marihuana cigarette.

I looked at him indignantly. 'Oh, God no. He didn't do drugs.' He made a face like I'm not buying it.

'No?' He seemed surprised.

'No.'

'No?'

'No!' I was getting angry.

'Really?' He said, head in an all-disbelieving tilt. He leaned in close, whispered, 'You can tell me.'

That did it. I wanted to shout, 'Well, my earliest memories are of women on all fours posing nude on our kitchen counter while I tried to eat my puffed rice and apple juice in peace. And of naked men in various yoga postures hanging off my goddamned jungle gym. Or the fact that I couldn't distinguish which ones my dad wasn't fucking. Or, how about this little gem, that, in fact, my father and I never shared a meal together alone, ever, once. The one time we were scheduled to have dinner alone for the first time ever, just the two of us, a crazy stalker-type fan, like you, sir, came over and my father took pity on him and let him dine with us, which is probably why I chose such a narcissistic asshole for a boyfriend and why I have no boundaries with a stranger like you.'

Instead, I just smiled politely and said, 'It was nice, may I please have my receipt?'

'Go, my fire-end,' he said, tearing up the little yellow slip of paper. 'It is my gift. Take it. A gift to the sad daughter of my mentor.' He waved me out, shouting, 'Goodbye, my fire-end, goodbye!'

I sort of half ran and half limped back to my car like a bad guy with a leaking bloody bullet wound, away from the red and white and green fluorescently lit tribute to my father at the corner of Tujunga and Ventura.

The fax lay crumpled up in my empty passenger seat. I picked it up, peeled it apart, smoothed it with my chocolate fingers and reread it. It was worse the second time around. It called for both bags of donuts.

Driving north on Laurel Canyon, brown bag on lap, I reached into my goodie bag with the hand that wasn't collecting snot on my sleeve and began cramming chocolate in my mouth like the scene in that TV movie where Meredith Baxter Birney has bulimia. Then I turned onto the 101 and looked for the sign that said Interstate 5.

I gulped in air with every bite, chewing and swallowing like a cartoon of a mad dog with pinwheels for eyes and a foamy chocolate beard around its mouth. As I drove I ate so much chocolate that the sun had no choice but to set. I watched it be snuffed out and disappear behind a massive row of mountains. Blue assaulted by orange and deep purples and rosy pinks, a real shiner.

I sped west on the 101 freeway past palm trees and the middle-class, safe in their suburban homes, conveniently located massive shopping centres and movie complexes. With my windows rolled down and Tori Amos blasting on the CD player, my Saint Christopher danced frantically in time to the music while I went over my strategy.

My plan was to drive directly to Jasper's house and just talk things through calmly, face to face. I knew if he could see the sadness in my eyes, the pain he had caused me, he would surely understand what he had done, and would change his mind. I popped another Reese's into my mouth, stepped on the accelerator until the needle said ninety, and lied to myself. Besides, a long drive might do me some good.

It was almost completely dark now. The valley and its hillside began to twinkle. I pressed my foot firmly on the accelerator, while applying red lipstick and dialling my home phone number on my car phone to check my messages. Maybe Jasper had called to say he had come to his senses. It would sure save me the trip. I couldn't get a clear signal so I sped up. Then I thought about Tulie and about how no one had a spare key so no one could feed her or let her out. That's when I realized I had missed my chance to merge on to the 405 heading north, so I honked and signalled my way to the Sepulveda exit.

There, I couldn't find the proper on-ramp I needed, so I made an illegal U-turn across an island and five lanes of traffic. That's when I saw the cherries.

'Ma'am? Ma'am, can you hear me?' said the doughy police officer with the blond buzz cut who tapped at my car window. He lightly touched the gun at his hip. 'Ma'am, can you tell me what happened?'

I was parked on the corner of Ventura and a liquor store with a green neon sign that said, Joe's. It made a terrible buzzing sound overhead. The J was missing. 'He, I . . . He hates my dog . . . His cats . . . Maybe in a few years . . . Bad timing, *ha! Understatement,*' I muttered in between heaving, runny-nose sobs. 'Like *he's* the *spiritual* one.' I handed him my licence, registration and the fax I still had wadded up in my hand.

I couldn't think straight, so I just stared blankly into space while my mind played the rewind game. I just wanted some air, I just wanted some room to breathe. That is what I wanted to say to the nice officer with the childbearing hips, that I was suffocating, you see, that it was vital I get some air. To tell him that, even though it looked like an illegal U-turn across five lanes of traffic into a bus zone I was not allowed to park in without wearing my seat belt, in actuality a bit of breathing room was what I was after, but the words wouldn't come.

I just sat there thinking about the Incredible Hulk. I thought about the alienation he must have felt, keeping himself contained like that and the satisfaction he must have felt truly letting go. I worried I might let go like that this very minute, and never come back.

'Ma'am, can you hear me?' Of course I could hear him, but I was miles away, trying not to burst out of my clothes.

Protect and serve, protect and serve, his hips and legs announced as he walked back to his car. People in cars slowed and stared as they passed. A handsome man wearing a western shirt with red, embroidered roses on it appeared out of nowhere, looking at me out of the corner of his eye as he walked by. Then the handsome guy stuck his hands in his jean pockets and disappeared round the block.

I just kept my eyes fixed on the officer as he smoothed the thermal paper flat in the palm of his hand, glancing sideways at me from time to time, shifting his weight from one enormous leg to the other. He could have been a football player.

The officer got on his radio, spoke, listened, spoke some more and waited. Then I heard a woman dispatcher's garbled mumblings. The officer spoke into a black hand radio and waited while she spit out more incomprehensible info. Finally the officer looked down at Jasper's letter and read. Then he looked back at me, looked away, and, passing a leather toe over the asphalt, folded the white thermal paper in half, in half again, and walked towards me.

He leaned his arm on the roof of my car. 'I'm still gonna have to give you a ticket.'

'OK,' I said, but it wasn't. He handed me the ticket along with Jasper's fax.

'Sorry about your loss,' he said, leaning in close enough for me to smell his aftershave. The word 'loss' blinked in time with the turning lights on the top of his sedan. Gee, they're pretty, like the little chilli-pepper lights in Jasper's bay window. Jasper, oh, no. Tears shot out of my eyes like missiles. 'Any relation?' he said, handing me back my driver's licence.

'Cocksuckingfaggotasspieceofshit... He doesn't even believe AIDS is real!' I said, nodding in the affirmative.

He gave the roof of my car a comforting pat, then winked at me. 'Things will look different in the morning, just take it easy.'

When I got home, I pressed my forehead into the door frame and stayed that way for a while. The wailing didn't stop just because the sun went down. It continued like it was a business day and this was my job, to grieve. It came out of me in desperate hurls, a kind of soundless frozen scream followed by a spattering of deep, guttural growls, and then the moans, like a ghost. I was being haunted, yes; I was haunting myself, because a ghost is what I had become. A fat ghost. That is what Jasper Husch had made me in the blink of an eye, or however long it had taken him to craft that fax. A chocolate-eating, fat phantom.

The wood felt cool against my skin. The decorative edge of the wood around the peephole dug into my flesh and made little indentations. I leaned into it a little more.

Did he have to go to Kinko's to Xerox it? Did he have time to browse through a couple of books before selecting the perfect passage to let me know our entire relationship had come to an abrupt halt? Did he not understand that a year and a half equalled a lifetime in this disposable world?

I thought, a facsimile, how fitting because Jasper was an extreme likeness to a boyfriend, but not an actual one, not any more. I thought we had figured it all out. I thought we had resolved his fears about our differences. I mean, he had a key to *our house*. Didn't that mean anything? I pulled at a wet strand of hair and put it in my mouth and locked the door. Click, click and I was in jail, just like that. That's when I named the place. For fun. I nicknamed the adorable little cottage we were *both* going to live in San Quentin because my entire house was now a cell, a prison of aloneness, and Jasper Husch was my jailer.

Tallulah stared up at me with her big, bulgy eyes. She sniffed my leg before giving it one light lick. I knelt down and pulled her face close to mine. 'I was going to let you starve to death and die, for what? Fucking asshole.'

Then I made my way to my big, empty bed, picked Tulie up and let her burrow herself deep under the covers. I climbed in, lay there, perfectly still, stared at the ceiling. Lights out, Prisoner 1-0-7-3-3, Red Fern Hill Drive. Lock down in cell one. Guilty of loving a manchild in the first degree, sentenced to life without him, no parole.

My head filled with the sound of my own heartbeat, the heart Jasper was breaking. If I had known that yesterday was the last time we would ever make love, I would have tried to enjoy it more. Tears streamed down my cheeks. Time to sleep, Mer, you can do it. Just get through the night. Things will look different in the morning. 'Yeah, worse,' I said out loud.

I promised myself then and there never to call him again. Who in the hell did he think he was? I didn't need him, he wasn't good enough for me. He'd have to beg me to come back. And even if he did beg, I vowed never to take him back, ever, not after what he did.

In the distance, crickets and coyotes and owls and dogs began to howl. The canyons are like that. They all sounded like they were crying. To me, anyway. Then I heard the sound of screeching brakes coming to a sudden halt. I wondered how I could kill Jasper and get away with it. Or how many ways I could kill him and not mind not getting away with it. I wondered what he was doing that very minute.

I pulled the covers up, smelling the last particles of Jasper I would ever have access to, and pulled them around me like so much lead. Anyone will tell you the first three days of the break-up are the hardest. I felt that if I could just get through these next few hours without calling him, it would be smooth sailing.

SIX

Black Sunday

'Mother stands for comfort.'

— Kate Bush

But my mother phoned. At 6.19 a.m.

I had left the ringer on silent, but the message volume at eight, in case Jasper called to reconcile, and now I was being assaulted by my mother's shrill soprano.

'Good morning Mer, this is Camilla calling!' I hated it when she called herself Camilla, acting like my friend instead of being my mother. This was a tactic she had been using since my early twenties, to get me and Spoonie to treat her like we were all terrific pals. Pals that obeyed her. 'I just wanted to let you know Spoonie is playing a concert this evening.' I thought, a concert? Try 'gig', mother. 'Oh! A birdling just landed on the railing! Well, I'm not entirely certain it's a bluejay, but it is undisputedly blue. You know that blue sweater thingy with the tassels and the shiny fringe your aunt gave your grandmother that she hated but wore anyway when your aunt visited, because she felt guilty that night they had dinner at the Magic Castle? It's *that* shade of blue. Yesterday two of them appeared and ate the new cat food I put down!' I buried my face into my pillow while my mother blabbed on and on.

Since my father's death, my mother has become an early riser. Maybe this made her feel like she could get a jump on things. She

45

enjoys the peace, the light, the ozone, 'All of the nutrients your lungs will ever need are all right there.' She likes the fact that no one else is up and that the whole world belongs to her, ignoring the fact that other people are sleeping and might possibly be going through a very painful break-up and did not have time to call and explain that to her, and certainly do not need to be reminded of it first thing so as to get a head start staying awake *all day* thinking about it. The machine cut her off.

A few minutes later the machine made a series of clicks, then came the booming voice again.

'Hello? Mer? Oh, I thought I heard you pick up. *Harumph*. It's Camilla, darling. Anyhow, Spoonie is playing a concert tonight at The Butterfly Club, and I am going to need the guest list. OK, love you, bye bye.' It's the Dragonfly mother. She finished up the endless call with one large, wet smacking sound. I closed my eyes, anxious to get back to my sorrow, knowing full well that the grieving process can take up to more than half the time you were actually together. Only, a few minutes later, the machine click-click-clicked *again.*

'Jesus!' I said out loud. Didn't she understand I was on the soul-mending clock? I rolled over onto my side and pulled a pillow about my face and ears like a bonnet. I tried to close my eyes but the sun was stinking up the place with too much sparkly happiness.

'Mer? Did you just try to call me? No? Well anyway, I forgot to tell you I need that guest list by four, so let me know who's coming. I just need to know so I can let them know by four. OK, love you, bye bye. *Mmchwa!*' She wasn't this organized before. When my dad died she took it upon herself to do whatever she could for our careers, especially when we do not ask for her help. And especially when we ask her specifically *not* to. In fact, asking guarantees it will not happen.

'Oh, also, I wanted to let you know I set up a lunch for you and that agent I was telling you about. I told him you are not at all happy with your current agency, and he said he'd be willing to help you find better representation as a favour to me. I never liked that agent of yours, anyway. His ears are too small. Bad listeners, men with small ears.' I looked at the clock: 6.27, then rolled on to my back, groaning.

I slammed my palm into Jasper's side of the bed, then reached for the pale blue princess phone on my little yellow nightstand.

'Mother!' I said loudly straight into the phone, without putting the earpiece next to my head, 'I do not *need* a new agent! I just signed with this one, and I've already been out on at least seventy-two auditions!' A lie. I tilted the phone to hear her response, but she was gone. I slammed the phone back in its cradle and curled my body into a fist. The answering machine clicked again. Guess fucking who.

'Oh, and bring Jasper.'

I sat straight up, held the phone with two hands. 'Mother, I am asleep!' I was yelling now.

Calmly she replied, 'Mer, how can you be asleep if you are talking on the phone?' I rolled my eyes.

'Why are you calling me at this hour?'

'I thought you'd have your machine on.'

'I do have it on, Mother. What do you want?'

'No, I mean I thought you'd have your phone turned off, it's so early.' I closed my eyes, tightened my jaw, exhaled loudly through my nose.

'It's just that—'

'What's the matter, do you have a cold?'

'No, Mother,' I said slowly, softening somewhat, 'I've been crying. My eyes have practically sewn themselves shut.'

'Oh. Do you have a plunger?' My eyes blinked open.

'It's too early for mind games, Mother.'

'Don't talk to me like that. I only called to say it would be lovely if you and Jasper could attend Spoon's performance this evening and show your brother a little support. I don't need to be treated like an animal just because you're sad and want to take it all out on someone.' I heard the sound of running water, then a sandpapery scrubbing, Brillo against porcelain. It made my teeth ache. I pulled my comforter around me.

'What do you mean, "like an animal"?' Tulie made a scraping

sound from inside her crate. 'Shut up!' I shouted over my feathery barricade. I scrunched back under the covers, held the receiver very close to my mouth. 'Jasper and I broke up.'

'Well, good riddance. How about Sadie, will she be coming tonight?'

I pulled the phone away from my ear. Stared at it, then my eye caught sight of one of Jasper's vintage button-down shirts hanging limply from a wooden chair in the corner of our room.

'Ooof,' my mother said suddenly as though wrestling something large, and losing. Then I heard a sound, metal grating against metal. 'Nobody really liked him anyway. His forehead was too small. No imagination.'

'What do you mean, nobody?' I roared, 'He had a massive forehead!'

'Ooof,' my mother said again.

'Jesus, what exactly are you building over there?'

'Don't Jesus me, you sound like an inner-tube tyre. I don't need abuse from you, madam, not when there is a lovely, civilized little bluejay perched outside my window waiting for his breakfast. Goodbye, Mer.'

Don't hang up! I feel dizzy. 'Mother, I'm sorry, it's just that I'm very upset about the break-up.'

'What for?' Scrape scrape.

'What do you mean, what for? *For kicks, Mother. I'm upset because it's fun! What in the hell is wrong with you?*'

'Goodbye, Mer,' she said curtly.

'Mother, Mother, please don't hang up! Please?' I pleaded. 'I can be calm, I can be calm.' I listened to a waiting silence on the other end of the phone. Tentatively I said, 'It's just that I would really appreciate it if you would be careful never to mention his name to me ever again. Ever. Like, as long as I live.'

'Mer, the Dalai Lama says our sole job is to be happy, so I ask you, why waste your energy being upset?'

I stared at the phone. 'Because, because.' I was stumped. 'Because I feel *shitty*? I mean, if I just lie down and accept this, Mother, why not join the army or a cult, or, or, or . . .'

'Now you're just being silly, which I prefer by the way, but don't take this all out on me. I am an innocent bystander, simply calling to ask my daughter and her boyfriend . . .'

I tightened my hands around the receiver, pretending it was a very thin neck. I watched my knuckles turn white, then gently held the phone back up to my ear and calmly asked her, 'Are you trying to kill me, Mother?'

'I didn't say his name.'

I poked at the holes in the phone. 'I mean, are you trying to drive me absolutely insane!'

'Spare me the melodrama, America, I need to know who you are bringing *before* four, if you are coming. I know Spoonie would really appreciate the support, so if Jas . . .' I felt my face go bright red. I was surprised the phone didn't catch on fire. 'I mean, if anybody changes his mind it would be nice to see you *both* down at the venue.'

'It's not a venue, Mother, it's a divy bar!'

'Good morning to you, too. Goodbye, Mer.' She hung up.

I held my breath and pressed the top of my head into the bed as if preparing for a somersault, and stayed that way long enough to calm down. Tears rolled into my hairline in great buoyant drops.

Goddamnit. Every time I want to hate her outright, I always picture two things. Her suddenly clutching her heart and dying, or her face that day as we watched the men in rented light-grey suits lower my father into the ground. I picture how the muscles around her mouth tightened and pursed, and how her chin jutted out and quivered. The blue of her eyes flat, eerily dull, and how the tears fell down her cheeks in perfect streams, like rain on a pane of glass. That was the only time I ever actually *saw* her cry. A woman who sheds no tears? What kind of a life is that? Oh, I heard her a few times, when I was little, behind closed doors, when we had no money, or when my father went away for long trips and she found a hotel receipt for a Mr and Mrs Throne when she had stayed behind to watch us, or discovered a scarf she did not purchase for him stuffed in a jacket pocket, scented with expensive, powdery, fruit-smelling perfumes. Evidence: My mother is a green-scented body type. Once, on my dead sister's birthday, I heard my father's murmurings, then a door slam and then his footsteps down the hallway, past my room, towards his painting studio. He didn't come out until my mother brought him something hot to eat.

I sat up and called her right back.

'Hello,' she chirped, 'this is Camilla speaking.'

'Mother, why did you hang up on me?'

'I didn't.'

'You did.'

'No, Mer, I didn't.'

I looked around the room, shook my head in disbelief. Abort, abort! She's in *New York Times* crossword-puzzle mode. Slowly I asked her, 'Then how did I end up with a receiver in my hand and no one on the other end of the line?'

'If you remember, I said goodbye,' she explained with equal slowness, enunciating every syllable. 'The conversation seemed to be over because you stopped talking.'

'I was *listening*, Mother!'

'Well, you made a snorting sound.'

'Breathing, I was breathing. That's what people do, they breathe. Jesus.' Silence on the other end of the phone, a stand-off. I wanted to say, what, no apology? Yeah, maybe Jasper and I can get back together so *Spoonie* will be happy. Just as soon as the break-up fairy pulls the stinger out of Jasper's ass he'll wake up and we can all live happily ever after so Spoonie has an audience. Terrific understanding of *my* feelings, Mother! But I didn't. Instead I rolled my eyes. 'I'm sorry, Mother.'

'Well, yes, OK, fine. I need those names by four.'

'I know, I know. By four.'

'Good. Well, I love you.'

I swallowed my pride. 'Well, I—'

'Oh, I almost forgot! I need to cut your allowance back, there's been a slight screw-up with the accounting, so you'll only be getting a thousand dollars a month I'm afraid, which I am sure you can manage, but now I absolutely must run, an exploding

sink calls. Bye byeeee,' she said, sounding victoriously chirpy, and
hung up.

'I . . . I . . . I . . . love you too,' I said to the dead phone in my
palm. I placed it on its cradle, calmly inhaled, then let out one
sharp, elongated burst of a scream. I looked at Tulie. 'What am I
going to do now?' I flopped on my back, stared at the ceiling,
pounded my fists into the mattress. I could tolerate my mother
when Jasper was around.

I was so tired I felt drugged. I crossed my hands at my heart and
tried to prepare for sleep the way a pharaoh might prepare for
mummification. Lying on my back gave me pause to consider how
much I hated the curtain ties I had made. There were other terrific
things to think about too, like how to afford my new place without
money or a job and what in the hell I even wanted to do for a
living, and what's so great about living anyway?

In a moment of sanity, I phoned my best friend Sadie to tell her
the news of my sudden impoverishment and loss of Jasper and to
go over The Plan with her: to live out the rest of my life from my
new *permanent horizontal*, and eventually to die in my new house of a
broken heart.

'Pick up, Sadie, it's an emergency. I need you to document this
for me and then forward it to Jasper so he lives out the rest of his
miserable life knowing he killed a woman by being emotionally
unavailable and, well, dumb.

When Jasper loved me, in my old house, he left poems
everywhere he knew I'd look: on my answering machine, in my
grandma's teapot, in the refrigerator by my half-and-half, next to
my computer, on my bathroom mirror, near the phone by my bed,
on my pillow. He would hold me until I fell asleep. When we
stayed at his place we would stay up and watch movies until the sun
came up, pausing to make love, or eat hippy TV dinners. Aflood
with memories of where we made love, laughed, cooked, danced,
fucked, painted, in window sills, on bathroom floors, and kitchen
table tops, where we made still more love, ate, made even more
glorious love, experimented sexually – I thought, I am so glad I did
not let you shit between my legs. Fuck you for even thinking that

was something even remotely acceptable to propose, but you found a way to shit on me anyway, didn't you, you fucking maggot!

I heard the phone make another series of small clicks. I leapt for it. It's him!

'Hello?'

'Do you have a plunger?' said Spoonie through a groggy yawn, 'Camilla's on a rampage.' I hated it when he called her that. I sighed loudly.

'Oh hi, Spoonie.'

'Do you?'

'What?'

'Have a plunger. Camilla wants to know.'

'You do realize I live eight miles away and that a plumber might be somewhat closer?'

'Camilla says it only requires a plunger.'

'Doesn't *Mother* have one there?'

'Just forget it. If you're not gonna help, I gotta go.'

'Uh . . . sorry. It's just that I feel like I am on the verge of a nervous breakdown here, and I really—'

'OK. So, are you coming tonight?' I shook my head in disbelief, thought, is my *entire* family insane?

'No, I can't. I'm suicidal. Jasper and I broke up.'

'So then you're *not* coming tonight?' I bit the inside of my mouth.

'Look, I'm just not feeling all that well . . .'

'OK, whatever.' He sounded disappointed.

I let out a sigh. 'But I'll try to come.'

'Cool! Try to come early, because I really think you'll like the opening band. They're called Rows Five Through Seven. They're really good! Kinda like fusion grunge mixed with symphonica, like Bach on an all-guitar-and-Twinkie binge.'

'I said I'd *try* . . .'

'Hey, I invited Sadie but maybe you could call her and remind her, and maybe get her to bring that actress chick.'

'What actress chick?'

'That *one*. The one she's working with. The one with the boobs.'

I rolled my eyes. 'Oh, and Camilla needs the guest list by four.'

I bared my teeth. 'Yeah, she mentioned that.' My mother called out to Spoonie for assistance. Suddenly I felt bad that the weight of her universe rested on his shoulders because he still lived at home. Then again, he got the same allowance as me and none of my expenses. *And* they got along.

'Bye,' he said, yawning.

'Bye.' I hung up, rolled onto my side, pulled my down comforter up over my face, and tried to relax. Just then I heard a loud-ass neighbour start up his loud-ass saw outside.

'*God damnit!*' I screamed. I kicked my legs. I was having a full-blown temper tantrum. I stood up suddenly and began to pace. I mimicked the sounds I heard outside and buzzed around my room, arms outstretched, like an airplane. Saw, saw, buzz buzz, right wall, left wall and back to the bed again while some new neighbour 'gardened'. I flopped back down on my bed and kicked some more. This time on my stomach.

The smell of gasoline wafted its way into my solitary confinement. I thought about permanent rest, about gas chambers and electric chairs and death by lethal injection and of course Jasper. Then it hit me: why should Jasper get to sleep peacefully if I couldn't? I mean, no one else was treating this like it was real or any big deal, so why should I?

'You have reached Jasper Husch Fine Arts and Illustration. No one is here to take your call, so please leave a message or push start to send a fax now.'

'Hey baby, it's me, are you around? Are you a square? OK, call me when you get in. No big. Love you.' I hung up and lay back and eased my head gently into my downy pillow. It felt good just knowing I had made contact.

I called right back.

'Baby, are you there? I really need to talk to you, so can you please pick up? Guava? OK, well, call me back, OK baby? I was wondering if you wanted to come down for Spoonie's show tonight, baby?

OK, well, let me know. My mom needs the guest list by four. Thanks. Bye.'

Baby, it's me. Are you up yet? Honey? Jasper? Baby, please pick up if you are there. Baby, are you there? Pick up pick up pick up pick up pick up. I know you can hear me. I know you are screening. No? Baby, it's important. I really really really have to talk to you. I was thinking maybe you'd like to fly down and see Spoonie's show tonight, and then we could sleep in late tomorrow and get up and have breakfast in our new kitchen together, and then we could drive back up together and pack your stuff up and drive it back down together, whaddya say? Baby? Baby, please don't do this to me. Jasper? No? Fine!'

I slammed the phone down.

'Pick up the phone, Jasper. Pick up the fucking phone. Pick the fuck up, you fucking piece of shit. No? Fine. Since I can't talk to you, let's recap. Two days ago we were in love. *Yesterday* I put you on a plane headed back for San Francisco after not the best, OK, fine, rather awful rushed sex, but I was stressed because I have exactly two hundred dollars to my name. Plus you *know* I don't like morning sex, plus I will have you know that my mother is cutting my allowance back so now I am *totally* stuck with this place and no money and no job. And I mean honestly, Jasper, I could not have gotten wet if I wanted to, not with only two hundred dollars to my name. Plus thanks to you I'm totally stuck. Maybe you are used to having no money, Jasper, but then another job always rolls on in for you and *leads* to something. Because your artwork is in demand, while I, an unknown freelance with no profession of my own, could starve to death in this town. Are you hearing any of this?'

The machine cut me off.

'Let me tell you why two hundred dollars is a bad amount of money to me. OK, so yes, I know *everyone* has concerns about money and career and such, but not everyone is a C-level celebrity, Jasper. Not everyone is a white, educated, daughter of a *genius* who had a head start and *still* can't pay her bills or figure out what to do with her life. You might expect this from a homeless lady or a grocery checker or whatever ... Hey, that's pretty funny, they are both bag ladies! Anyhoo ...'

'Fucking machines. Listen, I know this sounds weird, Jasper, perhaps even harsh, but I always wished I was raised a bottom feeder like you. Like my parents were. That way perhaps I'd understand better that the bottom isn't so far to fall. You guys don't seem to freak out over things like having no money. If I was raised with nothing, like all of you, perhaps then I'd be motivated to achieve, like all of you. When you are raised rich like me, you do have a desire to succeed because you have seen it all. You *know* money is not the answer, certainly not the key to happiness. The only reason to work is so that you can afford *not* to, so you can live happily ever after with the people who matter to you. That's where you come in, Jasper Husch. You matter. So while I was here busily trying to figure out a way to make money so you wouldn't leave me so I wouldn't have to rely on you so much so that I could have my own self-esteem so you wouldn't leave me, you decide to leave me. And because, why exactly?' The machine cut me off *again*.

'Baby, please pick up. I'm sorry I keep leaving these long messages, I just really love you and I really want this to work out, so call me, OK? Bye. I love you.'

I lay back feeling like I had been beaten by a pillowcase filled with oranges while dangling from a window ledge by my pinkie fingers. I sat up and called him right back. It rang and rang, so I hung up. Then I lay back and wiped my nose on my comforter.

Just ignore him, I thought. Yes, avoidance. Avoid all people. Avoid everything. Especially feeling. Try to sleep. Try to sleep it all off. But my stomach made a gurgling sound. I was starving.

I looked at the clock: 10.27 a.m. None of that rise-and-shine bullshit for me. I was up far too early for such a severe depression. I wanted to die, or at least fall back to sleep. I lay perfectly still and congratulated myself because I, unlike Jasper, could commit to things, like lying down.

A few minutes later, though, I had to get up to pee.

In the bathroom, I caught my reflection in the mirror and started picking blackheads instead. I tore a piece of toilet paper and began squeezing like a clean but demonic facialist. I bent my nose flat for more surface access. Twenty minutes and an inflamed face later, I looked like a heavy-weight boxer who had lost. I scolded myself: 'Stop it, Mer, you are out of control! You'll get through this. Just sleep it off, just make it through the next seventy-two hours and the hardest part will be over.' *Then* I peed and made my way back to my bed. Only, I ended up getting sidetracked at my living-room window.

There, from the corner of my eye, I saw a hummingbird. I stood still now and watched it hover outside the window near my lilac iMac, dip its beak into the face of a red hibiscus, dart away, move to another flower. While the little bird sucked the nectar from the veiny flowers, I wished Jasper debilitating mental pain and utter failure. Then, the hummingbird, representing joy in Indian folklore, paused by my window, held itself perfectly in place and crapped. It pooped out a massive hummingbird poop, a grunt about a third its size. 'This is *so* my life,' I said out loud.

I wanted to call someone, but no one would ever believe me except maybe Sadie, and she wasn't home. So I climbed back into bed.

Tulie came and sniffed my feet. I patted the bed to let her know she could come sit beside me. She burrowed herself under the covers, and gave my toes a lick. I twisted and turned in the bed of my own making. My fancy sheets with their fancy thread count mocked me. So I got up, dug the plastic applicator out of the trash and wrote 'fuck you asshole' in permanent marker and tucked it in the pocket of the shirt draped across the wooden chair in our bedroom. The one Jasper didn't care if he left behind.

Later, around dusk, after ordering, and then consuming, three sides of mashed potatoes, biscuits with molasses butter, a side of cornbread and a Caesar salad with caramelized pecans and fried okra from Why Cook, I would climb into bed and pass out; only to wake up in the middle of my brother's encore feeling jet-lagged and guilty for having missed Spoonie's show. I would then leap out of bed like a night fisherman checking his lobster traps to find *eight* messages!

Spoonie called to tell me that Sadie and I were on the guest list, plus one.

My mother called to see if I had any names for her.

My mother called to find out if I wanted to drive with her.

My mother called to see if I had left yet.

Sadie called to say she was very worried about me, was sorry she missed my calls, but thought I knew she was away all weekend and that she'd see me down at Spoonie's show.

Sadie called from a payphone to say she wasn't on the guest list, and where was I?

Sadie called to tell me she got in anyway, and where was I?

Sadie called again to say that she was home now, and that she loved me and that she was really worried about me. 'Mer Mer Mer? I'm really worried about you. Whatever you do, don't watch TV. Promise me you'll call me if it ever gets that bad.'

SEVEN

Radioactivate

'Cancer for the cure.'

— Eels

Public access is the only way to go.

For around fifty dollars, you can buy a half-hour time slot and make your own TV show, devoid of any content of professionalism, and beam it directly into people's homes. At least that is what I concluded from my living-room sofa hours after watching a lady marinate a chicken in orange soda, 'An old family recipe; it literally comes right off the bone!', after watching a guy sing songs about all the signs in the zodiac, and well after the lady who looked like a dancing bear dance like, well, a dancing bear.

I marvelled at the fact that although I shared the same desire to have my artistry be seen and appreciated, these pitiful outcasts were organized enough to take the three days of required training time, learning how to work the camera and lights and editing equipment, to pull all this mayhem off, whereas I waited around for my agent to call and tell me where my next rejection would be. Why hadn't Jasper called me? Was he home? Was he out? Was he dead in a ditch somewhere?

Presently, a man was making a belt buckle out of turquoise and found objects.

My phone rang. I thought, please let it be Jasper! But it was only Sadie.

'Mer? Mer? Mer? Mer??' I hated when she did that. She always says my name like a scratchy cat meow. She called it affection, I called it annoying. I didn't pick up.

Mainly because the man on the TV was smiling now. He was missing four teeth at the back. I hated happy people, and Sadie was always happy.

Sadie is my best friend. We have known each other ever since we both dropped out of a still life painting class at Parson's almost nine years ago. I wanted to impress my father so every Sunday a.m. I would trudge all the way out to Pasadena, set up my shitty easel and fail to capture the beauty around me. As it turned out, watercolours are a nightmare, but we both had massive crushes on the gentle instructor, Larry Gimmel. We confessed it to one another that first morning on the trek from the parking lot. I gave her half of a lemon poppyseed muffin, and in spite of our shared crushes, she told me I had some black things in my teeth. I trusted her instantly.

Once inside the gardens, we all began to feel the inspiration. Larry told us all to select a spot and paint, as best we could, exactly what we saw. The gardens were set up so that you had the opportunity to visit Japan or France or Brazil or merry old England via the plants.

We both chose England, and started with some climbing roses. My roses climbed all right, and then they kind of jumped, and ultimately ran. My painting seemed to be crying. I blamed the colour palette, which insulted real life, not taking into account that I had no depth perception, no sense of light or shadow play, along with zero perspective. Everything rested on the page with equal import and flatness. At least Sadie's interpretation expressed a bold commitment. She was not bound by the tradition of reds and pinks for the blossoms, she chose greens and greys, arranged them in abstract sort of blobs, and then selected black for the background, which she painted *after* the flowers were done. Her 'roses' sort of hung in a suspended blackness, a portrait of a sad infinity.

With his head cocked and his mouth in a half-pout, half-frown,

Larry seemed genuinely concerned. He gave us both the same note: start with one colour and get the relationship right with it first, before inviting other colours to join it. He demonstrated effortlessly with a little palette knife, and created a rich world using only *green*. He painted some foliage and a little winding path over my mess, and I swore I could see all the way down that road and into the depths of Larry's soul.

As we made our way back to the parking lot, covered in paint, I told Sadie that I felt like a failure because I could not interpret reality with my hands. I felt like it was an indication of my sanity and accuracy to perceive reality correctly. I wanted to be like my father, who could translate the world exactly as he saw it. Sadie confided she really had tried to paint the roses at first but then thought about her goal, Larry, and how sucking was a good thing. 'The worse the painting, the more the notes. The more notes, the more Larry?' Larry turned out to be gay, so we both dropped out.

Now she does set design for movies, mostly indie horror films. I like having her for a friend because sometimes she has no work for weeks at a time and we goof off. It's much better than having friends with real jobs.

'Mer? Mer? Mer? Pick up, I know you are there.' I didn't pick up. I watched the guy with the old-man hands show his belt-buckle mastery off in an extreme close-up. It was truly ghastly, that belt buckle, a tangle of twisted metal, like a small bus accident but with a coral and turquoise inlay.

'Look, Mer, I know you tend to isolate when you are upset, but I can't help you unless you reach out and pick up the phone. Mer? Mer? Mer? You're not in front of the TV are you, Mer? Because if you are, just turn it off and reach out.' I moved closer to the TV, an empty setting was being prepared for another assault of semi-precious stones. They cut back to another shot of him smiling.

'Mer? Mer? Mer? No? OK. Tallulah? Tallulah? Tallulah? OK, well, tell your owner to call me back when you get this.' The machine cut her off.

The phone rang again.

'Mer? Mer? Mer? Please pick up, I know you are there. I know you can hear me. You are probably just sitting there listening to this. Mer? Mer? I've thought about it. You are probably just experiencing pre-thirty jitters.' I stared at the machine, tried to send an electric shock through the wires, hoping to singe off her perfectly messy bangs. Failing, as she kept right on talking, I faced the TV and watched an ad for baby lasagna with renewed interest. Little layers of noodles and tomato sauce and something brown stuffed in tiny jars. For newborns. 'Promise me you're not watching TV, Mer? Are you? Mer? Mer? Mer? Please call me. OK?' She was silent for so long, the machine cut her off again.

He's probably at Benny's. I imagined him at Benny's little shit-hole apartment in the Haight now. I hated Benny. Benny was a gay musician with dyed blond hair that reminded me of a scalp disorder, in looks and smell. Plus, he had a scalp disorder. Not to mention I was convinced he was secretly in love with Jasper, who of course denied it endlessly.

Or maybe he's at DebiGlen's, an inseparably happy married couple I liked only slightly more.

I aimed the remote and switched channels, landing on a skinny man in a purple unitard with long stringy hair and an equally skinny beard. I watched him show off his 'invention', a custom-crafted Velcro hippy apparatus which he boasted 'perfectly duplicates the experience of floating in water while remaining on land'. He assured me that by making minor adjustments to the fifty or so 3D foam circles, squares and parabolas, 'a baby or a legal giant could feel like he was floating on a distant ocean, while safe in the comfort of his own home'. Then he encouraged me to order it on the number you see on the screen. I wondered why he invented it. I wondered if he was allergic to water. I wondered if a person could get seasick in her living room. Then and there I made a pact with myself to avoid men with beards.

I changed channels again, caught the end of a commercial for Huggy Bunny soft-smelling sheets.

Ha, ha, ha! My belly shook with mirth just thinking about how much Jasper would have enjoyed this, and how much power I had over Jasper by not calling him to tell him about it, and how much enjoyment I was having without Jasper, on my own. Big salty tears cascaded down my somewhat scabby, picked-at cheeks. I pointed the remote and channel surfed as though my very life depended on it.

The phone rang again. It was Sadie. This time on a staticky cellphone: 'I'm really really really really worried about you. I really need to talk to you. Mer? Mer? Mer? Look, just promise me something, and this is vital, America Throne, just promise that you will not under any circumstances call him. Do you understand me? Do not not *not* call him. Call me before you even think about calling him. Have I made myself clear, Young Miss Thing? I mean it, Mer. Mer? Mer, please pick up.' She was silent for a moment. 'Mer, reach out.'

I stared at the answering machine, then at the remote in my hands. I massaged the rubber base at the end with my thumbs. Impulsively I picked up the phone. 'Sadie?' I said, but she had already hung up. I let out a deep sigh.

I turned the machine and ringer volume off. Time to focus on checking out.

On the boob, a man from India with thick grey fingernails that curled and curled and touched the floor. He had been growing them since 1956. He kept the creepy, gnarled Hand in a long black sack. His wife had to turn the Hand over every half-hour when they slept so it didn't cut off his circulation because his precious, useless Hand was so heavy. I got mad at her devotion to his insanity. She reminded me of myself.

I looked around my new place. The whole house seemed dead, like all the air had been sucked from the rooms. I thought, being broken up isn't so bad. Losing all desire to work or eat anything other than items extracted from the cacao pod seems to be working out just fine. There's lots of great stuff on TV that I would have normally missed had I been burdened by a healthy, loving relationship. Now I could catch up on a bunch of stuff being a happy twosome had kept me from, like doing my taxes and getting a job and alphabetizing my CD collection. I couldn't catch my breath.

I aimed the remote and kept flipping channels. Why cry over

love, when I could watch reruns of Dharma and Greg?

That's when I felt it, glurp, a warm wetness between my legs and the dull ache in my lower back and ovaries. On the TV, a lady was running on the beach in a white bathing suit and smiling.

Quickly, I wiggled out of my undies and kicked them over to a laundry pile I had started in the living room, the one that Tallulah had turned into a little nest for herself. 'Off!' I snapped as I gave myself a quick wipe-down with a kitchen rag. Then I pinned the receiver between my shoulder and my ear, wadded up a bunch of towels, and held them in place with my legs to catch the flow.

I was ecstatic!

EIGHT

Radioactive (Dance Remix)

'Take the L out of Lover and it's over.'
— The Motels

'Hello?'

'Jasper? It took you so long to pick up, I was worried that something had happened to you.'

'What do you want?'

'Uh, I just wanted to call you and tell you that I just got my period.'

'I don't want to do this.'

'Well, what I wanted to say was that that's probably why I have been such a bitch lately. And, anyway, I just wanted to say I am sorry and I, uh, really hope we can work things out because I really want us to get back together. Jasper? Well, anyway, I just thought you should know. About my period. And my bitchiness. Jasper? I really wish I was saying all this to you in person. I just really miss you. I love you so much.'

'Are you done?'

'Why are you being like this?'

'Are you forgetting you left about a thousand evil messages lately? This is hard for me, too, you know.'

'Why are you crying? Are you fucking someone?'

'I gotta go.'

'I'm sorry. I just don't understand why you are doing this to me. I just don't understand why you are doing this. *Please* still love me.'

'Stop torturing me.'

'I'm sorry. Jasper? What do you want me to do?'

'I want you to say goodbye.'

'I'm trying to make sense of things, you asshole.'

'I really have to go. You obviously aren't in a place to understand or listen to me so I am going to put the phone down now.'

'Excuse me, but I would appreciate a little respect, seeing as how we just spent practically two years together, so just tell me, are you fucking someone?'

'Mer, please. I can't deal with your screaming. It's abuse, you know. Your abusive treatment of me is part of the problem.'

'Am I screaming now? No, I'm not. Are you referring to the fact that I express anger at *all*? Because in the entire two years I have known you, you have never raised your voice once, and you know something, you wear it like a fucking badge. You smoulder and say nothing and things eat away at you and then you suddenly dump me for no reason, or at least none you can articulate, and yet I'm the abusive one? Are you gay?'

'Why can't you accept that sometimes things just don't work out?'

'Just answer the question. Are you gay?'

'Why are you doing this? You are ready and I am not. We have gone as far as we can go. You are ready and I am not. That's all.'

'Stop saying that!'

'It's over.'

'But I said I'm sorry!'

'This is just too painful for me. We can be friends sometime, but just not right now.'

'Friends? *Friends*? Are you a fucking crack smoker? Just answer that one question, are you high? Are you a crack-smoking base-head? I am not your friend, *I am your girlfriend!*'

'I have to go.'

'What about this house? What about your stuff? I met your fucking parents and could still have sex with you afterwards, for Godsakes. This *has* to work!'

'I never told you to get the house in the first place.'

'You never told me not to!'

'You never gave me the chance! I have to go, Mer.'

'Is this about the sex toys?'

'It's not about the sex toys.'

'Because if it is, I'll be experimental if that's what you want. It just seemed like the type of thing you'd introduce ten years into a marriage that's falling apart. But we can do it if you want to. We can do it tonight! Jasper? Are you still here?'

'I gotta go.'

'Fuck you, Jasper. You are going to need a fucking restraining order, mister, because this thing *ain't over!!*'

I slammed the phone down before he could, slumped back down on the couch, and buried my face in my hands.

NINE

Sadie to the Rescue

'Running down a dream, that never would come to me.'
— Tom Petty and The Heartbreakers

On the TV they were showing footage of brave men who flew into the middle of deadly hurricanes to gather data about their severity. 'Storm chasers', the narrator said. They showed some shaky footage of a guy inside a noisy cockpit. I could see that he had a wedding ring on.

My own hand was shaking as I hit redial. He let his machine pick up. I called back around eight hundred more times, only getting his answering machine. My calls ranged from manic to dangerously calm. I hit redial like a pro, like I was perfecting a dance routine, ra-pa-ta-ra-pa-ta, jazz hands! Until finally the machine didn't pick up anymore. He must have unplugged the phone. I wondered if I was going crazy. I wondered if it was really possible to die from a broken heart. I wondered how long it might take.

The amazing thing was that I was proud of Jasper for listening to and following his inner voice because I know that's the hardest thing in the world actually to do. I just didn't understand why his inner voice wanted him to dump me, while my inner voice was convinced we should be married and have a batch of children, asap.

I decided I wasn't only mad at Jasper, I was mad at God, too; I felt abandoned by both of them.

I could really feel the cramps starting up. The paper towel rubbed the soft flesh of my inner thighs, and made a scratching sound as I made my way to the bedroom. Penguin-like, I flung myself on my bed.

Get a grip, Mer, I thought, think only bad thoughts. Remember his meat BO, butt acne and the male patterned baldness on his legs, not to mention the actual legs. How about the crust in his eyelashes; are you going to miss that? How about his reign-of-bathroom-terror stench? Can he cook? No, he can't. We know he doesn't bathe. What's so good about him? I screamed at myself inside my head, 'Shut up! I just love him, OK?'

I rolled over and lay perfectly still. There and then I decided not to brush my teeth ever again. If I couldn't be with Jasper, I didn't want to be with anyone, so who cared if my teeth rotted out of my head?

That's when the doorbell rang.

'Open up. I know you're in there. I can hear the TV, Mer, so open up.' Sadie.

I tiptoed back into the living room, and quietly slid the phone a safe distance away. Evidence. Then I made my way to the front door, the tips of my bathrobe ties dragging across the polished hardwood floors. Tallulah followed me with a wagging tail. At the door I adjusted the paper-towel wad between my legs, wrapped my robe around me tight and opened the peephole. Sadie cocked an eyebrow. I pulled on the brass handle and opened the door. My eyes stung from the brightness of the daylight. I blinked and squinted and tried to keep them open.

'Hi, Sade,' I said, forcing a smile.

'You look like shit.'

'I know.' I let my head fall forward.

Sadie rushed the short distance and gently rested my head on her shoulder and began stroking my hair. Her blonde hair smelled like honeysuckle. She let me stay like that until her red cardigan was soaked. Some strands from her sweater made my raw nose itch. I backed away.

'How's the transitioning going, Mama?' she said, holding my

chin in her hand. 'OK?' I nodded. Sadie pushed past me and threw her purse on the couch, and spun around to get a good look at the place. She looked at the TV, looked at me, and slapped the poor defenceless OFF button. I watched a soap opera hunk with a blond pompadour beg forgiveness and suddenly disappear into darkness. 'Really, Mer.' Then she beelined past me and headed for a box in the hall. She dumped out the contents: mismatched socks, a pair of tan suede roller skates I've worn twice, a kazoo, a box of cotton balls, a tin of Band-Aids, a broken, wire hanger, an empty CD case. She put the empty box in the centre of the living-room floor and headed for the black flannel fitted sheet I was using as a curtain.

'What are you doing?' I shrieked.

'Letting the stench of death out.' She threw open a window, more light came in. I recoiled like a vampire. 'Aaaahhh!'

She scanned the room briefly and headed for the bedroom closet. I followed her. Tallulah followed me. She began gathering up Jasper's T-shirts and boxers and trousers. A pair of green and purple Argyll socks fell to the floor. Even with the growing stack in her arms, she knelt down to retrieve them. She wasn't fucking around.

I windmilled my arms. 'No, Sadie! What are you doing?'

'I came over here to redecorate and to help you find the will to live.'

'That old thing? I lost it a while back.' I sounded like an old, soused, embittered movie actress from the forties.

'Why don't we look for it?' she said, pulling Jasper's clothes off their hangers. 'We can just make divining rods out of wire hangers like your mom used to have you do when she couldn't find her car keys.' I swung at her and missed. She ducked, and the clothes fell to the floor. That was the most exercise I had had in days.

'You know the rules. Number one, throw away everything that reminds you of him.' She counted the information out on her bony fingers. 'Number two,' she made a backward peace sign, 'throw away any article of clothing that you would not want him to see you in.' I focused on her knuckles. I never noticed how pink her hands were. 'Number three, pay attention, Mer, do something new every day, something that you've never done before. Today, I suggest washing your hair. With shampoo.' She emphasized the poo part. I wanted her to read aloud from *Winnie the*, and call it a day. 'And number four, *no TV*! If we must turn to the outside, we deal only in cinema.' She swept her palms together, swish swish, like she was dusting them off. 'I suggest you merely pretend your life is a movie, and recast. What you need is a nice rebound screw with a new leading man.'

'You're disgusting, you know that?'

'Why, because I tell you the truth? What you need is a great orgasm from a new guy, or a great orgasm and no guy. Either way, this calls for screaming Os.'

I glared at her. 'What I *need* is Jasper back.'

'For Godsakes, Mer, he's a Cancer with a Virgo rising and a Gemini moon. You knew it was only a matter of time.' She headed unflinchingly towards my bulletin board. I flipped her the bird behind her back. She started extracting photos of him I had tacked to the cork, and along my desk, haphazardly throwing him in the cardboard box.

'Whoa whoa *whoa!*'

'Now, now, trust me on this one, Mer. We are going to have a nice little funeral for him. I will not stand by and watch him suck the life force out of you. From now on this box is a coffin.'

'Wait a minute!' I rushed towards her and tried to pry the photos from her dainty fingers. 'I don't like the way you're manhandling him.'

She fought back hard, guarding them close to her chest. 'I never thought he was right for you, anyway. Too passive. Screw him.'

I stepped back. 'What's that supposed to mean?'

'It's not like anybody liked him. Your family only put up with him because you were *in love*. Please! You put up with this kind of bullshit from someone wonderful, Ben Affleck maybe, but not Jasper Husch.' She deposited the photos in the box and headed for the kitchen. I followed her. I could hear Tallulah's little nails trailing behind me.

'But, but . . .'

'The truth hurts,' she said, dangling the little teacup Jasper had hand-painted for me for my birthday last year (when he still cared), from her pinkie finger. 'But don't kill the messenger.' She dropped it in the box.

'Not the cup!' I collapsed in a dramatic heap. I lay down on the cool linoleum of the kitchen floor with black and white squares like a chequerboard. Tallulah licked my hair. I pushed her away. She nudged her sticky chew toy my way and I sat up and leaned against the stove. I thought, why, God, why me?

'At least he lives in another city. You can make a clean break.'

'That *other city* was my salvation from this hell-hole. *That* city is real life. *This* city is illusions and lies.' I stood up and followed her around like a basketball safety.

'Please! What are you talking about? You told me your self-esteem plummeted every time you got to that city because everyone there is gay.'

'Well, um, yes, that's true. I do feel like no guys want me there, but still! It's an incredible city, with a ton of opportunities to—'

'Then why didn't you move *there*?'

'Because, because,' I stammered, 'my work's *here*! I mean honestly, Sadie.' She shot me a look that bore straight through to the core of me. We both knew I could do voice-overs anywhere. Maybe she was right. Maybe I fucked it all up. Should I have tried life there instead? Maybe Jasper wasn't the one who was afraid of commitment. Maybe I was. I don't know how long I was silent. 'Just get out,' I said wearily.

Sadie made a face and started to say something, but then thought better of it. She just turned, walked into the living room and grabbed her purse off the couch.

'Sorry,' I said.

'That's OK,' she said, pretending to be interested in her car keys, 'maybe I'm being too rough.' I watched her study the teeth of a shiny silver one, fingering the edge of it. Then she put them in her sweater pocket and looked at me. 'I just hate seeing you like this. You're too good for him. You deserve someone who's going to see what I see in you, what everyone sees. He's a fucking loser, Mer.'

She looked at the white plaster ceiling and wiped mascara from underneath her lids with her middle fingers, then examined them for damage. 'Of course, if you guys get back together again, I fucking love the guy.'

I managed a small smile.

She took a tiny step towards me. 'Just promise me, if you can, promise me, whatever you do, you won't call him. At least let him come to you.' I looked down, noticed a knot in a floorboard. It looked like a woman screaming. 'OK' I said.

'Promise?'

I looked up at her. She was staring into my eyes now, searching for weakness or potential betrayal or at the very least some squirrelishness. 'Promise?'

'You will feel so proud of yourself if you don't call. If you give in, you'll feel like shit and he'll be the winner and he doesn't get to be the winner, so we have a deal, OK?'

I looked outside my kitchen window, saw a dead butterfly in a spider's web. 'OK, OK, I double-promise.'

She ran over and hugged me. 'I gotta get back to work, but I will check on you when I get a free minute.' She giggled, 'I'm supposed to be on a run for paint thinner.' Then she pulled a small parcel out of her purse. It was elegantly wrapped in heavy-looking brown organic paper, twine and some dried purple flowers. She tossed it on my couch. It landed upright. She turned back to me, a big, mischievous smile spread across her face. 'Did I mention how happy I am that we are both single together?' She was actually jumping up and down.

'Sadie, uh, hello, painful break-up alert!'

'I know, I know, but whenever you are ready to hit the town, just say the word.' She hugged me again, and we both heard a wet thud. We looked down. The home-made pad had reached its zenith and lay bloody-side up on the floor. 'What the hell is that?' Just then Tallulah came over to sniff the bloody mound. We both burst in hysterics. 'No!' Sadie shrieked gleefully.

'Off!' I snapped, still laughing. But Tulie picked it up and nearly made a clean getaway. I grabbed her by the collar and she dropped it. Sadie kicked the thing with her foot. It flew under the sofa. We erupted again. I held my sides. Sadie brushed away streaming tears from her cheeks. With Sadie's help moving the couch, I was able to retrieve it with a hanger and deposit it in the trash.

'This is so *Happiness!*' Everything was a movie to her. She air-kissed me on both cheeks. 'I gotta go. Try to stay cinematic, Mer. And for Godsakes, *don't* call him! Make this *your* decision.' And she was gone, a rainbow after a hard rain.

I stared at the door for a moment. I could do it. With Sadie's help, I could do it. The *new* plan was to make him come to me. He'd have to sweat out *me* not calling *him*.

I climbed back into bed.

'Jasper, it's me, are you there? No? OK, I love you.'

For a moment I berated myself about being weak, but I only let myself feel awful for a few minutes. Instead I reminded myself to stay cinematic about all of this, and decided, cinematically speaking, that I had been in the equivalent of a terrible car wreck and gone through the windshield and was now hospitalized in critical condition, and if, in my dementia, I cried out for my dead husband, so be it.

Then I went and picked up the package Sadie had tossed on the couch, climbed back into bed, unwrapped it, turned on a light, and began to read.

TEN

Hell or Highwater

'I am the widow of a living man.'
— Ben Harper

According to the book with the wedding ring dangling from the thorn of a rose, I was in bad shape. Sadie had given me a book entitled *How to Get Your Mate to Marry You or Move On*, and had bookmarked it with three outlined pages' worth of adventures she had planned for us over the next three months to keep my mind off one Jasper Husch, super-villain. The list of activities ambitiously included white-water river-rafting, karaoke, tap-dance lessons, horseback-riding, a cooking course in Italy, a painting course in Spain, an archaeological dig in Israel, miniature golfing, go-karting, therapy and yoga. Ick. On the inside flap of the flimsy paperback, in pink sparkly ink, she had inscribed, 'This book is my *Bible!* Love Sadiepop'. I adjusted the giant sanitary napkin between my legs and burrowed a little deeper under the covers.

In chapter one of The Book, written by Dr Karl Sage, Ph.D. — see smiling photo of plump doc inside back flap — it stated, 'If the person wishing to make positive change to repair broken bonds and restore The Love Within™ cannot show three simple days of self-restraint, i.e. not calling long enough to Let Love Lick Its Wounds™, then the fractured relationship is indeed irreparably doomed.' I read on.

His programme was a one-two punch: Out With The Old And In With The You™: 'you must be on strictest watch for ninety days.' I thought, can I give Jasper Husch ninety days? No problem. 'In addition, try new things! Do something you've always wanted to do Once And For You™. And for both your sakes, have fun because a happier you means a better weeeeee!' Next to all this was a tiny photo of the jolly doctor with someone whom I presumed to be Dr Karl's wife, on a roller coaster with their hands in the air. I scratched at it with my finger, smelled the cheap paper. Jasper and I never did dumb fun stuff like go to amusement parks. I read on.

In chapter two of The Book, it stated that there needed to be a masculine giver, a feminine receiver or else both parties had to remain androgynous in order to ensure Lasting Love™. The FemRe was supposed to respect her mate's ideas and *wait* for the MasGi to cherish her feelings. It made no difference if the receiver was male or female, but no relationship would work if you had both. I thought, of course! I had been the masculine giver *and* feminine receiver all along. It was uncanny, I was a *type*! If only I had found this book sooner, Jasper and I would be sending out applications to pre-schools. If I wanted to be the girl in the relationship I had to relearn certain things, like how to sit around and *wait* for the MasGi to give; in other words, I had to make *no* overtures of any kind and *wait* for Jasper to come to me. OK, can do.

I would know if the relationship was salvageable within nine weeks. Perfect, I thought, secure in the knowledge that Jasper would crumble, because even if Jasper managed to avoid me for eight and a half weeks, my birthday fell within the nine-week window. He wouldn't be able to resist my birthday.

Several testimonials in The Book bolstered my confidence because 'literally dozens' of the RMs™ (retrained males) actually turned around and proposed within the first month when they felt their female counterparts retreat. Ah, but would I say yes? Maybe yes, maybe no. Maybe yes. I let out a little squeal.

When you broke it down, all I had to do was get over the initial hurdle of three short days, and the next eight weeks and twenty-seven days would be eazy-breezy-telekinezey! When you broke it right down, about three thousand complete listens to an Alanis Morissette album, plus sleeping in late, would pretty much do the trick. I skipped to the end and read on.

In some rare but extreme cases, Dr Karl recommended total abstinence for The Wounded Heart™ in the form of lengthy silent retreats to derail and totally incinerate those feelings and patterns which magnetized only pain. I shuddered, thinking about all the losers that had it that bad. Out loud I said, 'That will never be me.'

I closed the book, held it to my heart and let out a deep sigh of relief. Then I called Sadie and left a message on her machine thanking her up and down, saying that it was just the kick in the ass I needed, and that I could completely see why it was her Bible, because now it was mine too and weren't we lucky to have Dr Sage and each other. Then, without hesitation, I got up and ran to my bathroom to look at myself in the mirror, to look myself straight in the eye and make a promise that very minute: America Ludmilla Odin Throne, you will get Jasper Husch back come hell or high water, even if it means having the discipline *not* to call him to win him back. You will find the strength to have zero contact with him at all costs.

I got goosebumps! I felt like a spy on a secret, important mission to save the world. I felt like I had a purpose. Then I kissed the mirror, spotted and dealt with a blackhead I had missed that needed extracting, climbed back in bed and called Jasper.

'Hello?'

'Hi!'

'I asked you not to call me.'

'I know, I know. I just called to tell you I won't be calling you any more, well, at least, not for a while.'

'You're calling me to tell me you aren't going to call me?'

'Well, uh, yes, when you put it that way ... I just ... I just don't want you to think I'm abandoning you because I'm not. It's just something I need to do for me.'

'OK.'

'I mean . . . I just need to disappear for a while . . . Also I thought you might want to get an extremely helpful book called—' I looked at the book now, turned it over in my hand, shitty font in shitty ink on shitty paper; it all seemed so pitiful, suddenly. I felt all the blood drain from my body. 'Well, it's kind of got a cheesy title, something like Getting Love or Moving On or something by this guy Dr Karl Sage . . . Anyway, never mind, but, yunno, it's pretty helpful . . .'

'Well good, thanks.'

'So how are you?'

'I gotta go.'

'Yeah, well, OK, me too. Well take care of yourself.'

'Yeah, you too.'

'Well, bye.'

I slammed the phone down so hard Tulie jumped.

I sank down under the blankets, covered my eyes with The Book and decided to sleep it all off like a bad dream, but not ten minutes later my mother stopped by, out of the blue, 'just to say hello, as I was nowhere near your neighbourhood!'

She was wearing a dress with a Chinese dragon print and red lace-up high-heeled shoes. She managed to look somewhat dressed up, save some blotches of pink cream all over her face. 'What the hell is that stuff?' I said, climbing back under the covers.

'Calamine lotion mixed with calendula and aloe. Camphor is great for tightening the pores. That's a terrific book you're reading. Really helpful,' she said, pointing. Then she pulled out three chocolate cream puffs from a wax paper bag, three because she was superstitious and could only eat things in odd numbers, and arranged them on a china plate which she had retrieved from my kitchen. She sat down on the edge of my bed. Her roots needed dyeing. Since my father's death she had made a commitment to a certain shade of auburn. Firehouse Red, I believe they call it.

'You went out like that?'

'Who do I have to impress? Fuck 'em if they can't take a joke.' She bit into a cream puff and recoiled like she had been socked in the stomach, trying to catch the white goo that snuck out the back with a cupped hand. 'Mmm!' She held hers out for me to take a bite. 'Don't you want?'

I made a sour face and rolled over on to my side. I clutched the lapels of my bathrobe.

'I'd really love it if you came over and helped me organize your father's room.' I hated when she called it that. She meant his art studio. The way she said it made it sound like it was the fifties and they were divorced but still lived in the same house. I didn't answer her.

'America, you really have to pull it together here and stop being so selfish.' I heard the clunk of the cream puff as it landed on the dish and felt the bed give way a little when she stood up and left the room, taking the delicate china plate with her. I heard the fridge door open and close with a vacuum kiss, the jingle of car keys, her high heels against the hardwood floor, Tulie's nails click-clicking behind her, then the sound of the front door opening and closing and the engine of a car starting up.

Fuck you, I thought.

Then I made my way to the kitchen and retrieved the puffs. I set the dish aside and lined them up on my kitchen counter, leaned against my stove and ate them one after the other. That's when I saw the envelope my mother had left lying on the smooth white tile. Enclosed was an article she had neatly clipped from the *LA Times* about how the depression of one family member negatively affects the rest of the family, that and my blood-money cheque for a thousand dollars.

ELEVEN

August

'Thank you disillusionment, thank you frailty, thank you
consequence, thank you silence.'
— Alanis Morisette

Sadie brought more clothes than she needed for those first three
nights. Unsure as to whether or not I could endure the remaining
62 days, 11 hours and 48 minutes, I enlisted her expert help.

Dressed in grey sweats, a white tank top that said 'Bitch
Goddess' and blue Converse slip-on tennis shoes, Sadie transformed my living room into 'a safe workspace'. She lit a candle and
spread out a bunch of newspapers and art supplies, including a
blank spiral sketchpad, glitter, crayons, coloured markers, glue
sticks and a stack of magazines for collage making.

Sadie pulled two cushions off the couch and motioned for me
to join her on the floor. Reluctantly, I sat down. She put a black
disposable fine-point felt-tip ink pen in my hand and began.
'Chapter one, question one: what did your Primary Annihilators™
(your parents) teach you about love and how is this similar to what
you learned from your current partner?'

'I really don't see how writing any of this down will—'

'Just do it, Mer. See how I did mine?'

Sadie showed me her journal with the sparkly gold glitter cover.
Pages and pages of longhand answers to impossible questions. She

had graphs and pie charts and collages and quotes and affirmations and articles and photographs and dried leaves and a calendar of tasks including things she had eaten, a happy-face sticker for good days, a frowning-face sticker for bad days. She had gone the extra mile and had a little gold star on the pages for the days she masturbated, pink shiny hearts for what she called 'duty dates', red ones for 'real dates', and silver hearts for 'wink-wink, nudge-nudge' dates. Mostly her book had all four. 'For extra credit,' she said wickedly, 'it just helps take the edge off.' It's strange how you think you know a person; Sadie with her book and Jasper with his lies.

'Ready?' asked Sadie, book poised.

'Wait, what was the question again?'

She rolled her eyes. 'Just write down what you hate about Jasper on one column, and what you hate about your father on the other.'

'Sadie, this is bullshit.'

'How do you think I got my amazing job, and why do you think I have the patience to hold out for my dream man? This isn't just about dating, it's about finally living.' She flipped her hair behind her ears. 'Now start writing.'

I stared at the black page, took a deep breath, then wrote:

The Things I Hate about Jasper Husch:
1   His slowness
2   His silence
3   His underground anger
4   His selfishness
5   His false self
6   His false love, e.g. Guava
7   His lack of communication
8   His lack of honesty
9   His starfuckerness
10   His timing
11   His fear
12   His lack of cleanliness
13   His covertness

14 His wishy-washiness e.g. money hoarding
15 His lack of commitment
16 His lack of loyalty
17 His lack of follow-through
18 His spiritual cluelessness, dishonesty & false piousness
19 His lack of sensitivity
20 His sex toys
21 His cats

Then, on the other half of the page, I listed:

The Things I Hate about My Father:
1 His cheating
2 His lack of attention to me in my life
3 That I heard my parents have sex all the time and that
he never made noise during sex, but my mother
sounded like she was dying while my father had no way
of communicating I mean I couldn't express my disappointment, anger, or joy and so as a result we never had
any time together, just the two of us (not even dinner
as a family) except, wait, that one time in NY, but the
restaurant owner sat with us so I don't think that
counts, in addition, I have no personal photos of him
because I knew how much it bothered him when fans
wanted his photo so none of us ever asked besides he
thought he was ugly and I look like him so I thought I
was ugly and he didn't think my mom was pretty or
valuable or why else would he cheat on her so much
and I look like her too and he cheated on her so I
chose men that needed to be babied and coddled and
felt weird when they tried to do things for me I mean
we had zero boundaries anyhow so how could I be
grateful for tiny gestures like the time I gave Jamie Nye
a blow job out of gratitude because he pulled a chair
out for me and got my coat he wanted sex and I wanted
him to leave so I blew him. Thanks dad.

I looked up at Sadie seriously. 'Next question, please.' My arm felt like a wind-up toy that needed to keep going.

That night Sadie slept beside me in my big bed built for two and I managed my first restful night's sleep in days.

The next day Sadie phoned from work every eleven seconds to make sure I was all right, and to monitor my every move to ensure I did not even think about phoning Jasper.

By day three we had already been to the museum, miniature golfing and spent a drunken evening karaoking Billy Idol songs until 3 a.m. I got a standing ovation from three Korean businessmen after a heartfelt rendition of 'Rebel Yell'. Even though I was sad and missed Jasper like crazy, I just kept thinking, 'Let love lick its wounds, let love lick its wounds'. I imagined Jasper licking his big lazy-ass paws after eating the fucking gazelle I killed.

I carried that book with me everywhere I went. All the while I read and reread and dog-eared and highlighted and underlined so I could master that sacred book.

The rest of August went like this:
Tuesday August 15: Go to batting cages with Sadie after work.

Wednesday August 16: Go to voice-over audition for more leg-room on commuter flights.

Later, go on duty date with self and play Miss Pac Man at local bowling alley. Get hit on by guy who sprays disinfectant into returned bowling shoes.

Thursday August 17: Get manipedi with mother in fancy salon. End up buying 120 dollars' worth of skincare products I'll never use.

Friday August 18: Go roller-skating in Venice. Start to feel like old self a little. The self I was before I ever met Jasper.

Later, go to pier to ride Ferris wheel. Catch obnoxious couple making out in front of me. Feel like piece of shit because Jasper doesn't want me; despise sloppy couple in precariously dangling car for being in love. Wish their death, fear my own for wishing theirs.

Think about Jasper's hairline, behave.

Back on ground, eat cotton candy, feel better.

Saturday August 19: Have picnic with self in park. Finish rereading section on Trying New Things. Deeply understand importance of putting my energy back into *me*. When get to part about starting with things I've always secretly wanted to do but was too afraid to dare try, realize answer is *art*.

Decide to keep journal chronicling all the hours Jasper and I endure apart complete with watercolours, photos, and favourite poems. Take entire weekend to work on with impunity because in heart *know* that someday Jasper and I will be together again, and he would more than appreciate how I kept the faith alive, in spite of hardship of time and distance apart.

Take (and later glue in) several Polaroids of myself. Start to get a little crush on self. Under sexy photos of self dressed like Vegas showgirl, write: 'You may be seeing this now and feel bad you hurt me, but don't because making this journal has helped me love *me*. PS Can you believe you wanted to leave all this?' Feel, thanks to The Book, I am really changing for the better in ways I cannot see.

Monday August 21: Zip over to casting office on Sepulveda for voice of Morticia Adams-type widow on black-comedy cartoon kid show called *Good Mourning!*.

On way home, stop by Spoonie's work at paint store under guise of saying hi, when really need to pee before facing rush-hour traffic. End up helping him mix paint colours and hearing endless details of show I missed. Bo-ring.

Pop in nearby crappy frame store, buy and later glue postcard of Chagall's *The Lovers* on top of journal. Get brainstorm! Decide to *send* said journal to Jasper, to remind him of how happy we once were. Remember vital to keep secret from Sadie. Congratulate self because not phoning. Remind self to suggest we both keep one and send it back and forth to keep our love alive together.

Go to Staples and spend rest of savings on necessary materials. Stay up all night making damn thing. Stare at and glue in photos, saved notes, movie and concert stubs, etc. Fall madly in love with him all over again. On the inside flap of the top-secret love vigil *livre d'or* write and even mean, 'No matter what happens, even if we are not together, I just want you to be happy.' Sign it, 'Bugs and Fishes Mer'. Fall asleep with smile on face.

Tuesday August 22: Have awesome sex dream that we are back together. Get up in best mood for the first time in weeks. Go to Kinko's to Fed Ex *it*. Do *not* tell Sadie.

Wait by phone for reply.

Wednesday August 23: Wait by phone for reply. Wonder if he is out of town? Wonder if it got lost in the mail? Wonder if someone stole it and saw the naked Polaroid? Call Jasper and leave message asking if he got it.

Later see Spoonie's band and secretly check messages from club 72 times. Come home to *no* messages. Eat chocolate. Pick skin. Scream at Tallulah. Fall asleep in pool of snot in too squishy pillow.

Thursday August 24: Wait by phone for reply.

Later have coffee with Sadie at French café on La Brea. Notice bald girl there is so pretty. Bet Jasper would want her. Bet Jasper is fucking someone exactly like her now. Hate her. Spill guts to Sadie. 'Writing is contact. Now you have to start the whole nine weeks over!' Fuck. Fuck Fuck. Fine. Cry so hard on drive home, almost get in accident.

Come home to a steaming pile of shit. Wonder: does my house smell like dog? Is that why he left me. Drive to store for ammonia. Eat entire bag of miniature Reese's. Refuse to brush teeth. Fall asleep watching late-night talk shows.

Friday August 25, 4.00 a.m.: Discover Jasper has switched over to voice-mail. Leave screaming message demanding return phone call even though cannot disturb his sleep the way he disturbs mine. Burn. Fume. Plot. Become murderously irate. Bombard Jasper with messages, e-mail and faxes demanding collage love journal back, plus all previous letters, photos, etc. asap.

Call Jasper and apologize for screaming messages. Calmly explain he has until sunrise to put things right with me, otherwise no more me... ever. Reiterate he has until sunrise to accept my offer. Hang up and scream at Tallulah for making licking sound.

Friday August 26, evening: Go on dumb voice-over audition for Red Bull beer. Forced to say 'Aicarumba! It's double-hopped!' Imagine Jasper being speared to death by bull's antler or tusk or whatever, and hopelessly paraded around in coliseum somewhere in Spain. Hear sound effect of crowd cheers in headphones. Feel good about audition.

Go home, check messages. Finding none, poorly rig TV so I can watch from bed. Watch disturbing *Oprah*.

See ultra-sincere black-toothed guy with the 10-90, ten-per-cent hair on the top, ninety per cent in the back, discuss the willingness to love. Find it disgusting the way he fawns all over his Shelly Duvall-esque girlfriend. Become rotten with jealousy they look so happy, and because guy is more emotionally available than Jasper, and because he calls his girlfriend 'm'lady' and her private parts 'her radiant temple'. Then declares he is honoured to worship there and displays her name tattooed on his chest to prove it. Feel utter disgust.

Call Sadie and confess everything. Beg her to sleep over. While waiting for her to arrive, pretend I am a dead body at scene of very bloody crime. Pretend I am also the detective. Speak into invisible tape recorder in fakey Raymond Chandler-esque accent: 'The body has been identified as belonging to one America Throne, note the cellulite on the thighs, like the wing of an airplane caught in a severe hailstorm, and that the birthmark on her ass that looks like Italy. Pompeii maybe.' Get distracted by sudden influx of Pompeii imagery. Think about all the beauty that was lost and the fear and futility those people must have felt. Think: all that beauty and then *whammo*! Volcanic surprise. Recognize am in a severe depression when use phrases like 'whammo'. Wonder if I am going crazy.

When Sadie arrives, get extensive lecture. Resolve to focus on me, my work and to, gulp, try *exercising* for a change.

Later burn arm on oven rack trying to make baked potato.

Saturday August 27: Begin Day One all over again. Take small walk with Tulie around block three days in a row. Feel *strong*. Decide: will never take Jasper back, *ever*.

Hear Tallulah stretch and relax, letting out an adorable high-pitched little breathy yawn. Thank God for her. Cry because I love her so much. Hold Tulie close, even though making soul-crushing licking sound.

Later get phonecall, find out booked dumb beer voiceover. Thank God again. Begin working on Mexican accent. Eat Mexican food for dinner.

Tuesday August 30: Record radio spot. Feel like a human again. Smile at people. Take a walk for the first time in aeons. Notice the way light hits plants and trees. On drive home hear mine and Jasper's song. Sing along to Journey's 'Open Arms'. Go home to zero messages. Resist *strong* temptation to call Jasper and beg him to come back now that I'm making the sweet green again. Instead, doodle self-portrait in black ink on white paper:

I am a fat skeleton monster lady with spots and scales and flippers and pimples and ingrown hairs and rolls and rolls of stomach fat. I have squinty, piggy eyes with dark junkie circles under them and my teeth are rotted, blacked out and covered in chocolate. I am waving hello with one hand and clutching a wad of steaming shit in the other. A giant erect cock is sticking out of my ass, bloody at the end where I tore it away from Jasper's body. I stand under a childlike palm tree and some twinkling stars.

Underneath it all I had written: *Another Fucking Day in Paradise.*

TWELVE

Radioactivate (Radio Edit)

'Can you help me I'm bent.'
>   – Matchbox Twenty

'Hey, Jas, it's me. Are you there? Pick up if you're there.'

THIRTEEN

Rock Bottom Jesus

'It is time for you to stop all of your sobbing.'
— Pretenders

Madame Barbara's House of Mystery is shabby and white and located in Venice. That should have been clue number one. Venice! The next clue should have been the 'sign' that announced a mere fifteen bucks for a life reading, written backwards on the inside of the front window of a filthy, dilapidated beach house, ironically, in soap. Spoonie covered his hand with his T-shirt and opened the door.

Earlier that morning, Spoonie had received a threatening call from Sadie that I was on death watch and had to be monitored constantly. She informed him that it was his duty as a brother to take me out to have a good time. She had given him implicit instructions to take me to the best psychic in town, information she received from the ditzy lead actress of *Beddy-bye for Betty*, a horror film about a babysitter who gets stalked by the demonic children she sits for. Since Spoonie had a crush on the vixen lead, Sadie promised a meeting in exchange for good behaviour, i.e. dragging me to Venice. So, when he pulled up in his inherited cherry-red convertible T-bird and honked twice (a trade our father had made for one of his paintings even though he refused to get a driver's licence), I half-heartedly ran down the steps to greet him.

His wheat-coloured Beatles haircut was still wet. It framed his face in damp, photo-ready points. He was wearing big, droopy Hawaiian-print shorts and a white V-neck. It could be below freezing outside, and he would still be wearing shorts. I, however, was bundled in a grey cashmere sweater and a pair of jeans. For additional warmth, my long brown hair hung down my back like a shawl.

I missed my brother. We used to be close when I was the only female ally he worshipped.

'Hey,' he said.

'Hey,' I said.

'What's that,' I said, pointing to some boxes in the backseat.

'A bunch of stuff Camilla cleared out of Dad's closet that she wants me to take to Goodwill. Which reminds me, she wants you to come over and help her clean out the office. The house is a disaster area.' I snorted through my nose, opened his car door and hopped in.

I looked up in time to see Tallulah's head peering out through the living-room window, her front paws resting on the sill. Her ears stood straight up like little black windsocks. She whimpered, 'Don't go!' I thought, probably a warning.

'Bye, Tulie!' I said.

'Bye, Bongo!' Spoonie said. He just did it to annoy me since her sight was failing and sometimes she smacked into things. Whenever he said that it made me think she would die soon.

'Doooon't.' I hate it when you call her that.' I tried to slam my door but it wouldn't close all the way. Spoonie had to get out and open it from the outside and slam it for me. I thought it was funny that it forced my lazy-ass brother to have to be a gentleman. No wonder he didn't have a girlfriend. That's not true; he had one once, in tenth grade, Brittnie, but after that he played the field. Lots of girls whose name ended in '-ie': Lizzie, Kimmie, Sophie . . . At least he had the decency to be a serial monogamist. That's a trait we both adopted in the wake of our dad's exploits.

Now we sat side by side on a plastic-covered floral-print couch in Venice, next to some five-foot fake plastic trees. A sign on the coffee table next to the full-to-overflowing mother-of-pearl ashtray said No Smoking. The stained, light-brown carpeting had the faint odour of flea powder and watermelon-scented bubble gum.

The first visible door was closed and had a pilfered plastic hotel Do Not Disturb sign hanging from the knob. The second door had a *Blair Witch*-esque wreath of dried flowers and twigs hanging from a carpet tack, and a small wooden sign underneath that said 'Healing Room' in blood red.

Spoonie now had his T-shirt over his mouth so he wouldn't breathe in the bacteria-infested air that he imagined he was being exposed to. Spoonie is a germ freak. When we initially entered the place, a large cluster of bells announced us but now, sitting here for nearly eleven unattended minutes, we began to wonder if anyone was even home. Then we heard a muffled cry coming from behind the second closed door. A man's low moans. Spoonie looked at me then, and through his one-hundred-per-cent-cotton T-shirt announced, 'Mer, let's go.'

'I thought you wanted to meet that girl?'

'I do, but come on, this place is a shit-hole.' Spoonie stood up and his legs made a suction sound from the plastic against his skin. I knew the germs that now clung to the hairs on the backs of his legs were the only thing on his mind now.

Suddenly the Healing Room door opened and an elderly, crying man with a fedora in his hand was escorted out by a nodding woman who looked like a cross between a gag version of a Hallowe'en witch and a gag version of a gypsy. White Nike running shoes snuck out from underneath the hem of her 'traditional' black and purple fortune-telling garb. 'Your wife loved you very much,' she said, in a fakey-sounding Count Dracula accent. She had eyes like Nicolas Cage, eerie green with long black lashes. They flickered when she saw us – fresh meat. Spoonie and I froze.

She stood in the doorway, guarding the dimly lit room, then held her arm out, opening and closing her long-fingernailed hand for instructions. By aiming that hand at the front door, the old man knew it was time for him to go. As the cluster of bells announced the crying man's departure, she aimed that hand at the room behind her and bade us enter.

'Please seet down,' said Madame Barbara. We did, on two black metal folding chairs. The room was painted black and had a purple lava lamp in the corner, and a turning metal light that threw blurry stars around the room. Glow-in-the-dark orange and fuchsia flowers with lime-green leaves sprang up from the baseboards. On the wall in a glass display case was a collection of small animal skeletons and some larger animals' jawbones. The small round table in front of us was covered in black felt and heavy tapestry fabric. Before us, spread in a fan around a crystal ball on a black base, were some shark's teeth, a grey and white feather, a rose-quartz crystal and a Starbucks egg-timer in the shape of a coffee percolator, which she set for fifteen minutes.

'You vont life reading?' said Madame Barbara.

'Uh, yeah,' I said.

'The both?'

Spoonie chimed in, 'No, just her.'

'Bystander, huh?' said Madame Barbara seductively. 'Are you the boyfriend?' Spoonie managed to look frightened *and* annoyed.

'I'm the brother.'

She leaned in close to him. 'Oh, so I am right. Boy. Friend.' She laughed. We were so uncomfortable, we laughed, too.

She closed her eyes and began rubbing her palms together. Spoonie took this opportunity to glare at me. She made a sound like she had a bad taste in her mouth and then her eyes popped suddenly open. 'You 'ave question for Madame Barbara?'

'Uh, I guess I just want to know the status of my current relationship. When we're going to get back together.'

'Is over?'

I looked at her. 'That's what I want to find out.'

She nodded. 'I understand. Is over?' She aimed the hand at me, then closed it.

I bit my lip and looked at Spoonie, help! then back at Madame Barbara. 'That's what I'm asking.' I said it more slowly this time. 'I'm asking if my relationship's over.'

Madame Barbara rolled her eyes and exhaled. 'I'm telling you, is

over? You understand, over? Vinish? Gaput? No more? All gone?
Poof! Wanish? Ze end? Do you know zis? *The end*?' My face
reddened because I understood two things now: 'One, Is over?'
meant is over with Jasper, and two, she answered every question
with a question.

'Next information job?' Madame Barbara pointed the hand at
me again.

'What?' I said.

'Is *job*?' She peered into the crystal ball, looked at me, nodding.
'Is good job come?'

'*Is* good job come?' I asked her.

'I think that's her answer,' Spoonie translated. He looked at her.
'Is that your answer?'

She smiled at him. 'Yes? Is good job come?'

I got wise. '*When* is good job come?'

'Soon?' she said.

'Soon,' I said.

'Soon,' Spoonie repeated. I was beginning to get upset. Even
fifteen bucks seemed like a giant waste to hand over to the
charlatan scam artist with vague one-word queries.

'Oh, never mind,' I said. 'I don't care about work, what about
love? Can I win Jasper back?' Spoonie stared at me disapprovingly.
'Look again, OK?' I pointed to the crystal ball.

She forcefully slammed the whammy hand down on the table,
and the objects jumped. She picked up a shark tooth with the other
hand. 'Is over?' she said louder, showing me the tooth as proof
somehow. My lips began to quiver. Small waterfalls cascaded down
my cheeks. She put the tooth down. Madame Barbara pursed her
lips. 'I do you favour, you know sell mate?'

'What?'

'Sell mate? Sell mate?' she implored.

I looked at Spoonie. 'Is she saying cell-mate? Are you saying cell
mate?'

We looked back at Madame Barbara. She shook a scolding
finger at us.

'Sell mate. Yunno, maaanny mans?'

97

'Oh,' I said. 'Soulmate!'

Madame Barbara smiled. 'Yes, sell mate. Sell mate is come. Bat bee carfull. He is come vit rose. Maybe is mother? Maybe 'ee give? Maybe 'ee tell you story ov? *This* one is sell mate. The one vit rose is sell mate? But *most* important,' she leaned in close, 'you get real therapist to trace origin of childhood wounds.' Then she leaned back and shouted, 'Vinish.' The egg-timer went off. She smiled. Then clapped her hands once as if she were closing a book, then looked at Spoonie who had already stood up with a metal squeak. She pointed The Hand at him and aimed him back towards the squeaky chair – 'You?'

'No thanks.'

'You,' she said again. It was a statement this time. He put his hands in his pockets and sat back down. 'You vont eeling I give?' Before Spoonie could answer, Madame Barbara closed her eyes and made a scratching sound at the back of her throat. It sounded like a baby pig was trapped in her mouth. Spoonie held his breath. I bit the inside of my cheek.

Then, without warning, she began to belch loudly. A series of small burbles, followed by one thunderous, extended roar. Spoonie covered his mouth and pinched his nostrils shut. I bit my lip trying to stave off hysteria, and tasted blood.

'Ahhhhh,' she said, opening her eyes. Then she clapped her hands once and announced, 'Vinish. Very good beerp mean very good 'eeling.' She held out her palm, 'Fifty doll-hair.' Spoonie and I stared at each other.

'Excuse me', I said, 'but the sign said it was fifteen dollars for a life reading.'

'Plus 'eeling, plus exdra. Beerp is exdra.' She said shrewdly.

'But what exactly did you just do?' I asked.

'Eel your 'art.' She pounded on her breastbone, then held out her palm again.

'The beerp is exdra?' said Spoonie angrily. 'What if we don't want exdra?' I grabbed Spoonie by the arm.

'Exdra is for 'er,' said Madame Barbara wearily, 'to lift blanket of darkness.' My brow furrowed.

'Then what did I get?' asked Spoonie.

Madame Barbara beamed. 'True hop-penis.'

I forked over the cash and she escorted us to the door. 'No worry,' she said. 'Your father is protect the both. The flower too.' It sounded like flow-er. I assume she meant our mother. I got goosebumps.

Once outside, we ran back to our parked car at full speed. Our laughter travelled into a nearby parking garage and ricocheted back to us, and for a moment, it was true, I felt happiness. In the full light of day, in the fullness of my laughter, my darkness had indeed lifted. Spoonie started up the engine. 'Do you think she's right?' I asked as we turned up Abbot Kinney and headed towards Venice Boulevard.

'As far as Jasper's concerned, I know she is,' he was still laughing when he said it. I stopped laughing.

'Are you trying to hurt my feelings?'

He got in the left lane and turned on his blinker. 'Mer, Jesus, I'm not gonna lie to you. I talked to him. He told me himself.' His words were a slap.

'What do you mean? You talked to him? When?'

'It's over.'

'What do you mean, you talked to him?'

'You knew I was thinking about him for some album art.'

'That was when we were going out. He dumped me, so you're dumped too.'

He turned left on Lincoln, then right on to the 10 freeway. 'Don't be stupid. I wouldn't make you do that.'

I looked at him incredulously. 'Yeah, because I'd never put you in that position. Because I would never try to be friends with someone who ripped your heart out.'

'Get a fucking job.'

'Fuck you.'

'You know what your problem is? You have no purpose, no vision for your *self*. You take money off Camilla and define yourself by whoever you're dating.'

I crossed my arms at my chest. 'What the fuck are you talking about? You get the same allowance I do, you just have a job at the dumb paint store to *hide* the fact that you're just as privileged as I am.' My hair whipped around me like a stampede. I tried to wrestle it into two knots about my ears.

'At least I save my money for my real career, thank you very much. While you're out buying furniture or ordering food in, waiting around for someone to give you a job, I'm investing in myself.'

'That's totally not fair! You always knew what you wanted to be.' It was true, too; while I drew pictures of ballerinas and hula girls and hearts and flowers and unicorns and princesses locked in towers, Spoonie had drawn two things – cars and musical instruments. They gave him piano lessons at age five, a guitar at seven, by twelve he had a saxophone, drum set, a bass, a keyboard and was practically running the high-school band.

'I'm just saying, get some job until you figure it out. If nothing else, it'll boost your esteem.'

I faced him now. 'If I'm such a fuck-up and you're so great, why don't you move out!' He tightened his grip on the steering wheel, wouldn't speak.

I turned away from him and rested my chin on the passenger window. I could smell the leather oil from the side panel. The ends of my hair snapped at the corners of my eyes. We drove past a mural of anguished faces and raised fists; in the painted crowd I could pick out Rosa Parks, Malcolm X, Dr King, Che Guevara, Ghandi, and that guy with all the grapes. They knew what I was talking about.

'What?' he said.

'I didn't say anything.'

He changed lanes, exhaled loudly. 'Look,' he said calmly, 'I didn't take time off work to fight with you.'

I turned and struck like a cobra. 'No, you just took time off to meet Lila. The whole world stops for a beautiful woman, doesn't it, Spoonie? You're just like Dad!' A lie. His jaw muscles tightened.

Suddenly he changed lanes, careful to avoid rear-ending an Alfa

Romeo that darted out in front of us, then downshifted. 'All I'm saying is get over it, Mer, the guy's totally moved on. Sometimes things just don't work out.'

'Excuse me?' I said, trying to pry my car door open somewhere around the 405 interchange. Spoonie reached over and pulled my hand away.

'What the hell's the matter with you? Are you trying to kill us both?'

'Say you're sorry,' I said, swallowing hard.

He alternated between keeping his eye on the road and glaring at me. 'For what? I didn't do anything wrong.'

I stared at him incredulously, then crossed my arms tightly across my chest and sank down hard in my seat. We drove in silence the rest of the way downtown to Sadie's set for his lion's-share end of the bargain.

I closed my eyes and felt the cool of the wind against the stinging heat of my cheeks and tasted salt.

When we arrived at the set, I hopped out of the car. Without looking back I said; 'Tell Sadie I'll be right back.'

'Where are you going?'

'Nowhere.' I needed coffee.

I headed in the direction of a little place around the corner I had spotted as we pulled up. I wandered past a silver and white meal truck where a bunch of people collected lunch on brown plastic trays. Past the rented trailers with the humming engines parked near the train tracks; past big corrugated metal doors and big cement-slab walls and cracked windows and abandoned warehouses.

My father used to have a loft space down here. That was in 1979, when I was ten, during his loner phase. He used to get dropped off and stay for weeks at a time. I would help my mother prepare picnic baskets of goodies for him to take with him: liverwurst and mayonnaise sandwiches on sourdough toast, cans of tomato soup, sardines and smoked oysters in oval tins with a little key. Sometimes he would only eat one thing for weeks so he wouldn't get distracted, like spaghetti O's or tomato soup. No phone. Not when he was working. While he was gone I pretended he didn't exist, or lived in Siberia. We had the house to ourselves. That's when we could make all the noise we wanted. But when he came home we had to 'Can it, kiddos,' during the day because he was too sensitive to light and sound and needed to sleep. The art show was called *One*. It was a flop.

A plastic bag blew past me. I kept walking.

Past old lamp-posts and alleyways strewn with trash until I came to the Mom and Pop Koffee Haus, a trendy art gallery slash coffee house. A welcome mat was embedded in the sidewalk. 'Come on in,' it said. I did.

Inside, mounted on the back wall, was a giant painted portrait of a punk-rock mom and a biker dad with a handlebar moustache. Their eyes glowed with tiny flickering orange lights. On a little gilded plaque underneath it said: Mom and Pop. The floors were polished concrete. The light picked up the odd stone or splash of spattered paint. A local artist's tribute to the human vagina, in dried beans and pasta, was on display in a crudely made plywood frame. Derivative, I thought, probably a fan of my dad's. In the corner, Billie Holiday made the jukebox's neon rainbow blink on and off.

I walked up to the counter where a handsome dark-haired guy in a tattered woven cowboy hat, grey T-shirt and army pants made a perfect pitcher of frothy foam. He looked familiar. I couldn't help but stare.

'That's for here, right?'

'Excuse me?' He caught my eye and I blushed.

'Oh, I thought you were the other guy.' I noticed a massive wad of black chest hair that was protruding from his neckline. 'What'll it be?' he said as he placed two large cappuccinos in blue ceramic mugs on the counter.

'A hazelnut latte,' I blurted. It came out sounding southern, so I pretended to be looking for something in my purse, sneaking a look at the hot guy behind the counter as he ladled thick, white foam with a teaspoon without watching what he was doing.

Just then a skinny man in painter's pants, John Lennon glasses and saddle shoes put a wad of money on the counter next to the tip jar that said Support Counter Intelligence and scooped up the two cups. 'Keep the change, man.' His voice was higher than I thought it would be. 'By the way, dude, your band completely rocked the other night.' The hot guy behind the counter smiled and nodded and said, 'Thanks.' Any crush I could have on either one of them dissolved with the utterance of the word 'dude'.

The bespectacled stranger smiled at me as he turned to go. Out of the corner of my eye, I noticed he had a rose patch on the butt of his pants. I felt faint. Why wasn't I wearing make-up or something less boxy? Could either of them see my sweat stains? Could they tell I'd been crying? I pushed the thought away. I did not want to feel new feelings about guys.

'Two fifty,' said the hot counter guy as he faced me.

'You look familiar,' I said knocking over a sugar dispenser. Fine white silt covered the counter. 'OhmyGodI'msosorry. I was aiming for my drink.'

'Whoa,' he said, scooping it into his cupped hand, 'No problemo. Do you need some sugar?'

I thought, more than you know. 'No, I'd better just drink it like this. I don't really trust myself. I've had a pretty rotten day. I've had a pretty rotten month, actually. My boyfriend just dumped me.' Idiot. The words hung in the air like the stench of rotting meat. Like that time a squirrel got trapped in the bush outside Jasper's back window. We found it upside down, tangled in a patch of thorns. It must have struggled for hours before it died.

'Then this one's on me.'

'No, that's OK.' I reached inside my purse.

'No, really. Maybe that way you'll come back and you won't be a stranger next time.' He put the blue ceramic cup on the counter, along with something wrapped in a napkin. I pulled a strand of hair from one of my loopy ponytails and blushed some more. He smiled. On the juke Janis Joplin belted out, 'Freedom's just another name for nothing left to lose'. I took this as my cue to go.

I got as far as the first table when he said, 'Oh, hey, take a flyer!' He was stretching sideways across the counter. His shirt pulled up a little and I could see a small patch of black hair against the smooth, pale skin of his stomach just below his belly button, and a massive sweat stain under his right armpit. He smelled like metal. I leaned in. 'Here,' he said, handing me a small red piece of paperboard with black writing on it. I grabbed the corner of it, careful to avoid skin contact. He smelled like a man. I blushed. 'My band is playing Thursday night. Come check us out.' He slinked back in place. He rested his elbows on the counter and flopped his chin in his hands. He tapped his face with his long fingers and smiled again. I blushed some more and put the flyer in my purse without looking at it. I smiled quickly, then looked at my shoes, which were now pointed towards the door.

'Bye,' I said, when I was safely outside.

'Bye,' he shouted back.

The sun was beginning to set and made the dirty buildings look like they were made of gold. It made me think of the colours in the little paintings my father made from his trips to Italy. I walked back with my testosterone-infested cappuccino and the little wafer the cowboy gave me for free, and realized I had accidentally stolen the blue cup. I wasn't even about to go back there, not after all the dumb stuff I said about being dumped. I really missed Jasper.

'There you are! Shit!' Sadie said, loud enough for people with walkie-talkies to stop and stare. I could tell Spoonie had told her everything by the way she embarrassingly fawned all over me like a cuddly octopus.

She grabbed the napkin with the remainder of the wafer out of my hand and stuffed the treat in her mouth. 'I was looking everywhere for you. I wanted you to say hi to that producer I was telling you about, but he already left. He totally wants to meet you. I showed him that photo of you in my wallet.' Then she leaned in close and whispered conspiratorially, 'Divorced.' I was insulted.

'I happen to still be in love with someone, Sadie. I can't even *think* about someone else.' I let a punishing silence pass between us, then smiled.

I showed her the flyer from my purse. She read it through and tossed it in a large, nearby trash can.

'Sadie! I haven't even read it yet!'

'Ick. Musicians. No money!' Then Sadie looped her arm underneath mine and pulled me towards a standing wooden structure at one end of the massive, darkened, echoey, converted sound stage. 'Come along.' Just then a hot guy wearing a massive tool-belt sauntered past us and smiled.

'Jesus, it's guy central down here.'

Sadie smiled and waved at him, then pretended to be waving away something smelly in front of her nose. 'Passaroo, I tried. He's Ack Dack.'

'Sadie, as if! What's Ack Dack?'

She rolled her eyes. 'Ack Dack. AC, DC. Yunno, he swings both ways, which is slang for don't bother because he's bi.'

'Sadie!'

She swatted me lightly. 'Sheesh, don't get your knickers in a twist,' she said, leading me over big extension cords held down to the concrete floor with thick black electrical tape towards a large plywood structure. We peered around the side of it. 'Voilà!' she said, showing me the set she masterminded: a children's bedroom dripping with a thick, red, gloppy syrup, over twin bedspreads and clothes and children's books and brightly coloured building blocks.

The bloodbath had other sentimental touches like strewn shredded teddy-bear parts and limbless Barbies and a pink music box turned on its side. Its tiny dancer clumsily twirled in time to the sad, twinkly droning. The overall effect was haunting. I was impressed. It looked exactly how I felt. Thrashed.

Through a window with breakaway glass made of sugar, a lone tree branch hung from a wire in front of a giant light perched on a metal stand near a fat man eating a donut. Sadie explained that the light was covered with black mesh so that when it was lit, the branch in front of it tricked the eye and made the room appear as though it was on a second storey on a nice middle-class suburban tree-lined street.

Sadie then led me through the fake-seventies-style blood-coated living-room set. There we ran into two more hot guys in paint-splattered overalls, painstakingly making two chalk outlines on the blue AstroTurf carpeting. Two actors dressed like plain-clothes cops smoked while they waited patiently to dust for fake finger-prints.

'Wanna sit down?'

'Sure.'

'Not here, this is a hot set.'

We headed towards the catering truck now where we found Spoonie deeply engrossed in a conversation with the double-D, slightly more attractive female version of Peter Lorre in a powder-blue sweater set. She had a bloody knife sticking out of her right shoulder, which really complemented the gash above her eye and blood-drenched hairline of her shoulder-length black hair. They looked nauseatingly adorable.

Then, in a loud whisper, Sadie said to me, 'I really think you might like Jym, at least for a rebound screw.'

'Sadie!'

The actress turned and spoke up now, soft as whipped cream. 'A-B-C, 1-2-3. You always have to replace a someone with a someone.' She smiled warmly and offered up her hand for me to shake. Instead, I shot her my most evil look and, before I could be introduced, said loudly to Spoonie, 'I'll be waiting in the car.'

Later, as Spoonie and I drove away from the faux massacre in silence, I realized that my life had been reduced to hocus pocus and fake blood. I looked over at Spoonie. He looked peaceful in his twenty-two-year-old, hormone-infested rock 'n' roll universe as we sped along the ten heading west.

'That wasn't cool back there, Lila is really nice.'

'Why don't you just date Tulie, at least she has a personality.'

He looked at and through me, as evolved people who happen to be your wonderful, smarter, more together, handsome younger brother tend to do, and said, 'I see someone's in a better mood.' I just stared straight ahead.

FOURTEEN

Camel Gateaux

'F-U-C-K, is that how you spell "friend" in your dictionary?
Black on black guidebook for the blind . . .'

— XTC

The view outside my window was a pointy, pagoda-like roof and a guy banging away at an old car. That's what my neighbour does for a living. Hits that car. At least, that's what I deduced on my first day of being thirty, as I watched a shirtless, ultra-tanned, white-haired French man test to see if the metal on the one side of his maroon Ford truck from the forties was as loud as the metal on the other side.

It was.

My plan was to stay home and pamper myself, that way I'd be close to the phone in case Jasper called. He couldn't resist my birthday.

As I listened to the infernal pounding, my hopes of sleeping in late were dashed. I sat up on my knees, rested my elbows on my window sill, reached under my nightie and pulled the left side of my white cotton undies out of my ass.

At least it wasn't alarm day. That's when he enjoyed playing the 'what if' game. What if I jiggle the door handle, does the alarm go off then? Yup. What if I put my foot on the back bumper? Yup. What if I sit on the hood? Yup again. I didn't know much about car thieves, but I couldn't imagine them casually leaning against the passenger window, which, as it turns out, also set it off.

My head throbbed in time to the automotive beating. Bang bang bang. One for every day Jasper had not called or written or faxed. It didn't matter, though, because today was my birthday, he'd call.

I watched him several more minutes while he pumped away at a jack to give his truck a lift. His sixty plus breasts with the spattering of white chest hair jiggled every time his elbow came up above his shoulders. I did not need to see this at that hour. Not at 9.17 a.m. Not on my birthday.

Entering thirty with a bang, I thought, as I made earplugs out of Kleenex and sunk down onto my belly. My pillow smelled like my new peony-and-seaweed-scented shampoo, a recent purchase on a me date at Fred Segal's, along with a pre-birthday impulse pair of shiny yellow patent-leather trousers I planned to wear to dinner with my family later that night. I had bought them without bothering to try them on.

I rolled onto my back, lifted my butt, smoothed my shortie nightgown past my hips under the covers, and closed my eyes. The sun beat down on my eyelids. While the banging continued, I tried to think about peaceful things like the human heartbeat, like rain on a roof, like the ocean, then about air-hammering my neighbour's head to the fender of his car and pushing him and it off a nearby cliff.

The phone rang. Jasper!

'Hello?' I said, accidentally jamming Kleenex further down my ear canal. 'Ow!' I said, pulling the tissue free. 'Hello?' It was only Sadie, calling on a staticky cellphone.

'Am I the first?'

'Yes,' I sighed, 'you're the first.' I examined the twisted, pointy end of the tissue for any amber-coloured residue.

'Oh, goody, then I'll sing! Happy Bir...' Her cellphone died. I stared at the phone for a moment before placing it back on its cradle. I waited, then picked up on the first ring. 'Mer, I'm heading over the canyon, this phone's about to die, so what's the deal? Are we still on for seven?' I set my dirty tissue on my bedside table.

'Yes.'

'A real seven? I know your mother's involved.'

'Yes, a real seven!' I was shouting now because she was.

'What are you going to do today?'

I patted down some air pockets in my duvet. 'I'm probably just going to hang here and spoil myself rotten, yunno, stay in bed, read, take a bath, maybe . . .'

'You're not waiting around for anyone to call, are you?'

'No,' I said, sing-songy, tipping my hand.

'Because he probably won't, and you might want to prepare yourself for that possibility. Because I mean, he hasn't called you in over—'

'Well, I think he will!' I said defensively, pulling a loose thread from the edging of my pink cotton nightie near the armpit.

'Yeah, and it might rain Popes. Anyway, I'm just saying . . . Why don't we go out bar-hopping and get you laid?'

'Sadie!'

'Hell, get us *both* laid. Have you been masturbating regularly?'

'Sadie!'

'Semi-regularly?'

'Sadie!'

It was true, I had been wholly unable even to think about pleasuring myself. For what? I'd only fantasize about Jasper, and what would be the point? It depressed me, but mostly I feared I'd die of heartbreak *and* be caught in a gutter with my hand down my pants. I stared at the peeling pansy sticker on the little yellow chest by the side of my bed. Inside that drawer was a small purple and white tube full of lubricant Jasper had brought home once, when he tried to talk me into letting him fuck me with a coke bottle.

'Are you still there? I guess that's a *no*. Mer, do you even want to get better?'

'Yes, I do, but—'

'Well, eventually you're going to have to *kill* that super-piney feeling and the only way I know how to do that is new boom-boom. Yunno, replace a cock with a cock. Like those squirrels. How 'bout a male prostitute?' What squirrels? Her phone was so crackly she sounded like she was in a popcorn maker. Her phone cut out. She called right back.

I watched my neighbour drop a wrench. It made an echoey, tuning-fork sound. I bet they could hear it all the way up the canyon.

'Goddamnit, cellphones are annoying! Sorry, Mer, I'm analogue now. Oh, come on, let's at least go out and have some fun tonight. Be single together. After dinner with the fam. We'll hit the town. Or I could organize drinks with that producer I've been telling you about!'

'I don't know, Sade . . .'

'You don't have to sleep with anyone tonight, we could just get some new drive-in-size fantasy going . . .'

'I don't want a new fantasy, I want . . .'

'I can't hear you, the phone's about to die. I'm telling you,' she made a vibrating drilling sound, 'take your womanhood back. You'll feel a lot better. I'll be by to pick you up at seven!'

'I—' The phone went dead. I lay there staring at the peeling pansy sticker. I ran my finger over its surface and felt the difference between the paper and the painted wood, then I absent-mindedly tore a small corner of it off, put it in my mouth and quickly spit it out. I opened the top drawer and reached my hand in. I fingered the small tube of lubricating gel.

Suddenly I'm seven and I have just fallen in love with a blue and white rubber-soled round-toed sneaker. I like the front nub; its hard, round, flat surface pressing against my soft and bony peeing place. Bonk, bonk, I kind of smack myself with the front end of the shoe, which, only a few moments ago, was a convertible car that Barbie was driving in to meet Ken.

As I knew nothing about sex, save the sounds I overheard in my parents' bedroom, it was merely an awkward bumping that made me feel a little tingly down there. It would be years before I would discover the pool heating jets while attempting to push off the side like an Olympic swimmer. I dropped the tube of clear goo back in its tomb and closed the drawer.

I clasped my hands in prayer. Aloud I said, 'Please God, please make Jasper call because I don't want to boink-boink diddle-diddle myself, not on my birthday.' Tulie scratched at the inside of her crate. I got up to let her out. I felt a little ill.

'Good Tulie, pottie pottie pottie,' I said as I watched her find a spot on the ivy-covered hillside through my kitchen window, while I poured dry dog food into her chipped ceramic bowl. 'Good potty.'

I filled the kettle with water, set it on the stove. I put loose Earl Grey in my grandma's fancy pot, chose the cobalt-blue cup I accidentally stole from that coffee joint, pulled some dead leaves off a plant I was murdering slowly in the window sill, and waited for my water to boil. My eyes burned. I watched Tulie sniff the base of a tree, then get distracted by a white moth while my neighbour alternated between drilling and banging out his Morse-code message of depravity out front. I didn't have to cross back to the front window to know that by now he had dismantled the entire vehicle and was just beginning to put it back together, like a puzzle.

Then, without warning, it stopped. The kettle shrieked. I quickly turned it off, made sure I left the back door open for Tulie and sped off to my bedroom and climbed right back under the covers. I lay there on my belly listening to actual birds. I felt myself sink into the mattress. Perfect. In a perfect world I would be spending this birthday much like my last one; making love with Jasper all day. Then, bang bang bang. My eyes popped open. They landed on the peeling pansy sticker. I thought, what the hell.

I reached over, grabbed the tube from the drawer, wriggled out of my undies, bit the plastic top off the purple and white tube with my teeth, spit it across the floor, squeezed some clear gel on to my fingers and reached my hand down underneath my night-gown. Sadie would be proud. At first, my hand half-heartedly probed my dried-flower arrangement like a clumsy left-handed seventh-grader. After a while I got the hang of it again, and peeled back the soft folds of skin between my legs like they were petals, and lightly traced circles around the small, fleshy, arid hills with my gooey index finger. I kept my eyes closed, ground my hips into the mattress in slow circles. The phone rang. I let the machine pick up. It was my mother.

'Happy Birthday, baby girl! It's Camilla calling and I have a surprise for you! Are you there, birthday girl? Pick up if you are there. Mer, darling? No? Darn. I wanted to pop by with your surprise! Oh, I'm giving it away.' I got nervous just thinking about it. She was kinda hit-and-miss with the whole surprise deal. Once she surprised me with what turned out to be my favourite birthday of all time and brought China to me: she hung little paper lanterns in our backyard and served my favourite, greasy egg rolls and stir-fried rice, topping it all off with a home-made white cake covered with green cream-cheese buttercream frosting and little paper umbrellas. And once she surprised me and Spoonie with a sudden trip to Connecticut to stay with Grandma when she wanted to surprise my dad with an empty house and no more family.

'Baby girl, are you screening? OK, well, I'll just see you when I see you. I'm not going to tell you what it is, but you are going to love it. Bye bye.' Maybe she was picking Jasper up from the airport! I resumed probing.

But the phone rang again. 'Mummy loves you.'

I buried my face in my pillow. Slight turn-off.

I am full-on masturbating when they arrive. My mother and her 'surprise' – an unmarried Oriental couple dressed like bankers, and a whorey-looking younger female counterpart acting as their translator. They had come to assess where the energy in my home was blocked because, for my birthday, my mother had organized for my house to be feng-shuied.

I had no time to wash my hands, only to leap up too quickly, slip my undies back on and blushingly let them in. They tried to insist on 'Western handshake', but I managed awkwardly to offer up my sinless hand instead.

'May we come in?' asked the hooker translator. My mother mouthed the words, are you all right? I blushed, nodding I'm fine, as I led them into the living room.

With a guilty-handed game-show reveal I said, 'Welcome.' The couple walked around, tapped out numbers on a flat black compass as big as an atlas and calculated the four directions in relation to the exact hour of my birth. They kept tsk-tsking at one another as they peered into every nook and cranny of my home, opening and closing doors, studying ceilings and corners, walkways inside and outside the house. After a half-hour of intensive snooping they stopped to inform me of the first of several pieces of 'goo' news'.

'They want me to tell you, you will never have a goo' relationship unless you cut down tree in front of house. Otherwise you always single lady,' said the slutty translator with the drawn-in mouth and teased-up brittle orange-ing hair.

'I'm sorry, they want me to what?'

The translator made a scissor cutting gesture with her index and fuck-you finger for clarification. 'Cut tree, or you single lady forever.'

I turned to my mother. 'They want me to chop down a more than a hundred-year-old tree so I can date again?'

She smiled, nodding.

The translator made the scissor gesture again. 'Cut then you happy in man love.' They all looked at each other and smiled and nodded. They had all contributed to ruining my life, and they were smiling.

'Arso, in bedroom must get rid of bed. Arso, must keep bathroom door close at all time. Arso, if possiboo, sleep in closet if you want have career success, otherwise bedroom fine.' The translator bowed. I was outraged. I looked at my mother. She looked serene as though pleased the wisest of elders were completing a more than helpful transmission.

The banker couple said something else in Chinese. 'Arso, said the translator, 'buy fountain and get rid of mirror.' The couple looked at one another and shivered, then looked back at me and smiled. 'Arso, your Neptune in Scorpio say no no alcoho'.'

'That's true!' my mother shrieked. 'We are all allergic to alcohol. It runs in the family!' My mother smiled proudly. The three strangers huddled together and whispered something else. I waited for the translator to garble out some more helpful news. Her eyes widened, she looked at me with what I perceived as real pity.

'What? What is it?' I said.

Solemnly she said, 'They want me to tell you so sorry, but Neptune arso rule anaesthesia, so no no plastic surgery.'

I glared at my mother, then looked back at them. 'Anything else?'

She smiled warmly. 'Most important cut tree, otherwise no husband. No husband, no kids. No kids, no reason be alive. No reason be alive, no happy grandma.' She bowed at my mother, which started a wave of them all bowing at her. My mother blushed and clutched at her heart like she had just won an Oscar.

'Yeah, I get it,' I snapped, losing all sense of decorum. I wanted to throttle my mother. Didn't she mind that these scam artists were throwing me deeper into calamity? Didn't she agree that all of this was a depressing pile of fraudulent insane? A giant, stinking sack of untrue? Or worse, maybe they were dead right. Maybe they all knew what I couldn't admit to myself: that I was destined to be alone for ever.

'Do her fortune!' my mother pleaded. 'What about her career? Any chance of success in acting?' They had already got almost three-quarters of the way through the front door to leave. The old man took my hand before I could refuse. 'What about her acting career?' my mother said again.

'Oh, no, very bad. She bad at business and she bad at acting. She bad at relationship and she bad at know how to be happy.'

My mother's face dropped. 'That's what I always thought.'

I stomped my foot, 'Well, is there anything I *am* good at?' I heard myself say, giving *all* my power away. 'What *should* I be doing?'

'Work with colour. You very goo' talent for art – paint bedroom colour of rose, very healing for you.' I thought, Un-fucking-believable, what it is with these con-artist people and their fucking roses? 'Goo'bye!' they said, bowing and bowing at me.

'Goodbye,' I said, smiling. This time they insisted on a Western handshake and won.

I wondered if I would go to hell, or if it was justified payment for such awful information. I actually thanked them before they drove away, but not before overhearing my mother confess that she, too, always thought working with colour would be very therapeutic for me. Since fucking when?

★ ★ ★

By two o'clock I had transformed my house into a mini day spa. I had steamed and scrubbed and cleaned my pores, shaved my legs, painted my toes and was still feeling a little cute, in spite of the fact that Jasper still hadn't called. Yet. Then and there I courageously decided that feng shui is for Chinese people and not for America the country or America the person.

By four o'clock, still in my bathrobe, I had cleaned my floors, sinks and toilet bowls spotless, curled my hair, and begun to apply my makeup.

By six o'clock the sun had begun to set and Jasper still hadn't called. (I must confess I was starting to get a bit worried.) I picked at an ingrown, ate a loaf of bread and an entire stick of butter in the name of toast, and looked up 'break-up' in the dictionary: 'Dissolution. Separation of things into its parts. Decay, esp. death, the termination of an assembly or partnership.' One word away from 'break out': 'to become infected with a skin eruption', the thing I couldn't seem to stop doing over Jasper and, oddly, exactly next to 'break-through', the thing I wanted with Jasper more than anything in the world.

To counteract my depression I made a mixed tape. The plan was to do a collection of powerful female role models, yunno, Tori, Alanis, Joni, Ani, Sinead. Instead it ended up being a weepy, oestrogen-rich collection of only sad songs.

Finally, Sadie and seven o'clock rolled around. And, even though there was still no sign of Jas, I slid into my new pants as Sadie had given me implicit orders to wear something sexy. Sadie kept saying the words 'duty-dating' like she was the General in the Dating Army in the war against Being Single. To improve the odds, but hoping for some evens, I slapped on a little shiny, red lipgloss.

'How do I look?'

Sadie covered her mouth with her hand. 'Oh, my God.'

'What?' I said as I speed-walked over to my full-length mirror. My plastic thighs rubbed, causing slight friction burn. I took a long look.

'Very action-based, very *Matrix*-esque,' she said enthusiastically. 'Now what shoes?'

All I could see was that they made my hips flare, that my stomach drooped over the top and they went straight up my crotch. 'I don't know, Sade.'

'Well, I do. Come on, you look gorgeous!'

She took me by the arm and led me into the closet, grabbed a pair of high-heeled purple boots I got downtown for ten dollars, and off we went.

At the fancy restaurant my mother chose, Chinese, I spotted her and my brother and the girl from the set sitting in a large black leather booth. My brother and the actress stood up to let me and Sadie slide in. The actress introduced herself. 'I'm sorry we didn't get a chance to meet on the set the other day, you seemed a little distracted. I'm Lila.' I smiled politely and shook her hand, then glared at Spoonie. Then Lila bent around me. 'Hi, Sadieface!'

'What's up, sistamama!' said Sadie, somewhat nervously.

Lila pointed. 'Did you see that our produ—?' Sadie coughed, shook her head. 'Oh . . .' said Lila, winking.

I could not believe my eyes. How dare Spoonie bring her to my fucking birthday dinner. A fucking winker. How dare Sadie, too, for liking her.

While Spoonie and Lila cooed away at one another, my mother attempted to make pleasant conversation.

'Isn't it remarkable that we're all single? You, Sadie and I? Spoonie will probably end up married before either one of you two!' said my mother. Lila blushed. I squeezed Sadie's hand. That's when my mother's cellphone rang. My mother just handed me the phone, nodding knowingly. 'Are you and that nice Jasper engaged yet?' It was my grandma. Calling from her boat in Hawaii.

'No Grandma,' I said, dying of humiliation and embarrassment to be on a cellphone in a restaurant, 'we broke up.' In the background I heard someone yell, 'Gin!' then what sounded like some elderly men fighting loudly, followed by some hacking coughs, and then some commotion with squeaking chairs.

'Men are bastards, always taking their halves in the middle before turning around and dying on ya. Get him some water, will ya, Joe? OK, Grandma loves you, happy birthday.'

I wanted to call my machine to see if Jasper had called yet, but I was completely surrounded, so I just handed my mother back her phone.

Around and around went the lazy Susan. Spare ribs and fried seaweed, orange-peel chicken and beef and broccoli in oyster sauce, fried rice and egg rolls and wonton soup. I was so upset about Jasper I accidentally ate a helping of kung pao shrimp even though shellfish gives me a rash and abdominal cramping. I spit it out.

Then came the presents. I got a journal and coloured pencils and a DVD of Lila's last movie, even though I don't own a player. The card said, love Spoonie *and Lila*. From my mother I got a red-knit blouson with capped sleeves and a dragon on it (that I'll never wear), a cheque for thirty dollars ('One for every year!') and a hummingbird feeder ('To feed the birdlings!') Sadie gave me a giant, translucent, purple vibrator. As I tried to stuff it back in its velvet pouch, Sadie loudly announced, 'It's called the Grape Ape! I got it at the Hustler store!', just in case the people in the back of the restaurant couldn't see it.

When the chocolate crème brûlée came with the single candle in it, and I recovered from the shock that I would not be eating actual birthday cake, I leaned in to blow it out. I thought, I have had some colossally bad birthdays but this one seems to be going for some kind of record. I blew, wishing for Jasper back.

When I opened my eyes I saw wisps of smoke rise up past the blackened candle stem. Then, slowly, tiny sparks began top flicker and the candle blinked itself back to life. I blew it out once more, praying that it would not be so, that I would not have the type of family that would think I would find this remotely funny. The more I blew, the harder they laughed. Lila took mini-Polaroids. That's when my mother announced, 'If I ever date again, the next boyfriend I have is going to be black.' We stared at her, especially Spoonie's new girlfriend, who couldn't tell if my mother was joking or not. Instead she just snapped another photo.

Sadie attempted to fill the awkward silence by announcing that, for my real present, she had signed me up for ballet classes, to which my brother replied, 'I didn't know ballerinas could be fat.'

I excused myself, and waddle-ran to the bathroom. Sadie followed too closely behind me. The way those pants were rubbing I could have started a goddamned fire. Sadie grabbed my arm. 'Wait, Mer, I want you to meet someone,' she said, waving to a blond, gangly giant with clunky black Elvis Costello glasses and a soul patch at six o'clock. 'Look! It's Jym Court, the producer I've been telling you about. Isn't this a coincidence?' Jym waved back and motioned for us to come over.

I shot her a look. 'Yeah, it sure is a coincidence. How come he brought a date?' Sitting next to him was a gorgeous amazon. I recognized her from the magazines. A model.

Sadie bit her lip, then blew it off. 'Who cares about her? Remember, at least three seconds of eye contact lets him know you are interested. Come on.' As we zigzagged past the ultra-hip in comfortable chic, the pants made an awful friction sound causing people to turn and stare.

'Jym, this is America. America, this is Jym.'

'Nice to meet you,' he said.

'Nice to meet you both,' I said. The frail girl's hand went limp in mine, but her eyebrows were perfect. Then we all smiled politely back and forth at one another. Sadie squeezed my hand three times, indicating the duration of eye contact she required of me. I could only stare at the ground and cross my legs because I was suddenly desperately aware of how much the model wanted us to disappear and how the fabric of my trousers was creeping up inside me like a karate-chopping hand in reverse.

'Well, again, it was nice to meet you *both*,' I said, and beelined for the bathroom with Sadie in tow.

As the bathroom door swung open, Sadie whispered, 'Now can I fix you up with him?' I don't know if I burst into tears because she was treating me like it was really over between me and Jasper, or if it was because she wanted to fix me up with a guy who dates models, or if it was because I caught sight of the girl in the mirror who was out publicly and could easily win the award for the deepest camel-toe contest.

I feigned illness and waited in a stall until Sadie was gone. I rested my head against celadon-painted walls. Jasper shouldn't have set the bar that high. He shouldn't have painted my dream; that's the kind of stuff people don't recover from, not if they are me. Then I checked my messages on the payphone in the bathroom. I wanted to see if Jasper had called yet. He hadn't.

'Do you want me to come up?' Sadie asked when we pulled up to my house just before midnight.

'Sure,' I said, meaning no. Even from the window I could see that the red light from my answering machine was *not* flashing.

We sat cross-legged in silence on my living-room floor, her with a pillow and me with a battery-operated digital clock and the phone in my lap. Sadie looked at me like I was dying of a massive gunshot wound to the chest and didn't want me to find out.

'He might still call,' I said.

'I know,' said Sadie.

We watched the clock. Eleven-fifty-six, 11.59, then, 12.00.

'Are you OK?' she asked. I nodded. You could hear crickets all the way up the canyon. 'Well, I should probably get going.' I nodded again. Sadie stood up and went to the kitchen to grab her car keys. I followed her in on my knees.

'Please call him for me, Sadie, for my birthday. I just want to hear his voice. Pleeeease?' I clasped my hands together.

She paced around in my tiny kitchen, then swung around to face me. 'What do you expect me to do?'

'I expect you to be my friend. Just call and hang up, that's all I'm asking. I just want to hear his voice. I don't even care if we get his machine.'

She crossed her arms across her chest. 'What if he answers?'

'Hang up. Pleeeease?'

She began to pace again. 'This is all a little too *Girl Interrupted* for me.' Then she stopped, put her hands on her hips, and looked up at the ceiling, then back at me. 'OK, I'll do it on two conditions.'

I stood now. 'Fine, yes, anything.'

'One, you go on a duty date with Jym.'

I crossed my eyes. 'Fine, yeah, whatever, and?'

'And two, that you see Dr Karl Sage in person and do *exactly* what he says.'

'What if he says hang in there, Mer, Jasper is totally right for you?'

'He won't.'

'What if he does?'

'Fine.'

'Fine,' I said. Sadie shook her head. 'Come on, Sade, I just have to hear his voice. I can get over him if I just hear his voice.'

Sadie rolled her eyes, held her hand out for the phone. 'What's the number?'

I grabbed my portable, punched in the crazy maths and handed her the phone. We leaned in close. He answered on the fourth ring. 'Hello?' he said. He sounded happy. 'Hello?' he said again. In the background I could hear a giggling female voice. Then the voice said, 'Who is it, baby? Come back to bed.' It had a German accent. Sadie hung up.

The room was spinning. Not only could he live without me, he preferred it. I clutched at my stomach. The muscles in my belly cramped. I felt a rush of hot liquid in the back of my throat. I ran to the bathroom, locked the door, and puked my guts out.

When Jasper loved me, on my last birthday, he put a whole universe together for me complete with my favourite music, tiny hanging lights and the scent of geranium oil. He had lined the floor with a trail of tea candles that I followed to the bedroom. Jasper had covered the bed in rose petals. In the middle of the bed lay a single gift, a painting he had made in secret, just for me. Of Tulie wearing a queen's coat and holding a sceptre. Then we made love until the sun came up.

Sadie knocked on the door but I didn't answer.

I pressed my forehead to the cool of the tile wall, listened to the flushing toilet settle itself. For round two I let my hand rest on the rim of the toilet. In my head I watched a speedily edited movie trailer that was a cross between *Eyes Wide Shut* and *Saving Private Ryan* starring Jasper and his slut: writhing bodies on satin sheets in our bed, me kicking the door in and spraying them with machine-gun fire. I thought, now I'll just have to pretend you are M.I.A. Jasper. You are dead and I'll never get to see the body to say goodbye. Only you aren't dead, my father is, but not you. I wanted to scream but no sound came out.

Instead, I knelt forward and threw up dinner and my entire existence. Sadie just kept knocking on the door. 'Mer, open the door. Mer, please answer me, are you OK in there? Maybe he'll call you tomorrow,' she managed brightly. 'Mer?'

After a sharp intake of air through my mouth, my breath plateaued, hung suspended like a trapeze act and settled in small aftershocks of air. I fell still. Finally I stood, opened the door.

'He's not gonna call,' I sniffled, turning a piece of toilet paper in my hand over and over.

'Well, maybe he'll—'

'Sadie ... don't.' She just nodded her head and looked at my shoulder, brushed my hair behind my ear. 'Are you OK?'

I stared at the floor, wiped my nose and mouth with my already damp paper-thin tissue, then folded it into a perfect square. 'Yeah, I'm OK.'

PART TWO

Let the Healing Begin

FIFTEEN

Boo Who

> 'With my naked eye, I saw the falling rain, and I knew if I
> said it all, I would be free again.'
> — Luscious Jackson

The bearded man with pointy shoes came out to welcome me. I
hated him on sight. Pointy shoes? Please. No wonder they only
took photos of authors' heads. Plus, he looked much more jovial in
person, all shiny, waxed-apple smiles and dimpled cheeks. His eyes
were actually twinkling.

Waves of disgust washed over me as Dr Karl Sage, Ph.D. guided
me into his 'office', which consisted of a forest-green couch with a
lot of pillows, a navy-blue single bed with a lot of stuffed animals
and a roll-top desk with a lot of Kleenex. Under his desk, there
was a small grey metal filing cabinet. Against one wall stood a
sturdy-looking oak bookshelf. It bragged five shelves' worth of
dense-looking hardcover reading material; some of the softcovers
had titles like *In Search of the Shadow Self* or *Raising Your Own Inner Child*
or *Unearthing the Hero Within Using Dreams, Symbology and Garlic*. There
were rocks, seashells, crystals, dream catchers and a small god's eye
with red and green and orange yarn wrapped around two popsicle
sticks.

On another wall, a large window revealed three neat rows of
bustling streets and a glimpse of the Pacific Ocean. On the wall

near Karl, a couple of official-looking certificates, a painting of a ship on a stormy sea along with some cheesy aphorism about endurance, and a brass clock so I could watch the fifty spendy minutes tick by. On the table next to me a digital clock for the good doctor to watch himself grow a hundred and twenty-five dollars richer. The whole room had a masculine, nautical, hippy feel to it, not at all my type of setting. I preferred something womblike in varying shades of cream, egg and white, with pretty photos of tree-lined roads leading to a distant, far-off but hopeful future. Certainly some flowers, maybe even a teaset complete with a small tin of almond *biscotti*.

God, his shoes were pointy.

Plus he tucked his shirt in and wore a belt. That says a lot about a person, as far as I'm concerned. You'd never see my brother or my father or my boyfriend, rather, ex-boyfriend, wearing a tucked-in shirt and a belt. I would never pick this guy out of a crowd as someone I'd be even remotely interested in talking to, let alone *pay* to hear my innermost secrets. Maybe as a child, with trepidation, I would have told him what I wanted for Christmas. Sure, I had his book and read it cover to cover, but that was *me* dissecting *him*.

'How are you doing?' asked Dr Karl with the compassion of a weeping saint.

'How am I doing?' I said, adjusting my buttocks into the too-squishy confessing couch.

'Yes, how are you doing right now?'

I crossed my arms across my chest. 'I'm doing fine, just fine.' I said, inspecting the fabric of the couch. I traced the raised Paisley pattern with my mind's eye.

'You seem agitated.'

'Do I?'

'Yes.' He cocked his head thoughtfully. 'When we spoke on the phone you mentioned several things. Maybe we could start with the break-up and feelings of extreme depression, OK?' I nodded imperceptibly. 'So, do you wanna tell me what's going on?'

'What's going on?'

'Uh-huh. How's the body?'

I clenched my hands into fists. 'You mean, other than what I already told you? Other than I hate my life because my boyfriend dumped me, and I have no real career, and my best friend wants me to stay single forever, and my mother drives me nuts, and my brother's life is perfect because he's her favourite, even though I am the one who role-models sanity in the house, even though I am an utter failure in my own life, not to mention that I have fantasies of murdering my dog when she makes a certain annoying licking sound?'

'All right now,' he laughed. He had the most intelligent eyes. I could tell he was really listening to me, really seeing me, possibly without any judgement whatsoever. Gross. I fought back tears of gratitude by finding a little resting spot for my tongue in my back left molar. 'Anything left?'

Abruptly, I flung myself sideways on the couch. 'I want to die. I want my boyfriend to love me and he doesn't. He doesn't want me. Nobody wants me. Why, why, why?' I buried my face in the Paisley evergreen and just kept chanting *why*. 'This world is so fucked.' Karl placed a Kleenex next to my wet face. I looked at the tissue, then rubbed my nose into the couch. It smelt like carpeting. Then I sat up, suddenly thinking of how many other noses had probably done the same, not to mention the bottoms. I timidly reached for the tissue through a tangle of hair.

'And what does that remind you of?'

I looked at him, brushed my stringy wet hair behind my ears. 'What?' Karl handed me another Kleenex, which I took greedily this time.

'America, when we have a strong reaction to something, it's usually because it triggers piggyback feelings from another hurt in a long line of hurts. So what does "nobody wanting you" remind you of?'

I stared into space. My lips quivered. 'It makes me think of God and how He doesn't exist, and how even if He did, all He likes to do is ruin everything. All He likes to do is take away anything good.'

Karl scribbled something in a small spiral notebook with a fancy maroon pen. It was probably inscribed.

'What are you writing there?'

'This?' He looked down at the notebook. 'Oh, these are just my own personal notes, so I can keep track of anything that might bubble up to the surface. I keep them in this filing cabinet right here.' He gestured to the file cabinet under the desk. I squinted at him warily. 'But you can look at them any time you like. See?' He turned to show me what he had written on the powder-blue lined paper: 'Depression over loss of male love, probably dad', in loopy chicken scratch. 'All right now, you were about to tell me what that reminded you of.'

'Is that supposed to make me feel safe, you showing me those notes? Fine, my father,' I said coldly, hiding my nose and mouth behind the damp tissue. 'That's who it reminds me of, my *father*.'

'Can you tell me a little bit about him?'

'Who, Jasper or my father?'

'Let's start with Dad, since that's where the imprinting first occurs. Did you know that's where it begins?'

'Uh . . . yeah . . .'

'What's your father like?'

I eyed him suspiciously. Hadn't he heard of my father? Didn't my name sound familiar? Didn't he know who I was? If he knew who my father was, surely we could get this over with in one session. 'My father's dead.'

'Oh,' said Dr Karl warmly. 'well, what *was* he like?'

I stared him down. 'He was only a brilliant genius, that's all. He painted a bunch of stuff, got a bunch of awards, wrote a bunch of stuff, got a bunch of awards, built a bunch of stuff, got a bunch of awards, then dropped dead, leaving us all behind.' He scribbled something down on his little pad. 'Boris Throne. Ever hear of him?' I kept my arms crossed, eyes at half-mast.

'Oh, OK, so he was the famous painter. I'm sorry, I know very little of his work. I remember seeing something about him once on PBS, or hearing something on NPR. His work was very graphic, very sexually explicit, is that right?' I nodded.

'Some of it.'

'You seem angry. What did you mean by "leaving us behind"?'

'Nothing.' I brushed the steel-blue carpeting forward with my foot, brushed it back.

'It doesn't sound like nothing. Did you like his work?'

'What work? The painting, the writing, the elaborate stage designs, the performance art?'

'Sure, any of it.'

'You mean as a kid?'

'Yes.'

'Well, as far as the art went, I liked some of the colours. Mainly they embarrassed me. The early stuff anyway.'

'How do you mean, embarrassed you?'

'Well, yunno, close-ups of vaginas and anuses, people copulating, penises being inserted into vaginas or anuses or ears or whatever. It freaked a lot of people out, including me, and still I had to behave *nice* in public and be *supportive*. At age seven. Some of the butt-holes were so close up they looked like flowers, so they didn't bother me *as much*.'

Then he asked me about his creative process, so I told him how he'd have his friends come over and sit. Well, not really friends, because my parents didn't have any, so students or models really. Well, not really sit. Mostly they'd be naked on all fours on our kitchen table or stuffed in the dishwasher naked in some yogic posture. Then my dad would photograph them from all angles and they'd either come back and 'sit' some more or become his 'friends'.

They'd work long hours so I'd be downstairs helping my mom prepare food for all of them. His studio is behind the house I grew up in. It's like a tree house with a big redwood deck, and I'd come up there with fancy sandwiches we had painstakingly made on a silver tray and I'd find them naked all over our stuff because my dad had decorated the 'set' with things from around the house, like my toys, blow up sex dolls, porn comics, the American flag, our dishes and blankets and forks and clothes and whatever. Once he did a series of acrylics based on nude photos he took of me and Spoonie, when we were tiny. He painted these tiny nude children on everything. Household stuff. Soup spoons, plates, a baby doll of

129

mine, an old TV, a can of bug killer. Me, tiny and nude on an old black phone. I used to just adore pretending to talk on the telephone, probably because I saw my mom on the phone so much. I'd use anything and pretend it was a phone, hairbrushes, stuffed animals. It totally freaked me out that someone else was going to buy a tiny me and take me to their house. Of course, critics thought it was some deep commentary on the decline of communication and commodification of society, or something. 'It was pathetic.' I laughed. 'I wanted to be a secretary when I grew up.'

'What else?'

'Nothing else. Just big, droopy, naked-ass bodies all over all our stuff. Just your basic all-American orgy scene.' I thought I detected a slight frown beginning on Karl's face. I crossed my legs and shifted my weight on to my right hip. 'We didn't have a lot of money then, so we kind of had to use stuff from around the house, yunno, share stuff.' Karl's shiny pen moved across the paper. I scratched at a non-existent itch on my throat. Did Karl think I was weird? Did he think my parents were weird? Was my upbringing weird?

' "Stuff that was just laying around". You mean like your own personal toys and personal belongings?' My face reddened.

'Well, I mean, all for the sake of art, yunno.' I nodded and smiled uneasily. Dr Karl just continued to look at me with a blank face.

'Were your parents naked too?'

'Oh, God, no. Never!' I thought, phew, I'm in the clear. I continued confidently, 'The only time my parents were ever naked was when we were all alone in the house. *Then* they would walk around naked.' I smiled.

Karl frowned, shook his head and began scribbling violently.

'Hey, what did you just write? Is it bad?'

He put the pen down on the desk behind him, swivelled his chair back around and faced me. Then he held the writing tablet up and turned it around for me to see: 'Negative response to explicit visual stimuli, not protected from inappropriate stranger nudity, inappropriate parental nudity, no object constancy, narcissistic parenting, improper reality mirroring.' The room began to spin. I felt claustrophobic, like the walls were closing in and squeezing my helpless history self right out of me. I wanted to run outside and get some air.

'How did all that make you feel? How did sharing your toys with strangers make you feel?' Dr Karl asked, handing me a stuffed koala bear.

'I felt, uh, angry, is that what you want me to say? I felt angry?' I said, unconsciously pulling at the bear's ear. I was angry with Karl now.

He rested the tablet on his knee. 'America, I want you to tell me whatever is true for you. I'm just here to help *you*.' Dr Karl smiled. 'If you felt angry, then that's how you felt. Is that how you felt, angry?' I wished he'd stop smiling.

'Yes!' I snapped. 'I felt angry. Angry that he had all this time for all these freaky naked people who touched all my things and rubbed their stupid smelly-ass, fat cocks and cunts all over everything. All over *my* things. I didn't ever want to see those things or those people ever again. And there it was, The Finished Product. The horrible memory frozen in time for the whole world to see, and everyone that saw it said it was fucking wonderful, and, oh, how neat that your life was so free, not like society with its soul-crushing *rules*. Lucky you, America, to know true freedom all the time!' I had practically twisted the ear of the koala bear clean off. 'I wished everyone would die, and one day my father did. There. Are you happy now? Are we done?'

'Could you talk to him about your feelings?'

'No! Weren't you listening? I couldn't talk to anybody about anything.'

'Was there ever a time when you could? Tell me about reaching out to your daddy. Tell me about your daddy being there for you.' I looked outside the big window and stared into the vastness of a perfect blue sky I couldn't feel.

I'm twelve. I want to be an actress, so my father writes a story about a twelve-year-old girl named Amelia who wanted to be an actress. He used to call me Air-Heart because I pretended to flap my arms and fly around the room to get his attention when he was working too much. The girl in the story was so lonely she would cry herself to sleep and spend hours and hours alone drawing in her room because no one in her family had any time for her, which was quite a coincidence. It gets made into a movie but I don't get to play the part of myself because they have to shoot it in Canada to save money. Plus, no one had the time to be my guardian. But my father goes to oversee the production and has an affair with some eighteen-year-old who plays the part of me.

I'm twenty and still a virgin. My father writes a play about a girl who is twenty and still a virgin. It goes to Broadway where he fucks the lead actress so my family stays behind. My mother almost has to be hospitalized because he is never home, because his 'art' is more important than his family. In fact, when I move out a few months later, on his allowance, he doesn't even have my phone number.

I'm twenty-six. The men are wearing cheap grey suits when they lower him into the ground. The pretty lady I don't recognize can't get her umbrella to close. I don't say any of this to Karl, instead I push the feelings away and watch a seagull fly past, dropping something it holds in its beak.

'What does all this have to do with my boyfriend?' I said, tearing at the corners of a tissue.

'I don't know yet. What did your boyfriend do?'

My eyes narrowed. 'He's a painter.'

'Like your father? Look, America, I am going to save you a lot of trouble. What do you want?'

'What do I want?'

'Yes, what do you, America, want?'

'I want Jasper back.'

'Besides Jasper.'

'I want my father back.'

'Well, they aren't coming back, so pick something else.'

'What do you mean?' I roared, pounding my fists into the sofa.

Karl smiled. 'Would you like to do a rage exercise to move some of the blocked energy around?' Before I could say no, he motioned for me to move to the floor by the bed with all the rest of the stuffed animals. Somehow I did. 'Great,' he said. 'What I'd like for you to do is to lie down and slap your tailbone into the ground.'

I blew my nose. 'What?'

He turned to pour some hot herbal tea from a silver thermos into a coffee mug that said Number One Dad. 'I'd like to have you lie down on the floor and slap your tailbone into the ground.' He turned back to me now, smiling even more warmly than before.

'Yeah, no, I heard you, I just don't . . .'

'It's an exercise I have you do to help unblock some of the trapped first-and-second-chakra energy at the base of the spine. It's actually based on what little children do when they are having a temper tantrum.' While he spoke, I watched the steam from his herbal concoction spiral up behind him. It made a little wispy halo around the back of his head. 'Your survival and identity issues are hidden in your tailbone, and this exercise is sort of like turning a little key which opens up a little door there, and relieves some of the trapped negative feelings. Compacted rage, self-loathing, hope-lessness, despair.'

'But in the book you didn't say—'

'I work a little bit differently one-to-one. In fact, in extreme cases, I'll go so far as to recommend nine-day silent retreats to really purify the emotional body and face the dragon head-on, so to speak.' I thought I might faint. Did he think I was that bad off? Did he think I was An Extreme Case? 'Would you like to lie down and try it?'

'Look, you fucking voyeuristic pervert, I'm just here for therapy. I had no idea, you know, floor work would be involved. I don't even belong to a gym.' Karl reached out to hug me. I hissed like a cornered animal. Karl looked worried.

'Did we hit a trigger? I'm hearing a lot of fear.' I pulled my knees into my chest and inched away. I wasn't used to being spoken to with so much love and patience, not after being such a complete bitch, not by my mother, not by anyone. *Especially* not by a man.

He leaned in close, hands rested on his knees. 'America, I am on the board of an ethics committee. I take my work very seriously. I hear your fear and I would be more than happy to suggest another exercise instead. We could find out where "not good enough" lives in your body, or we could work on expanding your capacity to receive, or we can just sit right here and keep right on talking if you'd feel more comfortable.'

I buried my face in my hands and convulsed in big quakes. Karl handed me a new box of tissues. My hair fell down around me, protecting me like a cage. 'I just want not to be in pain anymore. I just want to be able to let Jasper go and be able to move on. I want a different ending, I want my life to begin.' I felt Karl tentatively rest his hand on my back. I wanted to swat him away, but I was in too much pain, so I let him rest it there. I just kept sobbing into my hair.

After a while Karl said, 'I'm sorry, but our time's up for today, but we can get right into this next week, if you'd like.' He stood up now and moved toward the door. I looked up, panic-stricken, then ran interference by blocking the door frame with my arms.

'But why is all this happening to me?' I said, eyeing him hungrily.

'America,' he said, folding his hands politely at his crotch, 'sometimes we choose prickly people to make us feel yucky feelings so we can uncover old hurts and be pointed in the direction of our wholeness. That way, we can start to feel our happiness sprout real roots . . .' he exaggerated his face to punctuate words, scrunched-up for 'prickly' and 'yucky', smiley for 'wholeness' and 'happy', '. . . because eventually we are only going to be interested in finally seeing our true selves, grounded, in an expectationless reality.' The way he said it I knew it was probably trade-marked, or would be soon. 'But we can talk more about this next week, if you'd like.

'But how am I going to get through *today*?'

'How 'bout a homework assignment?' he said brightly.

I made a face. 'OK.'

'One, make a list of all the things you love about Jackson, the positive qualities you associate with him.'

'Jasper.'

'Jasper. Then make a list of all the things you love about your dad. See if you can notice any similarities between Jameson and your father. See if you start to notice any patterns. This will allow you to see if you can have the positive qualities you associate with them in your life, on your own.'

'Jasper.'

'That's right, sorry. And, two,' he aimed his fingers at me like a gun, 'take long walks. That will keep the blocked energy moving until we meet again. And, of course, call me any time. You did great work today.' He unlocked the door.

'*Wait!*' I shrieked so loud he stepped away from the door.

'Shall we schedule another appointment?' I thought, never! I wanted to kill him.

While he extracted a business card from a well-worn imitation leather organiser and wrote down my appointment, I asked him if I had any hope of getting better. He told me the good news: that I'm pigeon-chested, my thighs are a warehouse of unexpressed rage, and the way my shoulders slump forward indicates I'm shut down in the heart region; also, according to my clavicle bones or something, I was ripe for being reparented because I obviously wasn't held enough as a child. Then, with enthusiasm, he added that he had the time and energy, so long as I did.

Before opening the door he said, 'America, if you continue to work like you did in this room today, in no time at all you won't even be interested in entertaining situations that aren't in your best interest.' Then he pressed the little grey card with silver writing into my palm, patted me on the shoulders, opened the door and held it open for me like a real gentleman and said, 'All right now.'

A man in the waiting room looked up from his magazine, Karl nodded at him and the new victim crossed past us eagerly. Karl smiled at me and closed the door. I heard the click of the lock, so I walked outside.

The bright sunlight stung my eyes. I couldn't stop blinking. The sun made little rainbows in my eyelashes where the salt had crystallised. I thought, so this is how it is: pay someone not to have enough time for me. Then, when I get better, in about thirty years, I will finally make good choices, for me.

I looked at the business card and wiped my nose on the fabric of my long, loose, flowing skirt. The sea air hit my nostrils once more and I felt like little sparkles of light were trying to burrow themselves into my lungs.

When I got home I checked my messages to see if Jasper had called. Habit, I guess.

I flopped down on the floor in the living room, unclipped the black disposable pen from the spiral binder of my journal, found a clean page and began to write:

The Things I Love about Jasper Husch:
1   his appreciation for music,
2   colour,
3   air,
4   trees,
5   eyelashes,
6   legs,
7   dancing,
8   eating,
9   sleeping,
10   not sleeping,
11   anything fun,
12   and, of course, my crotch.

Then, on the other half of the page I listed:

The Things I Love about My Father:
1   his humour,
2   his mind,
3   his commitment to himself and his creativity, no matter the distraction, his belief in himself, no matter the criticism, his focus, his kindness, the way he was so patient with his freaky fans, his ability to actually enjoy himself, the way he did everything so expertly, in his own way, in his own time, his smell, his hands, his hugs, the way he loved me unconditionally, and how happy I felt when he loved me.

Seeing Jasper and my father clearly spelled out on paper gave me a much-needed perspective on things. Did I think I could provide the same things I associated with being loved by them for myself? No, I did not.

SIXTEEN

Free Dumb

'Tossed into my mind stirring the calm, you splash me
with beauty and pull me down, 'cause you come from
out of nowhere.'

— Faith No More

'Based on Jasper's body type, the way his neck lurches forward and
the way his shoulders kind of collapse in towards on another, I can
honestly say that this relationship was doomed from the get-go,'
said Karl the following Thursday.

In the photo, we are sitting on a low stone wall. Jasper is wearing
a pair of ripped-up jeans and a too-small crew-neck olive and grey
vintage wool sweater and Birkenstock sandals with thick orange
socks. I am wearing a pink flowy dress with big red hibiscus flowers
and a pale blue knit beanie my grandmother gave me. I have my
arm around him. I am smiling broadly. Jasper's eyes aren't open all
the way, and he looks like he just got a whiplash brace off. It's the
best one I have of us together.

'Just looking at how skinny his calves are, I can see that he isn't
equipped to handle your anger and intensity. Eventually you would
have left him.'

'All right now, today we are going to find out where "*not good
enough*" lives in your body, so I want you just to breeeeathe.' I sat
up.

139

'Before we begin, I just want to say how great it is to realize that I have merely transferred my pain on to Jasper when really it was my father who caused it all along, and I'm totally willing to transfer it all on to you so we can get down to business.' I smiled. Karl looked at me with a straight face, thought better of saying anything and silently passed me the Kleenex box.

'Why don't we go inside and just breeeeathe.' I closed my eyes again, folded my palms in my lap and let out a massive sigh. 'Now, imagine you are on an internal jungle safari. You are walking through a dense, but lush, tropical jungle looking for where "not good enough" lives. You hear the crunch of leaves under your feet. You brush vines out of your way. Ooo-oo-wah, oo-oo-wah.' He made a distant jungle monkey sound. I peeked an eye open, arched an eyebrow, saw that Karl's eyes were closed, so I closed mine back up again. 'Where is "not good enough" hiding? Oo-oo-wah, oo-oo-wah. Come out, come out, wherever you are! Where does "not good enough" live in the body? Woo-hoo! Come out of your hiding place.' I bit the inside of my cheek. You can do this, Mer, just surrender... 'We are gonna pull you out by your roots today, so don't be shy.' I imagined it all right, me wearing a pith helmet, hacking through uncharted territory with a large machete, through the tangled vines of all my negativity to get to the glowing, bejewelled source, swap it for a bag of sand and run like hell so that the wrecking ball didn't get me on the way out.

'Just relax and keep breathing. Now, imagine an emotional Geiger counter scanning the landscape of your vessel.' I rolled my eyes, even though they were shut tight. I thought, sweet Jesus, he's obviously a quack who tricks you the first session and then completely snaps for round two. 'All right now, can you tell me where "not good enough" lives, America?'

'Uh, it's definitely in my belly.' I was feeling kinda bloated from lunch and was expecting a period, so it wasn't completely untrue.

'Great. Now just breathe into your belly and when you're comfortable, tell me what you see.' I didn't exactly know how to breathe into my belly, all the same, some images bubbled up, of my chicken

Caesar, half-order of spaghetti and three cappuccinos. Then another, of me putting his grandkids through college while my condition worsened came floating by right behind it. 'Anything?'

'Nothing yet.'

'You're doing great. Keep hacking!'

I opened my eyes. 'Are you sure this really works?'

'Well, you are a little tougher than most, so why don't we send for back-up, intensify the quest, so to speak. Why don't we have you stick your legs straight up in the air and point your toes towards your nose?' I paused, stared at the diplomas on his wall and swung my legs up above me.

'Good. This activates several meridians along the backs of the legs and inner thighs. Just let the blood gently cascade down your legs and pool into the lagoon in your belly.' I felt the blood moving towards my hips now. It made me feel a little queasy. 'Just keep breathing, America, breathing and pointing. Let me know when the images start to surface.'

'I'm seeing something!' I said suddenly. It was true. 'I'm seeing something kind of strange. A bunch of barbarians carrying dead deer on long poles. I see the ropes around their ankle joints. It's the olden days in a mountainous region. France or Iceland maybe, and I'm a slave, I've been bought on the black market too! I feel *doomed.*'

'Good. Go to "doom", only try to stay with this lifetime.'

'Oh, OK.' Suddenly I'm standing in the sun by the stairs near my old public-school classroom. 'I'm . . . ten. I'm running my fingers over my greasy forehead. I have pimples. A ton of them. They just keep erupting. I keep my eyebrows raised to stretch the skin so that the redness disappears. It makes me look like I'm in a constant state of surprise. Everyone notices that I am slowly becoming a large pepperoni pizza. The kids yell out various toppings whenever I walk by.' I heard Karl scribbling.

'Go on.'

'I'm so self-conscious I start wearing a baseball cap to school to hide the inflamed whiteheads and scabs. One day I hear my mom and dad fighting because my father is never there for Spoonie and me. I overhear her tell him to try saying hello to me for a change. I

141

sneak into their room to tell them I'm gonna be late. My dad pulls my hat off my head to kiss me and grimaces. He didn't know my skin was so bad.'

I told Karl I felt rejected, rejected like I felt when Jasper wouldn't pay for dinner or make love when I wanted to, rejected like when my mom accidentally told me she didn't want kids or this life when my dad stayed away too long, rejected like when my dad didn't make time for me, like when my dad died too soon, too fucking soon, like when Jasper left me for no reason at all and refused to speak to me. Karl stroked my hair and handed me a floppy, bow-legged stuffed camel and another box of Kleenex.

Before I left, Dr Karl said I should focus on me, on my perfect career, on my boundaries. Then he said he thought it would be great for me to stay open to duty-dating and practise being the girl and allowing myself to be nurtured. I was to let the man pay for dinner, no matter how uncomfortable it made me; accustomed as I was to going dutch or picking up the tab entirely.

Back in my car I felt defeated. I'd told myself, just hang in there, Mer, someday you won't feel anything for Jasper at all. Then it hit me. I rested my head on the steering wheel, thought, I am *alone* and *this* is my life.

And so it went. Week after week, little salty pools formed in my ear canals. Then Karl would say something brilliant like, 'Dads are supposed to support their kids,' or, 'Do you see how that might be connected to you choosing people who can't meet your needs?' or, 'You're doing great work.' No matter what I confessed – dropping out of school and not going to college like I wanted, sneaking food, lesbian orgasm dreams – he was always supportive. Then he'd always end the session by saying, 'All right now', and I'd leave, clutching a Kleenex at my leaking face, and drive home a slightly lighter wreck as new concepts began to fall into place like a train-station schedule board.

Over time, I hated Karl more than I hated anyone else in the world, even more than my father, even more than Jasper. 'What's going on, America?' Something about hearing my name said so lovingly, by a man. I spilled my fucking guts.

★ ★ ★

'Mer Mer Mer? Are you there? Pick up the phone, Mer, I gotta talk to you. Mer Mer Mer?'

I dropped my purse and ran for the phone. 'What? Sadie, what is it?' Tulie took this as a cue for playtime. She ran and grabbed her tennis ball, held it in her mouth, nudged it at my kneecaps.

'The girl at the restaurant with Jym?'

'Huh? Oh, yeah?' Tulie dropped the ball at my feet, looked up at me. 'Off, Tulie! Off!' I whispered. She scooped the ball up in her wide mouth and skulked off to her little bed to suckle her ball.

'The model Jym was with?'

'Yeah?' I said, with mounting impatience.

'It's his ex.'

'So!' I snapped angrily.

'So? So, we have a deal.'

'Sadie, he's fucking his ex-model girlfriend. Why are you calling me?'

'Wife. It's his ex-wife.'

'Whatever,' I rolled my eyes, began to look through some mail I had left lying on the kitchen counter. Bills, bills, coupons, missing children and a postcard from my old friend Michael with a Rumi poem and a stamp postmarked Tunisia.

'Apparently he dated *Rose* in college.'

'Wait, what? His ex-wife's name is *Rose*?' A rush of adrenalin flooded my system. I screamed.

'I know, I know! He's-in-NY-for-a-week-but-then-he's-coming-back-and-I-gave-him-your-number-and-I-hope-that's-all-right!' I screamed again.

'Sadie, what if he calls me?'

'He's probably gonna.'

'What if he's my soulmate? What if he's my husband? What if the reason Jasper dumped me was so I could meet—' My phone clicked. 'Hold on, Sade,' I clicked over. 'Hello?'

'Hello? America? This is Jym Court calling. Your friend Sadie gave me your number.'

'OhmyGod.'

143

'Is this a bad time?'

'No! *no*! I mean, I'm just on another call right now.' The phone crackled and echoed with fancy hotel long-distance.

'Oh, well, I can phone you back if—'

'No!' I shrieked maniacally. 'Hold on.' I clicked back over to Sadie. 'Jesus, it's *him*!'

'Oh, my God. Oh, my *God*!'

'What should I do?'

'Talk to him!'

'Now?'

'Yes!'

'What should I say?'

Lightning fast, she said, 'Just be yourself. Just be normal, then call me right back!' She hung up.

'I clicked back over. Calmly I said, 'Hello, Jym, it's good to hear from you.' What was wrong with me? I sounded like I was wearing a skirt suit.

'Uh, well, the reason why I'm calling is, I was wondering if you might be interested in joining me for some supper.' Some supper! *Supper*? How positively civilized! I held the phone to my heart, then put it back to my ear. '. . . if you're available then,' he said.

'OhmyGod, I'm so sorry. When?'

'Or another night, if that one's bad.'

'No, it's probably fine. I just need to know when you mean, exactly.'

'Well I meant this Saturday, but it could be next Saturday if you'd prefer . . .' And risk him getting a girlfriend by then?

'*No*! This Saturday's great!' My eyes went as big as saucers. Jesus, God I don't believe it, a date with two days' notice, like a gentleman, like in the olden days, like out of a fairytale, like out of a *movie*! Holy Christ! Calm down and breathe, Mer! I lowered my voice.

'Well, great, see you then, Jym! Goodbye!'

'Wait! Where shall we meet?'

'OhmyGod I'm sorry, I'm in the middle of eight million things . . .' I smacked myself on the head. Idiot.

'I could pick you up if you like?'

'Fine!'

'Great! Well, I'll call you Saturday morning to sort out the details. Are you a morning person?'

'I bit my finger. 'Oh, yeah, totally!' Tulie looked up at me from her little daybed, then put her head back down. Busted.

'Saturday, then!' 'Saturday it is!' When I put the phone down I screamed again and ran over to give Tulie a little squeeze. She hopped up on her hind legs and we danced around like a couple of maniacs. Then I flopped down across my bed without crawling under the covers and went over the call blow by glorious blow. I'd call Sadie soon enough, but right now the moment belonged to me! Jym Court called me. Jym Court called *me*. From *New York*! Jasper never would have done that.

Or if he did, I'd be worried the whole time that he was spending a fortune calling me from a hotel. Of course, if it were Jasper, he would have told me to call him back and pay so he could save his money. Not Jym. I wanted to call Jasper and tell him everything, but I knew he was not a friend to me. Not any more. I could be consumed with thoughts of Jasper no longer, not when I had Jym to think about. Suddenly I didn't feel like staying home.

I was so excited and unable to sit still that I picked up my journal and took a drive. My plan was to find a coffee place and just write. I was so spaced out and drove for so long I ended up all the way downtown, so I decided to go to the Mom and Pop Koffee Haus.

It wasn't until I walked through the door that I remembered I had stolen a cup the last time I had been in there. I wanted to turn and leave but, before I could, the guy behind the counter recognized me and shouted, 'Hey, I remember you! Hazelnut latte, no foam. You stole a mug last time you were in here!'

They had changed all the art around since I was there last. Now it was all portraits of puppies, bunnies, kittens and a baby monkey with a cast on his tiny arm. The show was called 'Fluffy Things'.

'Wow!' I blushed. 'OhmyGod I'm so sorry, I completely forgot. How much is it?' I reached for my wallet.

'Don't worry about it, it's on me.'

'No, no, really, I'm not like that!' Then I thought about Karl's order to receive, and ordered an Earl Grey tea and said thank you instead.

While he separated the leaves from the tea with a white plastic and mesh strainer, he said, 'Yunno, I'm reading this really interesting article on the lotus blossom and all its uses, and about how scientists are studying its surface to learn how to make a better house paint because nothing sticks to their petals . . . That's why they were selected, for their spiritual significance. Did you know that? He smiled and put the tea on the counter. I smiled back when I noticed he had poured it into a paper cup. 'Milk and sugar?'

'Half-and-half.'

'It's really cool.' He put a metal thermos full of half-and-half in front of me.

'Huh?'

'The article.'

'Oh.'

He watched as I poured in three-ish sugars from a free-flowing sugar dispenser and stirred my tea. 'So, how's it hanging?'

I thought about Karl and his instruction for me to practice boundaries.

'I don't mean to be rude, but I don't really feel like company right now.' Karl would be proud.

'That's cool.'

I scooped up my cup, walking in time to Shelby Lynne on the jukebox, and plopped down at a small table and began writing in my journal.

America Court. America Court. I practised doodling my name with his last as my own. *Jym and America Court.*

It looked kind of awful, but who cared.

I worked on a hyphenated version instead. *America Throne-Court.*

While Bob Marley belted out 'Redemption Song', I perfected the transition from the capital J to the lower-case y. I didn't put a tip in the jar when I left, or even say goodbye. When I got home I found out I was booked for another voice-over. I thought, rewarded. For all my good growth.

Later that night, lying in bed, I thought, Jym with a 'y'. Jym with a why the fuck not! Then I thought about the lotus blossom, and about my parent's hippy friends who ditched their last names and took a whole new last name entirely. Jym and America Lotus, because nothing sticks to them, because they are untainted, like me.

SEVENTEEN

Owls

'Talk talk talk yeah, birds talk to me.'
— Crowded House

I called Sadie in a panic. If he was on time, he'd be there in less than an hour!

Earlier that day, Jym had called to square the pick-up time. I almost burst into tears when he asked, with real interest, how I was doing. To know that I was talking with a man who I was not paying, who still wanted to know about my feelings.

For the rest of the day that followed our nearly twelve-minute call — when I wasn't busy daydreaming about what our children would look like or wondering whether or not he'd make a good father (this I vowed to find out at dinner) — I noticed how amazing plants and animals and sky and birds were. But, by 7.22 p.m. it had all worn off and I was becoming more and more socially unstable with every revolution of the second hand.

Wholly unsure of how to behave or fill the remainder of time without my head exploding off my body, I realised that my entire life hung in the balance. If things went well with Jym it meant I was indeed moving on and away from The J.H.I., *but*, if things went lousy, I was destined to be alone and miserable for the rest of my life. Sadie gave me implicit orders to wear something sexy or she would personally off me.

A few things make me feel sexy: tights, not pantyhose, but tights. I love how they make my whole lower half one streamlined package (I feel taller, skinnier and sexier). A g-string under a flowy skirt also does the trick. Big balloony dresses with thick men's socks to the calf and clunky shoes, preferably platform, work too, as do overalls and really well-worn T-shirts. All of these things were in a large pile on my bed.

Finally, I put on a saffron-coloured blouse, hoop earrings, a favourite pair of bell-bottoms with a sixty-nine patch on the back pocket, and a pair of motorcycle boots and looked at myself in my mirror. Jasper always seemed to think this outfit was attractive too, so maybe Jym would, too. I did a three-quarter turn in every direction.

Then again, maybe Jasper didn't really like my clothes at all, and that's why he dumped me. Maybe at thirty I just wasn't sexy any more. I quickly changed my shoes, put on a pair of sexy strappy heels. They looked awful with the pants. I changed back into the boots. In the end I opted for a black silk slip, a black drapy shawl and ballerina flats.

Seven-fifty-two. Shit, shit, *shit*, Magruder!

He'd be there in eight minutes.

Fuck the producer guy. If he didn't like me for me, what was the use of him. But my hair!

I decided to appoint the remaining minutes of my nervous breakdown to wrestling a decent hairdo out of the ethers. I couldn't decide: up, down, low ponytail, high ponytail, braids, wavy or straight, sloppily swept up, sleek or loose. His ex had worn hers down in a wild mane. I could not deduce psychically or logically, though I tried, whether or not Jym preferred to stay with what he knew hairwise, or deviate from the norm. When the doorbell rang I decided on down, with a blue rhinestone barrette.

In a frenzy I checked myself in the hall mirror for stray threads, things in my teeth, deodorant balls and sweat stains. Finding none, I opened the door.

There he stood, freshly showered and cologned, in a light brown cashmere sweater, black tailored trousers and funky black boots with burnished buckles across the toe. I leaned against the door to steady my balance. He was more handsome than I remembered.

We stood in the doorway smiling goonishly at one another, while I pulled on the ends of my hair like a nervous schoolgirl. 'Are you going to invite me in?' he said. For a second I thought about vampires and how they can't hurt you unless they are invited in.

'Of course!' I blurted. 'I have zero manners. I'm so sorry. I'm so nervous, I feel like I'm getting diarrhoea.' Jesus, Mer, what is wrong with you? I blushed and bit my fingernail nervously to keep from saying anything else idiotic, but he just started laughing.

'I'm nervous, too. Maybe we could just hug for a while.' I could not believe my ears. 'Yes!' I announced, utterly relieved that a) we had feeling ill in common, and b) Jym, unlike Jasper Husch, was a problem-solver. It felt strange to have my arms around someone I didn't know, and even stranger because I didn't really mind. Probably because he smelled like *IsittoosoontomovetoFrance?*

In my arms he felt vulnerable and manly at the same time, maybe because I knew he had been loved and divorced. His body seemed to have absorbed the experience and was whispering it to me in soft wool and vetiver.

We stood like that and held each other until only the sound of our breath and our heartbeats and rushing blood mattered. I heard Tallulah's nails click-click-clicking against my hardwood floors. I could feel her at my ankle sniffing Jym's leg. I pressed my nose hard into his cashmered arm and deeply inhaled.

He let go first, stepped back and looked at me. 'You look really beautiful. I really like your hair that way.'

'My hair? Oh, God, it was driving me Brazil nuts about thirty seconds ago!' Brazil nuts? Jesus, Mer, who talks like that? I died all over again, fearing maybe now he knew what a complete moron I was, and was only waiting for the right moment to unapologetically do an about-face.

But he took my hand and asked, 'How 'bout a tour?'

As Jym opened the door of his white convertible Jag, and I slid into the cream-coloured leather seats, I learned an ugly truth about

151

myself: that in a heartbeat I had become the girls that Sadie and I hated most. The ones with the boyfriends that took them to fancy restaurants and bought them expensive presents and took them on all-expenses-paid vacations. I always thought Jasper made me stronger, but now I realized that he just made me feel unloved. I mean, I couldn't get Jasper to fold my laundry.

When the seat-belt form fitted itself snugly around me and Jym flipped the switch that made my seat heat up, I decided that no matter the outcome of my alliance with Jym, I was over struggling-poverty-art-boys entirely.

At the hidden restaurant in Malibu with Sol in the title, people could not help but stare at the attractive, glowing chemistry factory seated at table four, courtesy of a twenty-dollar bill slipped discreetly into a bloated maître d's hand. Jym ordered for me and kept calling me Dollface, and I felt like one instead of like an every-man-for-your-selfer, like when I was with Jasper.

Over the weird French appetizer with the tiny sweet pickles, boiled potatoes and hot smelly cheese, I discovered Jym, unlike Jasper, had a real job making real money. Jym worked for a company that made TV shows and low-budget, top-grossing teen horror flicks. Jym was in *Development*. His dream was to blend the teen format with adult content and make his mark giving the game-show world the legitimacy it deserved. Jym went to college. Jym graduated.

Jym didn't believe in astrology, even though he knew he was on the cusp of Virgo/Libra with a Scorpio ascendant and a Pisces moon. He actually had an office and a phone and an expense account and a personal assistant and an apartment with its own parking space and everything. Jym, unlike Jasper, drank caffeinated things and had been to therapy. Jym thought therapy was *important*. Jym had two cats, but loved dogs, too. Jym liked sex. Jym, unlike Jasper, was a real, grown-up, looking to be in a monogamous, committed relationship. When the shaved white radish and frisée salad with truffle oil and mango dressing arrived, and Jym said he hoped to get *married* again someday, I almost choked on my own saliva.

152

I thanked God for my body's amazing autopilot control system in charge of things like swallowing and breathing and beating my heart, because everything I wanted was seated directly across from me.

When the rabbit stew in the individual clay pots arrived, I wanted to tell Jym everything; that I was afraid all the time, that I wanted him to hold me all night long, and tomorrow night, and for the rest of my life, because he was a *man* and a man is what I needed, because he made me feel like a woman. I wanted to tell him I needed him, and how much I had lost, but that it was all worth it now because he existed. Instead, I said, 'The key lime pie sounds good.' But Jym ordered coconut crème caramel and apple and pear *tarte tartin* with caramel sauce. 'Trust me.'

When it arrived, he rocked in his chair like a big kid and smacked his lips and said, 'Scrumdidliumptious!' I really admired how totally unafraid he was to express his childlike wonder and dorkiness over little things like smell and taste and texture! I just smiled and smiled and beamed him love.

When the waiter brought the check, I repeated my therapy mantra. 'I am the lady, not the caretaker, not the eldest child, not the mom.' But I didn't have to worry, because Jym was Catholic and from Illinois, so, unlike Jasper, he reached for his wallet and paid with a shiny new corporate credit card.

'You little tax write-off!' he said decadently, while the little candles on all the tables flickered their Morse-code message, *he's the one, he's the one.*

I looked up at the ceiling and saw a big mural of a blazing sun. How many times had I cried over Jasper, when now it all seemed like a funny dream? What was I ever so upset about? That's when I figured out that 'sol' means sun. Sun, sol, soul. True love is what was allowing me to see the sun as soul. Sol. Sol mate, to be love itself, an ever-shining sun.

As he sensually sucked back the last of the warm, caramel-coated apples and flaky crust crumbs and waited for the waiter to return with his receipt, I couldn't help but wish it was me in his mouth. No, Mer, you mustn't rush things, I told myself. You are going to let things take their natural course, so, on the drive home, I brought up venereal diseases and suggested getting AIDS tests together, even though I assured him we would definitely be using condoms for the first six months. He looked at me and laughed and then said, 'You're reading my mind.' I was so happy I felt drunk, both hyper-alert and giddily anaesthetized. You could have performed surgery on me that minute and I would have felt no pain.

As we sped past a big moon shimmering on a certain Pacific Ocean with the top down and the heat on, Cat Stevens blaring on the CD player, I wondered if I had always chosen love over money because I had grown up with excess, and rebelled by choosing poverty. Or maybe if I mistook poverty for grounded reality because I had never found the two to be available in one package. Or maybe I chose love over money because my mother did, because when my parents splurged on us it meant my father had been fucking someone else. All I knew was that one night of being treated so well by someone who was interested in me for *me* made me think I had come a long way in a few short months of heartbreak and therapy.

I thought, if I die on the way back from the five-star restaurant *he* chose, I'll die a happy woman.

Jym walked me to my door and asked me if he could see me on the weekend. A moth circled the overhead light. I swept the wooden deck with my left foot. It made a sweeping sound. Shuffle-step-kick, shuffle-step-kick. I accidentally kicked the welcome mat out of place. A big black spider ran towards my foot. I jumped back. I shrieked. Tulie watched us in the window.

'So is that a yes?'

'Um, yeah, OK, I . . . sure, yes, I'd love to.'

'Saturday then?'

'Sure! Yes!'

He leaned in and kissed me softly on the cheek, like a gentleman. 'Goodnight.'

I giggled. 'Goodnight,' I said, all swoony, and slipped inside, closing the door behind me quietly. I pressed my back into the wood and smelled the dark with its night-blooming jasmine and magical unknown. 'Thank you, God, thank you, God. I have met the man I am going to marry, I am sure of it.'

'Sadie,' I said, kicking my feet free from the too-tucked-in sheet, 'he even said he wants to get married and everything!'

She groaned slightly. 'What's wrong with him?'

'Nothing's wrong with him!'

I heard her light up a cigarette, inhale. 'Something's wrong. He probably has a small cock. No man with a big cock wants to get married.'

I giggled. 'I don't think it's small.'

'You slut!'

'No! I sort of felt it when he hugged me.'

'Listen up, girlie, you are not allowed to have sex with him until you have seen his apartment, to be sure there are no Star Wars action figures in their boxes on display. To make sure he is a grown-up. Do you understand me?'

I bit my lip. 'I think he's the one.'

'The one what?'

'The *one* one.'

'Are you saying you'd stay with him if he was paralysed from the waist down?'

'I think I am.'

'Are you saying you'd stay with him if he was HIV?'

'Sadie!'

'Well?'

'I think I would.'

Long pause. 'Are you telling me you could eat his ass?'

I broke into peals of hysterical laughter. 'Yessss!!'

'Oh. My. God.' I heard her take in the seriousness of what I had just said. After some time, she managed, 'Well, I'm not paying for my bridesmaid dress. And it better not be ballerina pink.' There was panic in Sadie's voice, perhaps the fear of loss of girlie slumber parties and crushes on boys in coffee houses, or the fear that I could be moving on without her before we even got to be single together.

'Come on, be happy for me! You're the one who set us up.'

'To date, not to marry, to *date*.' I bit the edge of my duvet. 'And it's *our* generation's job to keep the population explosion down, so no kids. Ya hear me?'

'Not right away, anyway.'

'Jesus,' she said, utterly disgusted. 'Goodnight, Mer.'

I hung up the phone and pulled my covers over my head. They smelled all baby-powdery clean. The light shone pink through the hand-sewn flowers. Tulie made her licking sound and I didn't even mind. I reached my arm out from under the covers and turned off the light.

That night, I had a dream an owl landed on my shoulder. It is ancient times and I am a young woman being trained in the healing arts. Karl is there. He is a wizard. He is my teacher. When I look at the owl, I notice it suddenly has big squishy Mick Jagger lips. It begins kissing me all over my face, particularly on a few pimples and old scars. Karl tells me it is a great blessing from the Creator and that owls represent wisdom and deception because they have full sight even in darkness and thus represent the total truth. 'Light and darkness,' he repeats. 'A mirror of truth.'

I woke up right in the middle of it. Just then I heard an owl in the big old pine tree in front of my house. I had never noticed just how tall that tree was.

EIGHTEEN

Hope: a Tribute to the Colour Brown

'Jolene heard the singing in the forest, she opened the door
quietly and stepped into the night.'

— Cake

The next morning the biggest batch of white lilies arrived at my
door in a brown vase with a note, 'From your not-so-secret-
admirer. Love, Jym'. I hummed the wedding march while I put
them in water. Jasper who?

NINETEEN
Belly Button

'God have mercy on the man who doubts what he's sure of.'
— Bruce Springsteen

'Welcome to my Padarooski!' Jym announced the following Saturday night as he opened the door to his highly Ikeaed, two-bedroom apartment done in creams, white and light woods. 'Come on in and meet the freaks!' Two cats nearly immobilized by fat, meowed and meowed in steady unison on a well-worn braided rug. 'Freaks, Dollface, Dollface, freaks. The fat one is Messy and the fatter one is Bessy.' The larger of the two had an inspired Freddie Mercury-esque overbite. Jym knelt down and petted their bellies. I melted.

'How did they get their names?'

He coughed. 'Uh, my ex named them. Messy because her hair always mats up, Bessy because of Bessy Buckley. From the musical *Cats*.'

My face went hot. 'You mean Betty Buckley. The mom from eight is enough? Betty Buckley?'

'Yeah, she loved that show.'

'But ...'

'Yeah, I know.' He closed his eyes. He tried to shrug their history off by rubbing the smaller, shaggier cat with the clumpy dreads. She tried to scratch him but her reflexes were too slow. He stood quickly and moved towards the kitchen. I followed him.

159

The apartment was train-shaped; you moved from the living room through a spare bedroom he'd converted into an office, through the kitchen, then presumably a dining room behind a swinging door, and beyond that probably a master bedroom of some sort, from what I could make out anyway. Thus far, not a Star Wars action figure in sight. 'Do you want some water or beer or wine?' he said as he pulled two glasses from a cupboard.

'Sure, water would be fine,' I said as he poured a glass of '94 Merlot. He handed it to me and touched my hip.

I smiled shyly, giggled, 'No thank you.'

'You don't drink?'

'Actually, I'm allergic.'

'Oh? What happens when you drink?'

A wave of feral heat burned in my belly, butterflies on fire. 'Um,' I said blushing, 'for one thing, I get a little bit sexual.'

'Really,' he said, swirling the wine around in my reject glass. He smelled it. 'That doesn't sound too bad.'

'A lot bit sexual, actually.' He handed me back my glass, which I reluctantly took, smiled, took a sip from his own glass, then leaned against the door frame.

'Don't worry. I don't bite.' I blushed, then took the smallest sip. Then he pushed open the swinging door and I saw *it*, a chandelier! A grown man who wasn't gay with a chandelier! Below the big droopy crystals was an orange and white chequered tablecloth on the floor with about three dozen blazing tea lights. The candles made the chandelier cast starry rainbow streaks on the walls. Hearts and flowers shot out of my eyes; I was that cartoon skunk floating around that amazing two-bedroom apartment within walking distance to at least four Starbucks.

I thought, see you at the altar.

We ate takeout Italian with real silverware to classical music with a few too many crashing cymbals in my opinion, and then talked about his favourite movies and magazines. He subscribed to everything. 'I have to, to stay on top of things. Yunno, for work.'

'You obviously get the home magazines.' Stupid, stupid. 'I mean, because this place is so beautiful.'

160

'Yeah.' He looked around, took in his gift. 'I thought about getting it submitted to *Metropolitan*, or *Home and Garden* or *MS Living*, but...' he trailed off, looked at the floor, 'I just rent, so...' He topped off the final sip in his glass, stared at me. 'You look really beautiful in this light.' Jym touched my cheek. His hand felt moisturized, save one stray hangnail that dragged a little. I didn't say anything, I didn't want to spoil the mood. It was a good thing because just then he leaned in to kiss me. It was soft and a little wetter than I imagined. Fire-coated winged creatures danced in my belly. I panicked.

'I should probably get going,' I said suddenly.

'OK.' He said too quickly right back. It made me think he didn't like me anymore, but then he touched my hip and walked me outside. 'Goodnight, Dollface,' he said, lightly stroking my hair.

'Goodnight,' I said, like some mute, lobotomized Juliet. I turned to go, followed a little brick path that led to the street.

'Hey, Mer?'

I turned back. 'Yeah?'

'Do you want to stay the night? I promise I won't try anything.' He crossed his heart as proof. Adorable!

Mer, be strong, I thought, don't blow it, don't rush. I could hear Karl's voice in my head, like Obi Wan, 'Wait Luke, wait.'

'I just thought it would be nice if we just held each other tonight,' said Jym as he slinked toward me, softly rubbing his soul patch.

Mer, be strong, pace yourself, pace yourself... Besides, there's no one to let Tallulah out! Then I blurted, 'Sure, I'd love to!' Jesus, Mer, what an idiot. I heard submarine attack sirens in my head. 'But I don't have a toothbrush.' Good girl.

'I have a spare.'

'What?'

'Toothbrush. I have a spare toothbrush.'

'Of course you do, you have all those teeth.' I practically skipped back into his padarooski.

He let me wear his big flannel jammies to bed while he wore a T-shirt and some Abercrombie and Fitch boxers. Of course he left his calf-length socks on. He squeezed some blue gel toothpaste on my fresh new out-of-the-box red toothbrush and we brushed our teeth side by side, like a couple.

As I bent forward to spit I caught our reflection in the mirror, thought, we look good together.

In his big asthma-proofed bed with the feather-free down comforter and matching pillows, he stroked my cheeks and hair while I tickled his back underneath his T-shirt. 'I'm really glad you're here.'

'Me too.'

'I know we aren't in charge of life's little gifts, but I want you to know I am open to receiving them.'

'Me too.'

Suddenly his breath was on me. It smelled like those creamy pastel after-dinner mints. He tenderly kissed me goodnight and we hugged, pressing our pyjamed bodies close.

Nose to nose now, he said, 'Goodnight, Dollface.'

'Goodnight, Giraffe,' I said, just like that. I nicknamed him back, just like that. It just came right out. Dollface and Giraffe. It took me and Jasper ages to come up with Guava. It took us so long that we didn't have the energy to come up with another name, so we were both Guava.

I thought, holy shit, maybe my life is going to work out after all.

Even in the dark I could see he was looking at me and smiling, and I was flooded with the alarm one feels when one glimpses the entire rest of her life ... and likes it.

'Goodnight,' he said again.

'Goodnight,' I said. Then Jym just held me until we fell asleep like monkeys, a tangle of arms and legs and my hair.

In the morning Jym microwaved me some chai tea, bachelor-style, but poured it into a big, beautiful, aesthetically pleasing cup like a grown-up. Why does everything taste better when someone else makes it? Jasper never made me a cup of microwaved chai. Then again, Jasper didn't own a microwave.

After Jym showered, he told me if I ever wanted to leave things at his place, he would empty out a drawer for me in the bathroom. If I ever? I drove home in a moon-walking state of shock.

There, I found two puddles of urine and one steamer.

It was worth it.

'Does this mean he's my boyfriend? Do you think, Sadie, do you?' I said, as I damp mopped.

'Not if you only dry-humped. Dollface and Giraffe? Jesus, Mer, my stomach. You are making me physically ill. What about Jasper?'

'I'm totally over him. It's just like his fax said, people grow and move on. He's on a path and I'm on a path and that's just the beauty of life.'

'Euch.'

'Sadie, why can't you be happy for me?'

'Because you're nuts. You haven't even had sex with him yet, and you think he's your boyfriend. What if you hate him in bed? What if he makes porn face when he cums? What if he's a premature ejaculator?'

'Sadie!' Tallulah came traipsing in and nudged a chew toy in my lap. I was feeling generous, so I wedged the phone between my shoulder and my ear and tossed it, even though it was wet with her stinking saliva. It skidded across the kitchen floor and made a friction sound as it disappeared under the stove.

'I'm just worried about you, is all. You complain non-stop about Jasper, and then miraculously overnight you are planning your future with a guy who sounds like a high-school basketball PE coach. Can you say rebounding?'

Tallulah reappeared with the wet ropy chew toy. I bent down and tossed the damp horror east.

'You're the one who fixed us up!'

'To *date*, not to fall in love with. To be honest, I really didn't think it would go anywhere...'

Tallulah reappeared enthusiastically with the wet chew toy, then dropped it and sat panting, waiting for the next toss. I teased her by holding it over her head and lowering it every now and again. 'We know that Auntie Sadie is just a little jealous, don't we, Tulie?

163

You understand that I am not in charge of life's little gifts. I am merely open to receiving them.'

'Auntie Sadie is just gonna go throw up now. Bye, Mer.'

Tulie nipped at my hand. I swatted her down, put the toy on top of the fridge where she couldn't reach it. 'Bye Sadie,' I said, utterly fascinated with the communication device in my hand.

I thought, aren't phones amazing?

I knew I was in love because when my French neighbour started up his uncommonly loud leaf-blower and beat his car senseless, I didn't care. When Spoonie called to tell me he and Lila ran in to Jasper at a photo exhibit in Silverlake, I didn't care. When my mother called to tell me she was thinking about selling the home I grew up in, I didn't care. I only thought, if Jasper was a cosmic joke so that Jym Court could be the stellar punchline, I am laughing with the Almighty this minute!!

On Thursday I saw Karl. He didn't even have to prod or ask me how I was or anything. I just blurted out a monologue of unbridled joy. 'He can't stop buying me gifts. Sweaters, socks, bath products, soaps... He calls me Dollface and e-mails me from work non-stop, and when I call his office, even the receptionist seems happy for us. She always puts me right through, even when he is in the middle of an important meeting. He says adorable things like "scrumdidliumptious", and "what's cooking", and "*nada piñata*". He's funny and playful and masculine and smart and has an important job, and that makes me feel important. I mean, miraculously I am beginning to feel more like myself again. Only, I'm a me I have not known before. And the more I like myself, the less sense it makes that Jasper doesn't want me, that my father didn't want me, when I'm great. Only now I don't care that they didn't want me because Jym wants me and he's great, and, and, and...'

'What is it America?'

'I'm just really happy,' I said, only then really seeing Karl for the first time. I saw *clearly* that Karl had been re-parenting me all along, teaching me *by example* that I deserved more, because Karl gave me more. Karl cared about me. Karl listened to me. So now, as a result,

I had attracted someone else who cared about me as much as Karl did. Now I knew it was time to quit therapy.

'Did you have sex with Tim?'

'No!' I blushed. 'His name is Jym.'

'He nodded. 'Good, because the courtship phase is extremely important. Remember, you can't roast marshmallows in the power-struggle phase if you haven't built a fire in the courtship phase! That way, if you *wait* until you know who you are dealing with, you can enjoy *s'more* of him later on!'

'*I'll wait! I'll wait!*' I giggled. It made me miss my dad to be scolded like that.

He winked at me. 'All right now, our time's up for today. Next week, same time?'

I nodded my head. I didn't think Karl was ready to hear the truth. So on the drive home, I phoned him from my car, thanked him for all his help and cancelled the following week's appointment.

Later that night I saw Jym's pubic hair for the first time.

We kissed and dry-humped for a hot while, and I could feel him hardening. As he pulled at my shirt, trying to get it over my head, I thought, oh, God, he's going to feel my adult acne! Fine. Better to get it over with sooner rather than later. He should know this about me. If he is anything other than understanding, it's his problem. I would still accept him if he had a few zits. He said nothing, just continued to kiss me so deeply and so sweetly that all I could do was relax. Then he stuck his hand in my jeans and, checking for wetness, began to finger me.

I unzipped his trousers. He wasn't wearing underwear. I thought, how sixties of him. His cock flopped out like a lazy showgirl. Jesus, I thought, he's huge! I began to suck on him a little with his trousers still on. He fully stiffened. I tugged at his pants and he lifted his hips so I could pull them all the way down.

That's when I saw his pubic hair. It was shaved. He had almost no pubes, only razor stubble. Like Don Johnson in *Miami Vice*. He really should have warned me, although I couldn't imagine how it might have come up.

Try to maintain, I told myself, this is the same nit-picking that tore Jasper and me apart. Just try to accept him for who he is. He seemed to not care about your back; surely you can get over this. So what if he has a few kinks, you get kinks with everybody. It's just a matter of finding the ones you can live with. I didn't want to break the mood, so I did a kind of blow-drier technique on his stubbly balls to make the negative energy vanish.

He was moaning and gyrating then. Thrusting his exceedingly large cock in and out of my mouth. It whacked the roof of my mouth with the force of the end of an industrial flashlight. He was a gentleman, however, and pushed my mouth away before he came, and it mostly landed in his exceedingly large belly button, and my hair.

Turned out he was a screamer – also a bit shocking – but then these are the things that one can only find out by jumping in.

We lay there for a little while in his afterglow, me on his buttery chest, him tugging on the ends of my crispy hair. Then, suddenly, Jym sat up and started to cry. 'There is something I have to tell you that you might freak out about.' My mind raced. What could it be? Herpes, AIDS, cancer? We already talked about that stuff. Did he lie? Is he a sociopath? Did he kill someone? Is he still married?

'This is really hard for me, but I think I'm falling in love with you.' He nuzzled into my tiny bare breasts. 'I just feel so selfish for coming first. I wanted to stop but your mouth felt too good. I'm sorry.' I patted him on the back, then thought, wait, am I consoling him or mothering him. Either way *turn off*. 'It's just that it takes a really long time for my penis to get an erection again.' Penis? Erection? Was I dating an anatomy book? He leaned up and kissed my cheek.

I thought, you know something, it would have been nice if you had given me an orgasm first. Or at all. Or, say, *now*. I guess he's *kind of* tried, or is he just a lazy pig. I was angry now.

'Oh, baby, I'll make it up to you. Come here, Dollface. Whattsamatter, baby? Whattsamatter?' he kept repeating. Whattsamatter was my face was smushed under his sweaty pit. Only, I didn't say anything because he was crying and already felt like a big fuck-up.

'Please forgive me.'

'Of course I forgive you,' I said, even though I didn't.

I thought, why can't he just get over it and seduce me now? If he wanted to give me an orgasm so badly then why didn't he just do it? Why doesn't he just give me head right now? Or, at the very least, finger me. Anything, just do it now now *now*. Or is this some twisted manipulation so he gets out of it altogether? And how come I can't say any of this? Now I feel like I'm a freak for even wanting him to, and now he has kind of totally gotten away with it. And now it's too late to even ask, and anyway, why should I even have to ask, and now there is just too much pressure!

'Let's just hold each other,' he said.

We leaned back and he draped the blanket across us. I lay against his wide, flat chest listening to a revving engine nag and stall. I listened to Jym's breathing and his heartbeat. I thought, at least he was falling in love with me, and that was something.

After a little while he grabbed my hand and let me feel him hardening. 'Stroke me,' he whispered. I did. I was still a little crabby from before, but his passion for me dissolved my irritation, and before I knew it, gold foil was coming off an extra-large condom. Miraculously we managed to climax at the same moment. I started crying Jasper was truly behind me now.

'Come here,' he cooed and held me close.

I thought, first-time sex is so weird.

It began to rain as we lay in each other's arms. We listened until I felt Jym twitch himself to sleep. Overall, not the greatest but, I knew I would sleep like a baby, certain that there would be many many more opportunities to perfect our lovemaking.

In the morning I heard him get up and shower. I listened carefully to his bathroom sounds — wet feet on linoleum, the brushing of perfect teeth, the coughing up of phlegm, rinsing of the sink, tapping of the toothbrush. Soon I would have to move my car, which was blocking him in.

I thought, I can live with this. I mean, I think I can live with this.

TWENTY

Hit TV

'Why?'

— Annie Lennox

That first couple of weeks it was all faxes and phone calls and e-mail letters. Jym was literally healing me with his adorableness, like in this one:

Dollface,
Recipe for Happiness:
Seeing your face
Smelling you
Hearing you laugh
Hearing you cum
Holding you close
And 4 T. vanilla
Love always,
Jym the Jyraffe

(I liked how he did the clever thing with the tablespoons and the Jy in Jyraffe.)
And this one:

Baby, Sweetness, Honey, Love, Dearest, Angel, Peaches, Darling,

Gorgeous, Sexy Pudding Pants, I want to chew your clothes
off and make you squeal like, well, something that squeals!
Jym 'Barry White' Court

And this one:

Roses are red, violets are blue, I'm fully hard and want to
come over there and make pumpkin love to you.

(Pumpkin love, because for Hallowe'en we got a little naughty in
the middle of carving a pumpkin together!)

Then one day, out of the blue, he just said, 'I just think you
should have this,' and handed me a key to his swanky, high-tech
apartment *avec* chandelier.

The best part of any relationship, the only noble cause worth
aiming for, is the settling in. I despised the courtship phase, the
'Steely Dan' time of the relationship when you swear up and down
that you have the same taste in music, the calculated dispensing of
half-truths that eventually break down and give way to what is real.
It is only when one is truly brave, like me and Jym, that one is able
to let all the disguises fall away and be granted entry into the
glorious land of We. Jasper and I couldn't even find our keys to the
car in the parking lot near the entrance of such a place.

What I loved most was the regularity with Jym, the monotony,
the routine of simply being. The discovery of when we both
wanted sex or dinner or time to ourselves, and the careful
negotiating of it all without killing each other.

I already knew the mornings by heart. First, wake up and have
sex. After, Jym would shower and dress, then he would heat us up
some chai tea from Trader Joe's (bringing mine to me in bed), toast
me, take a sip of his, smack his lips and say, 'Scrumdidliumptious'.
Then, one of the cats would either spit something up or meow too
long, causing Jym to yell at them both. Now I'd have to get out of
bed and move my car, which was blocking him in.

In the evenings Jym would get home around eight thirty and
since I didn't like to eat late and Jym didn't cook, we'd usually just

order a fancy oil, cream and butter-drenched takeout and watch TV. I was careful not to cook for Jym because I didn't want to turn into his little *hausfrau* like I was for Jasper. I was hyper-aware not to repeat old destructive patterns that turned me into a mother or resentful lover.

Then, after I watched Jym watch his game show, sitcom or teen horror competition duke it out on the boob, we had sex.

On weekends the sex times varied in between watching Jym playing street hockey with the guys from work, watching Jym get a manicure for work, walking my dog, seeing movies and watching Jym snack on lunchable meats and mayonnaise straight from the package.

I would watch him tear the pink processed meat away from its neat stack and dip the wiggly square with the rounded edges directly into the mayo jar itself, getting dollops of white goo on his hand. I feared for Jym's cholesterol level, but praised him for having the courage to do it in front of me as, in my opinion, this was the type of thing one did on one's own time behind a locked door.

Jym astounded me. He was unafraid to pick blackheads, fart and listen to his messages in front of me. This was the beauty of Jym. Largely, it was through my acceptance of Jym's little quirks that I was beginning to realize how I was partly to blame in the demise of my relationship with Jasper.

I never really let Jasper be Jasper. I was too busy hating everything he did that was not related to me, because I felt threatened that Jasper's choices took him away from *us*. Like his love of porn, or his affection for seeing movies with me in the gayest hardcore neighbourhoods of San Francisco, when there were plenty of other theatres within walking distance to see those same movies. While I always thought he was stupid and secretly gay, now I saw that he was just a sensual, life-loving innovator. With Jym, I was willing to watch him eat processed meat and saturated fats and not even mind so much because a happy him meant a happy *us*.

For the first time I felt I was in a real grown-up relationship; mainly for the first time in my life I felt motivated to work out (partly because Jym didn't and partly because Jym was around models and actresses all day long). Plus, by the time he'd get home late at night, I'd have missed him a whole day's worth and actually *wanted* to see him again, whereas Jasper worked at home and we were always in each other's hair and space, never taking time apart, unless I was in LA for a couple of weeks trying to book a VO job. Doing stomach crunches on Jym's sisal rugs, I could not believe I was ever even depressed.

Picking up kitty litter and food for Jym's cats one afternoon, I ran in to the coffee guy. I apologized for being such a bitch the last time I saw him. He just said, 'No worries, mate,' in a fake Australian accent and handed me another flyer, which I promptly stuffed in my purse. He was standing near the catnip mice wearing a 'Jesus Saves, Gretsky Gets the Rebound and Scores' T-shirt. It made me feel kinda sorry for him, so I paid for the goods and got the hell out of dodge.

Later that night, curled up on Jym's sofa, he asked me why we hadn't made love in my bed yet, asked if it was because of Jasper. I told him maybe I was still holding on to a small part of him. I was so grateful to be busted: I had to have him that very minute, so we got in the car, drove to my place and did it, slow and missionary. Then it was official – Jym and I were for real for real.

Thanksgiving came and went without incident, even though it was the day before the anniversary of my sister's death and Jym and I couldn't be together.

His family had been expecting him home in Illinois, and he'd already bought the ticket before he'd even met me. And besides, he promised we'd spend Christmas together, and that was by far the more important holiday of the season, so no big.

I liked how Jym was totally willing to plan the future with me whereas Jasper, like my father, had always taken enlightened pride in just living moment to moment.

My mother didn't even bother me once the whole day, even though she talked at length about exciting upcoming events that were planned around my father: a retrospective in Prague, a nine-page spread in *Art in America*, a cover story in the *New York*

Times, and a touring slide show in elementary schools across the country. While she made the gravy and her world-famous (in her mind) cornbread, ginger and chestnut stuffing, I felt happy. I even helped make piecrusts because I actually had something to be thankful for.

I had a terrific chat with Lila. Spoonie talked about maybe going away to a spa for a long weekend as a foursome! Though I will admit I did get a little peeved when Lila said, 'It's so great that Jym's finally calmed down, yunno, because of his reputation for being such a player and all.' I just had another helping of turkey and all was forgiven.

Of course, it helped that Jym faxed me romantic mushy stuff about 179 times that day.

The next day, however, I was feeling particularly bloated and we had our first fight. I told him I was feeling a little lonely and a little fat. Jym told me bluntly he didn't believe in feeling sorry for oneself, to which I replied that I didn't feel sorry for myself, I was just feeling sad. (I also made the mistake of mentioning that I was envious of his work because he was gone so much.) He said I was just like his ex-wife and why didn't I just get a job, any job, and focus on problems I could actually solve. 'I mean, what do you even do for a living? All I see you doing is getting an allowance like a thirty-year-old child, just like my ex-wife, while the rest of the world works for a living.' And I said, 'You're just jealous.' And he said, 'Of what?' And I said, 'Not having free time.' And he said, 'To do what? Sit around and get fat?' Then I said, 'You should talk, what about your bagged-meat obsession?' And he said, 'At least I buy it with my own money.' And I said, 'yeah, and you'll pay for your hospital bills with your own money too!' So he said, 'At least I have health insurance!' That shut me up, because, no I wasn't sure if I was on a co-pay because I didn't even know what a co-pay was.

Then he hung up on me and didn't call me for two days, even though I had to go to his apartment twice a day to feed his cats. Apparently he felt perfectly justified not apologizing. (Then again, I didn't call him either.) I wanted to call Sadie, but she was still mad that Jym and I had progressed past the one-night stand she had hoped for, and I didn't want to give her a reason to celebrate. I thought about calling Karl. Instead, I just wrote it all off looking for ways to push Jym away because I was afraid of getting attached to someone so great.

I called Jym and apologized and we 'agreed to disagree'. Jym made me promise either to get a day job and/or not feel sorry for myself. That night we stayed on the phone and talked for hours; stories about pre-Christmas shopping with the family and first snowfalls and icicles and fireplaces and cider and drunk aunts and being snowed in. All in all, I counted only seventeen scrumdidliumptiouses.

By the end of the call he could tell I was still a little upset, so he told me that we could get a spare crate for Tulie and leave it at his place so the animals could start getting used to one another. I felt a lot better.

Then I drove to Jym's place, curled up with Jym's fat cats, listened to the rain falling on his roof, ate an entire bag of Oreos and fell asleep.

In the morning I smelled something putrescent, and traced it to Jym's closet, where a leak had caused the walls to fill up with a boil of mildew-filled stink.

It had been raining pretty hard since he left, and now his clothes had taken on the vile aroma, so I began the unpleasant task of salvaging things from the closet's cavernous toxicity and moving them to Jym's spare bedroom. Then I went out and bought two floor fans, but they only blew the stink around and back again, doubling the carcinogenic horror.

As I sprayed 409 on the infested areas like Jym's hired slave, I wondered if all couples endured the same kind of crap. Was I this depressed before I met Jasper? Would my life be simpler without Jym? Did I have this many problems on my own? If this were my place, would Jym be here doing this crap with me? I mean, here I was, scrubbing his floors, and I didn't even live there, for Godsakes. All this, followed closely by, why isn't loving someone enough?

Then and there I decided that awful things are always better when
you go through them *together*.

I sat back on my heels, pushed my hair back with the black
industrial-strength rubber glove and smiling, thought, maybe I
should have a baby.

Two weeks before Christmas, Jym and I went out for dinner and he
broke the news to me over oysters on the half-shell ('Scrumdidliumptious!)' that, unfortunately, he would be away in New
York. For Christmas.

'It's business, Dollface,' he said matter-of-factly as he sucked
back another hot-sauce-infested piece of sea slime. Some translucent liquid dribbled out of his mouth. 'Scrumdidliumptious!' he
announced again when his head recoiled. I frowned.

'But Christmas? You promised!' He handed me an oyster he had
prepared for me. I cupped the shell and its jiggling contents in my
palm, touched the hot sauce with my tongue, then put it back on
ice. I took a large gulp of water.

'Look, Dollface, we are courting these hotshot puppeteers and . . .'

I spit my water out. It hit Jym in the face. 'Hotshot puppeteers?'
People put their forks down and stared. Calmly Jym wiped his face
with his napkin and said evenly, 'I'm trying to make hit TV here,
Dollface, but I promise we will have New Year's together.'

I started laughing hysterically. He signalled to the waiter for the
check. I would have been scared but 'hotshot puppeteers' and 'hit
TV' repeated in my head along with a phoney laugh track. Jym
looked around the restaurant nervously.

'Why didn't you ask me to go with you?'

'Is that what this is about?' Jym said, patting my hand. 'I just
assumed you'd want to spend the holidays with your family. It
won't be much fun, Dollface.' He held my chin in his hand, made a
booboo face. 'Besides, we have two whole weekends before I leave,
for just the two of us.' I softened, leaned in to kiss him. He kissed
my forehead, wiped his mouth on his napkin and folded it in his
lap. 'Also, I need someone to watch the cats.'

We drove home in silence.

175

★ ★ ★

Since Jym was going to be away, he wanted to sleep at his place for the remainder of the month so his cats knew how much he loved them. To appease me he went out the next day and surprised me by buying Tallulah's little bed and setting it up for her in his living room.

That first weekend dedicated to just us, we went shopping at the Beverly Center and I helped him buy presents for all the people he worked with, and for some people he hardly knew. Whoop-dee-doo. The whole time he complained about how much money he had to spend, and how people were constantly taking advantage of him and his hard-earned money, so I ended up feeling guilty when he asked me if I wanted him to pay for a sweater I had already added to his gift pile. I was so shocked that he had put me in the position to decide whether or not he should buy it for me, that I said no thank you, even though he would and did spend almost seven hundred dollars on thoughtful gifts for people he wasn't fucking. Worse, Jym seemed genuinely grateful that I was not taking advantage of him the way they were.

My face burned with resentment and feelings of abandonment. I thought to myself, as the salesperson rang up the unflattering orange sweater I would forever hate and come to associate with the pain of this moment. He likes the people he hates more than he likes me.

In the evening he broke dinner plans with me because he was busy doing rep work on the sock-puppet phenomenon. His exact words? 'Dollface, I gotta stay here and make U.V. for the Flyover.'

'What's U.V.?' I naively asked.

'*Uber*-viewing.'

'Oh. What's the Flyover?'

Jym looked annoyed. 'Yunno, the people between NY and LA. And we know how America loves their Appointment TV.' At first I thought he was joking when he said he was blowing me off for the Flyover, then I realized he was *serious*, and that I was dating a mutant with a get-famous complex who worked with socks. My unstated fury turned to uncontrollable, borderlining-on-violent, laughter.

'What?' he said.

'Nothing.'

That night I slept at my own house, in my own bed, feeling more alone *in* a relationship than out of one. Then I called him an *Uber*-asshole in my head and made myself laugh out loud.

The following Saturday, before Jym left for the Big Apple, he took me to buy a Christmas tree, which we decorated with tiny purple lights, handmade ornaments I had collected over the years and tinsel galore. I accidentally broke a beautiful silver-glass ornament Jym had given me and he yelled at me but then apologized. I felt terrible. More than that, it felt mysteriously symbolic somehow (even though it came from Banana Republic and they still had about a million more left). I put dried rose petals I'd been saving in a wooden bowl into the shiny fractured half-sphere and we hung it up anyway. Though fragile and useless, it still retained something in its jagged beauty.

Later, we saw a comedy starring Pauly Shore. Jym laughed like a Mexican hyena at the misogynistic sex parts, so I scrunched down in my seat and pretended not to know him. We made love before we went to sleep and he had an orgasm, but I didn't.

In the morning, Jym screamed at Tallulah and then at me, because, overnight she had gifted him with a nice steaming pile of my disowned rage on his pristine hardwood floors. As he droned on and on at ear-splitting volume about how it would leave a stain and how now he probably wouldn't be able to get his deposit back, I thought, my, he really is quite the little rage-a-holic. Mom, much?

I tried not to add fuel to the fire, but he kept pouring on the gasoline. I told him that I was convinced the only reason I had a key to his place was because he wanted me to water his plants and feed his cats while he was away. By now he was screaming loud enough for the neighbours to threaten to call the police through the cracking plaster walls, while he intermittently paced and packed fancy ironed pinstripe shirts into a black Tumi garment hanging bag, while I ammonia-mopped his precious floors down on all fours.

That's when he announced, 'You don't respect what I do!' out of the wild blue. I assured him that I did, and he blurted, 'I bet no one ever stood up to you before and told you you're wrong. I bet you always get your way. I bet no one has ever told you no.' Like it was his personal duty to be confrontational with me.

'BLAAAAAAAA!' I shouted up at him, like a juvenile delinquent. He just stared at me. I started laughing and went to kiss him, and even though he let me, neither one of us felt resolved.

Later, when I drove home from taking him to the airport, I couldn't help but think how remarkably similar this felt to the last time I took Jasper to the airport. I shuddered.

Tallulah hopped in my lap as we drove up La Brea, past rows and rows of houses with wreaths and sleeping Christmas trees in their windows. Stopped at a red light, Tulie's funny face made some leathery-faced men in a beat-up pick up with a dancing hula-girl on the dash laugh.

I just smiled and drove on.

TWENTY-ONE

Merry Xmas

'Step right up, march push crawl, right up on your knees.'
— Nine Inch Nails

My mother cooks only one truly amazing meal a year, and that's at Christmas. We have this great tradition of taking in strays we know don't have families or can't make it home, but there is a price. We eat turkey and all the fixin's, like a normal family, but for some reason my mother insists on making dozens of tiny individual meat pies for the baby Christ's birthday.

Since our oven is too small, she can only bake so many at a time, so she tortures everyone by making us take numbers and forcing us to eat in a round-robin row, row, row your boat sort of way. While some of us sit others of us wait, smelling the scents of various fillings: curried chicken, minced meat, stewed fruits, and a vegetable medley for the vegetarians (that may or may not still be available by the time they are called to the table). In the meantime, everyone has access to an enormous pot of mashed potatoes and mulled wine.

Spoonie and I have tried to talk her out of the madness, but she seems to think this allows people to mingle, be free-thinking and casual. Thanks to therapy, I secretly think the reason why she likes it is because it prevents any real intimacy from taking place.

Since my father's passing, we begin Christmas around three-thirty in the afternoon (although the meal never actually gets under way until well after eight or nine), but it can take as long as six hours to make sure everyone is fed. Usually by this time they are hungry again for seconds.

While she torments guests in one room, Spoonie and I keep the others occupied in the room with *the tree* with made-up parlour games like 'Sing or Die'. In this game, you draw a subject (celebrity weddings, politics, last book read, dating, etc.) and musical style (jazz, folk, country, blues, punk, rock or whathaveyou) out of two hats, and you make up a song on the spot, while Spoonie accompanies on guitar, *or* be humiliated in some way to be determined by the group. Kind of like a musical Truth or Dare.

I had spent all day making small talk and piecrusts galore, intermittently checking my messages to see if Jym had called (he hadn't yet), anything to avoid watching Spoonie and Lila fall deeper and deeper in love. I called Sadie in Idaho where she was visiting family to wish her a Happy Merry, but she was out sledding with her tiny cousins. It was strange not to see her on Christmas. It made me melancholy. It made me think of my dad.

I missed not seeing him grouchily crouched in his favourite chair in front of the elaborately decorated sixteen-foot Douglas fir. And tonight, in walking through the two-storey, craftsman house I grew up in, outside and up the wooden spiral staircase that led to the addition in the back, I felt the smoothness of the wooden banister where my father rested his hand on nightly pilgrimages to his art sanctuary, and didn't push the feelings away.

I felt in the dark for the sconce Spoonie had painted monsters on as a Father's Day present when he was five, and flicked a light on. Paintbrushes in old tea tins, acrylics, oils, gouche arranged by colour from lightest to darkest, charcoal, gesso, scissors, palette knives, coloured pencils, glitter, glue, along with stacks and stacks of pressed paper on home-made shelves. Everything was just as he'd left it, just as my mother had preserved it for him, like the next museum tour would start in five minutes, like he was going to come back and knock off a masterpiece any minute now.

I looked at a painting of Cupid that rested on an easel. A favourite painting of my mother's from B. Throne's *Satirical Archetype* series. Dan Quayle as Mickey Mouse, Angelyne as Cupid, Fidel Castro as a bloated moon-walking Six Million Dollar Man and Bowzer from *Shanana* as Jesus. I studied the airbrushed Cupid hovering over Los Angeles, where a lonely-looking woman in a floppy hat and sunglasses lounged poolside waiting for her dreams to come true. It seemed the more Jym and I settled in, the more I saw that my old restlessness and depression weren't going away – they were only playing peek-a-boo while I was distracted by Cupid's little arrow in my ass.

Going through a stack of canvases propped up against a wall, my eye landed on one of my favourite paintings by my father. A large canvas with a very small camel and a bouquet of watering cans in dark and murky depths, done in oil. When I was nine I had tried to imitate him and this painting, working with crayon, ink and paper. I held it up and he said it was good but would be better in oil.

In the corner of the room, reams of dust-covered canvases leaned against the wall near a tilted maple and metal draughtsman's table where a light box rested. I moved towards it. On its milky surface lay three slides – photographs of my father that he had selected for a book about his latest (and sadly, last) works. I looked at him through a loop, up close. They had been taken a few weeks before he died.

My father hated Christmas. We would wake him moments after he had gone to bed after an all-nighter, and he would resentfully sit in his Papa Bear chair while we tore through countless presents my mother had spent weeks accumulating and wrapping. It must have brought him some joy to see us so happy over piles and piles of useless stuff, but he never let on. Maybe he was embarrassed because my mother picked everything out and he just put his name on the card. One year I got a particularly disturbing black lace and leather vest. It looked like something a dominatrix or a gay card dealer during cowboy times might have worn. That was the same year he was thinking about divorcing my mother. And the same year he made me a present for no reason.

In an airport overseas somewhere, he stuck a coin in some machine and made me a lightweight silver-dollar-size coin that said I love you or I miss you or something. It was supposed to bring you luck but I lost it. In some ways I didn't mind because he was visiting some dancer lady at the time, but I was still a little sad I'd lost it because he made it himself without any prodding from my mother.

Downstairs, in the living room, I could hear a blend of acoustic guitars and laughter drifting up through the floorboards. I picked Spoonie's out of the din and savoured it like a ripe berry. Then I turned off the lights and went back inside.

'Give me a hand with this,' my mother squawked, wrestling a large shiny brown bird on to a large serving tray while trying to preserve the drippings for gravy. I jumped up and arranged the garnish while she moved to the sink to strain boiled potatoes for mashing, the steam rising up above her like starchy apparitions.

With her back to me like this, her pale white neck peeked through a tangled mess of hair and I thought she looked vulnerable. She used to wear her hair tied up with toothbrushes and pencils when she cooked. I grew up thinking things that were long and slender were hair decorations.

I remember going to the grocery store with my mother. She'd hitch-hike with me on her hip. People would stop because she was pretty with long flowing hair and big doe eyes. Or maybe because of the way her hips leaned forward on her pretty muscular legs. No shoes. Definitely no bra. She looked fourteen. She still does.

My mother's feet used to be black and calloused from walking everywhere barefooted. She'd go to the grocery store with no shoes. She'd walk around on hot asphalt in the middle of summer with no shoes. She'd walk around my school without any shoes. Her feet were hard, like hooves, and her toes were painted magenta. I can't see magenta without thinking of my mother's toes.

'Let's eat!' she announces, and we do.

Later, watching the lovers exchange gifts, my heart melted. Spoonie gave Lila a red G-shock watch and Lila gave him a matching one in yellow. 'Thanks, Honey Boy!'

'Thanks, Money Girl!' they said in hushed tones of tenderness and surprise. Then they gave each other matching turtleneck sweaters, board games, journals, sheets, books, mugs, robes, slippers, facial products, bubble bath, socks, boxers and an enormous box of chocolates which they donated to me because I was eyeing it so completely.

Even though I was so full it hurt to lie down, I raced to squeeze or bite every chocolate to see if I was interested in it. Anything caramel and almondy, buttercreamy or mocha-esque I ate. Fruits, liqueurs, coconut, and nutty brittles I left up for grabs. When I was close to puking, I vowed to work out and maybe even fast for a day so I could button my pants when Jym came home the day after.

When I got back to Jym's to feed his fatcats there was no message from him, only a narrow inlet of other-worldly cat throw-up. I was just heading for the ammonia when I heard Jym's voice on the machine then, and, reaching for the phone, I slipped in the vomit, banged my head on his chandelier *and* managed to break a clear, hanging, crystal teardrop. Merry fucking Christmas.

I picked Jym up from LAX, and he was so happy to see me and looked so handsome in a new cashmere Dr Huxtable-style sweater and Santa hat, I forgot to stay mad at him. The plan was to head straight back to his house, have our own belated Christmas together and sex sex sex. 'Scrumdidliumptious!' he shouted, leaning out the window, as I paid the three dollars at the airport parking kiosk.

We took Century Boulevard, to Aviation, turned left and got

as far as Manchester when my little Audi lurched forward and made an awful popping sound. An even crueller hissing and a final lean to the right added up to a blown front-right tyre. 'I have a spare in the trunk,' I said, 'I just don't know how to put it on.' Jym shook his head and angrily got out to survey the damage, then climbed back in the car and said we'd better call triple-A.

While we waited for the tow-truck guy, Jym said, 'I never noticed you had a moustache before.' I caught my reflection in the rear-view and, in the winter light, the hair above my lip did seem a bit darker than usual.

When the skinny, sweaty guy in the red and white baseball cap and matching shirt showed up almost an hour later, he asked Jym why he hadn't put the spare on himself.

When we finally turned on to Jym's car-lined road, Jym said, 'Dollface, I'm tired.' My knuckles looked white from clutching the wheel so hard.

The tyre episode was certainly a buzz kill, but once inside I gave Jym his Christmas gift anyway, an antique robot that shot real sparks from his tiny raygun. It turned out he had no gift for me because he was so stressed about the puppet show that he got no shopping done. Then he said he didn't really have time to buy anything, then he said he didn't see anything he liked, then he said what do you give the girl who has everything, then he said he really just wanted to wait until he had more time to find the right thing. I would have preferred just sorry.

Later, in the middle of a great dream I was having about being a long-distance runner, Jym woke me by mounting me. I didn't open my legs fully or climax because I was too freaked about my moustache and the whole present thing. But not Jym. I just kept my hand on my lip and stared at the ceiling until he was done.

In the morning Jym told me it had slipped his mind that today was the day he had scheduled to have his house de-fleed. He told me the exterminator said it wasn't safe for me to be there while they de-bugged the place, and that it would also be wise if I took all of my clothes and belongings home, anything that I didn't want contaminated with the toxic foam. Jym brought me a box from the hall closet and watched me pack up, sweetly assisting me by putting Tulie's crate and toys in the car. When I came back in the house to help him with his stuff I saw that he had packed a box full of my bath stuff. I laughed. 'At this rate I'll practically be taking everything!' He just smiled at me as he zipped some of his suits up in a Gucci garment bag, saying, 'I'll just dry-clean the rest.'

At 11.17 a.m., in the middle of bleaching my moustache (and, while I was at it, bikini line) my phone rang. 'I have to tell you something I'm afraid you won't be able to love me for.' It was Jym calling from his office. I was sitting in a floral bikini, straddle-legged on the living-room floor organizing receipts by month, cash or credit, personal or business, just one of the many perks of dating someone who was so organized, while I waited for the white cream on my upper lip and bikini region to take. 'Do you have a minute?' I sat up a little straighter, furrowed my brow.

'OK...'

'I told you a lie. There was no exterminator. Actually, I called a locksmith.'

'Huh?' The bleach was starting to burn.

'I want you to know I respect you, but I am really not ready for a relationship right now. I thought I was, but now I realize I was just rebounding and I just want to get to know myself, since I have never really taken any time off for just me, and it all happened so fast and plus we don't really get along.'

The bleach was really burning now. I waved my hand in front of my face to cool my upper lip. 'I'm sorry, are you breaking up with me?'

'I guess I am.'

'On the *phone*?' At least it was progress. 'Can we at least talk about this, say, later, *in person*?'

'I wouldn't be comfortable with that.'

'WHAT?' I blew air at my crotch to cool the tender skin.

'I just feel that you don't respect me and what I do.'

'Well, uh, Jym, you do work with socks. Wait, wait...'

'We just don't get along,' he snapped with a grotesque finality.

'I think we do,' I said defensively, eyes watering from the intensity of the bleach smell.

'We don't.'

'Well, I think we do!' I was standing now, pointing at the receipts.

'Look Dollface, I don't want to argue any more. This isn't about you, it's about me. I gotta run.'

'But I didn't do anything wrong!' I was laughing now. 'You pursued me!!!!'

'It's just, I'm not done grieving my last relationship, and this all happened so fast. I was hoping for a friendship that would slowly build into something...'

I was up now, hopped from one leg to the other. The burning irritation had really intensified. 'OK, Jym, fine. Let's just take things a little slower...'

'I don't think you understand, it would just be too painful for me. I should really go.'

'But... but... but you have pre-teen breasts, for God sakes!' Manboobs hung up on me. I called him right back to ask him if he was bipolar, but he wouldn't accept the call. I stared at the phone, then made a dash for the bathroom.

I ran cold water over a well-worn rose-coloured washcloth. While I rinsed my skin down with the cool, wet cloth I thought, back to jail, do not pass go, do *not* collect two hundred dollars. Thanks for nothing Jym with a *why*. I felt like one of Jym's sock puppets. Like a hollowed-out sack of flesh with God's hand up my fucking puppet ass.

I was about to go into old me, leaving hostile messages on every one of Jym's numbers (home, car, office, voice-mail, email *and* pager) telling him he was a fake human, a non-person, a cyborg, someone who is only a façade of a man and an ass, but something happened. I realized that if he was freaky enough to organize a lock-out, he was freaky enough to be all wrong for me. Just like Jasper.

I heard a plane fly past just then. They seemed to be sailing overhead with increasing regularity. I thought, they must have changed their flight path.

Truth be told? I felt nothing, just like Karl said I would.

TWENTY-TWO

Not See Party

'You are witnessing a start, a new life, you are witnessing the
start of my fabulous life.'

— Katell Koenig

'Ben Affleck is going to be there!' Sadie meant the big New Year's
Eve shindig Lila had got us all invited to. Even my mother was
asked to come. Lila also organized for Spoonie's band to be the
entertainment, as well. It was some kick-off for a new magazine
called *Launch*. The theme for the party was, of all things, OUTER
SPACE! Lila had gained us all entry because she had secured the
much-coveted premier cover. It was a photo of her in a silver bikini
straddling a bullet-shaped rocket that said 'Uranus or Bust'.

I didn't want to go for the following five reasons: a) it was a party,
b) it was on New Year's Eve, c) my mother would be there, d)
Spoonie and his steady girlfriend would be positively adorable
together the entire night, and e) this would only further contribute
to reminding me I would never have the love I need, ever. I mean,
you don't put an orphan in a room full of happy families, do you?

Earlier in the day I had made my resolution and sworn off men
entirely. As women weren't an option either, I felt the evening
would be better spent preparing for a lifetime of utter aloneness.
But Sadie just said she would pick me up at nine, and that was the
end of that.

Of course, when she saw me she announced, 'You are not going out like that.' I had assembled a real man-get-thee-back sort of costume for the occasion, featuring a grannyish yellow and lime-green flora-patterned muu-muu housecoat, black and white Argyll socks and purple clogs. 'Why not?' I said in mock defiance.

Sadie rolled her eyes. 'Because nobody wears clogs in space. They are bad enough on earth, and you'll ruin my chances of hitting it off with Ben.' This from a woman in silver jodhpurs and a pink fluffy tube top. (Not to mention her silver strappy platforms that showed off her hand-painted silver-and-pink-flowered toenails.) She was back to her old self all right, now that I was single again.

'I need tenderness!' I crossed my arms and pouted. She sat on my couch and rolled her eyes. Please. 'Anyway, who am I gonna meet at a *party?*'

She jumped up. 'Exactly, no one so long as you're dressed like that, or worse, you'll meet the type of person who would be drawn to you in that outfit and trust me, you don't want that. Besides, you know the rules, A-B-C, 1-2-3.' Smugly, she pushed me towards my dangerously overstuffed closet and began to rummage through my tissue-thin summer dresses like a Valley-ite at a Barney's sale. Metal hangers scraped against a too-thin metal pole. I covered my ears with my hands.

'Thank you, but I have no interest in men. I am through with them.' Sadie held up a sheer lilac-coloured slip. 'You do realize it's the middle of winter.' She put it back in exchange for a plaid skirt and baby-tee combo.

'I'm tellin' ya, A-B-C, 1-2-3. Pose, counterpose,' she said again, making criss-crossing, karate-chop hand gestures. 'If Jym doesn't call, work out so your ass attracts someone who will. If Jasper's career flourishes, date his boss. If his boss doesn't want you, fly to Europe and have a fling with someone who does, like an emperor or something. Now, tonight you are going to look pretty and have fun if it kills you.'

'A European emperor? Hello! Bad listener alert.' She began physically to pull the balloon dress over my head. 'Sadie,' I said, trying to untangle my hair that had got caught on a button, 'what I

190

need is a purpose to continue living, something to believe in. What I need is to get over Jasper and *men* entirely.'

'You're the one who said you were *over* Jasper, that he's on a path and you're on a path . . .' She pulled harder. I was thrashing like a drunk in a straight jacket now.

'That was before Jym decided to dump me. It's his fault I'm thinking about Jasper. I just can't believe people think it's acceptable to love you one day and run out on you with zero answers the next. Jasper is probably with someone else in a loving, committed relationship this minute.'

'Please. What makes you think either one of them have the skills to actually be with *anyone*?' You are going to have a good life, missie, so let's hit it.' She chose my shoes too, black, patent-leather, high-heeled tennis-shoe boots, then coiled my hair in big loops about my ears, blew silver glitter on my eyes and spun me around to face my reflection in my floor-length bedroom mirror.

'That's a lot better,' I said, bored to my core.

'And don't think you are ever going to get any answers out of Jasper or anybody that would ever satisfy you anyway,' she said as we flew across Mulholland in her black Ford Explorer. 'I mean, the guy has the personality of a fucking radish, and no one likes radishes.'

'Rabbits do,' I said, squinting my eyes and staring out at all the city lights. They made rainbow tracers as we sped past.

After standing in a dangerously long line, hoping to get past the red velvet ropes just so we could be assessed by five ripped doormen as to hipness or space-agey costume and general validity of the statement 'I am on the list', I began to feel even less than enthusiastic about the whole thing. 'Who invites people to a party and makes them wait to see if they are allowed to come in?'

'Apparently Condé Nast,' Sadie said wryly.

I had almost persuaded Sadie we should leave when the coffee guy recognized me by my hair and pulled Sadie and me by the arm past the others who would spend at least forty-five more minutes shivering in the cold. He knew the doorman. I silently apologized to each and every Martian, astronaut and Venusian goddess as we slinked past – I know, I hate me too.

'How's it goin'?' said our grinning saviour in the baby-blue fleece blanket draped across his shoulder like a toga, once we were safe inside the silver, rotating room forty storeys high. For some reason, I was excited to see him (particularly his white skin and black chest hair hypnotizing me with their crop-circle patterns), until I noticed the thing he was attached to – an all-legs, blonde, drop-deader in Eskimo boots, headdress and fake-fur bikini. This set against bedroomy cat eyes and dark eyebrows. She looked like a Siberian husky, only a lot taller. I racked my brain trying to remember if we had ever exchanged names. Now I guess it didn't matter.

'There's Ben Affleck!' Sadie announced suddenly, and pulled me towards the bar with arm-dislocating force.

'Well, bye!' I said to the coffee guy. 'Oh, and thanks!' He did the 'catch you later' jerk of his head and sort of saluted as he disappeared with his Ice Princess beyond an enormous ice statue of a mythical, bald-eagle creature clutching the earth in its talons.

Sadie put her hands on her hips. 'Shit, we lost him!'

'I was talking to that guy, you know.'

'Who, future Caesar? Please.'

'Why is it fine for you to chase someone, but I can't have one simple conversation?'

'That's because you try and make one simple conversation your new boyfriend. *Fun only*, missie!' She chewed on her index finger and scanned the crowd. 'There he goes! Ben at six o'clock.' She tore off into a cluster of Spocks leaving me standing stranded to survey the futuristic onslaught. People roamed around like zombies, only shinier, with free coloured vodka drinks in tall glasses. Lots of women in their late thirties with tiny backpacks and sparkly barrettes, silver lipstick and matching tops. Lots of guys in jeans and boots with other-worldly sex appeal in lieu of costume.

My jaw ached from fake-smiling at people I had auditioned for or with on jobs I had not gotten over the years, in various offices around town. I felt queasy with loserishness as the bar made a new rotation around another voice-over enemy.

I thought, even if Sadie talked to Ben he'd never sustain her. Sadie is a chubby-chaser. They are her real weakness. Once she broke up with a guy because he lost so much weight that he actually shrank to a woman's size four. If you mention his name Sadie will convulse as if recalling severe food poisoning.

Just then a man with a perm and a blond moustache walked past me. He was an agent at my agency whose name I always forgot. Now I wondered if I'd *ever* forget him. He wore a yellow neon plastic pool life-saver around his middle and a T-shirt with puffy letters that spelled out Jewpiter. He was eye-level with a pair of silver spray-painted breasts he couldn't keep his eyes off. Surely she'd have her own sitcom by sunrise.

By the stage in the centre of the room where Spoonie would be performing in less than an hour, I overheard a freaky girl I lost a foot deodorizer ad to brag about dreaming the cover of *The Dancing Wu Li Masters* when she was only eight, *before* she ever even saw the book. 'It totally rewired my matrix.' She was hitting on a smooth-faced guy with a greying ponytail, held in place by Buddhist beads. It seemed to me, her pick-up technique was intimidating her victim into submission with a lengthy incomprehensible monologue about her obsession with sacred geometry and carbon-panelled speaker chairs. 'They adjust your chakras while you listen.' When 'truncated tetrahedrons' came out of her mouth my eyes crossed. I walked away.

Standing by a giant glass window that gave me a perfect view of hell, I suddenly ducked behind a fake ficus to avoid my mother, who was now arm in arm with Quentin Tarantino. I did not even want to know what that could possibly be about.

That's when Baby accosted me instead. Everybody called her Baby because she had a too-big head for her body, zero attention span and, moreover, because that's what she called everyone else. Baby was in PUBLICITY. My father worked with her for a stretch. Betty Boop on drugs my mother would say. She reminded me of those girls in school who bragged about how their thighs didn't touch at the top, even when their legs were crossed. Girls like this made me want to eat more, even when I wasn't hungry, just to punish them.

'Baby!' she said when she saw me. I tried to pretend I hadn't seen her, that I was interested in a fake plastic leaf instead. 'Baby!' she said again, kissing the air beside my cheeks. 'You just don't meet real men out here! Come visit me in New York, where you'll be a star on the bar scene!' Then she introduced me to a brooding, twenty-something actor she'd end up fucking on a motorcycle in an alley in about an hour. (Another reputation she didn't seem to mind.) 'This is my friend, Craigles,' she said, pulling at some silver-beaded elastic bracelets on her wrists.

James Dean raised a beer. I nicknamed her thug escort Lotsa Face, not so much for his Leno-esque mandible as for a special I had seen on Mount Everest. It had shown that one of the most dangerous parts of the mountain was a slippery ice sheer called Lhotse Face, a virtually impossible climb. This guy knew about 'the climb' all right. Baby wanted me to go to Bar Marmont with them for drinks.

'I can't because I'm here with someone.'

'Oh, is he here?' Baby asked, craning her neck and puckering her collagen-injected lips. 'Is he a celebrity too? Spoonie sure got a good one. Did you see the piece in *In Style*?' Craigles looked around too. It was like he was on a time delay.

'*He* is a she. And no, she's behind the scenes.' Did I just sound lesbian? Does a PR lady think I'm a lesbian?

'Oh.' She looked confused. 'I don't remember, help me out here, are you gay?' said Baby, eyebrow cocked. Craigles stared at me now, too. Suddenly her bracelet flew apart and beads scattered in a million different directions. Baby started to bend down, then thought better of it. Craigles now took his cue to be a gentleman and bent down. Baby grabbed him by the arm, pulling him back and said, 'Never mind, you can just buy me another one when you're a star!'

'No, I only meant my best friend who's a girl.'

'Pity', Baby said sadly. 'We were kind of hoping for a three way.' Craigles winked at me and they walked away.

I scanned the crowd for any sign of Sadie so we could make our escape. The bar made another rotation and I passed the coffee guy again. He held an invisible phone to his ear and mouthed 'call me'.

I laughed and gave him the Fonzie because he was such a giant dork. Then he and Attila the Cunt left the building.

In line for the restroom, I scanned the crowd for any sign of Sadie. There, a chest-first frat boy robot was telling a bored galactic cheerleader about his three dogs, a cocker, a 'nard and a 'weiler'.

'Pure beer,' Sadie whispered in my ear like a fairy godmother. 'Cosmopolitan?' She tried to hand me the pink drink.

'No, thank you. Where have you been? I want to leave!'

'Benland.' She swallowed her drink in a single gulp. 'Too skinny.' A tray of multicoloured Rice Krispie treats went past on a silver tray and Sadie went with them calling, 'It's not even midnight!'

'Sadie!' I called after her.

Alone again, I made my way to a nearby table where a set of twins in matching puce jumpsuits, accessories and headgear, sat staring at the empty stage, as though a show were already in progress.

'Hey, you look like Princess Leia!' said the shadow that loomed above me now. I looked up in time to see the most angelic human I had ever beheld. Olive skin and green eyes and long black hair tied up about his ears in two loopy coils.

'Hey, so do you.' It was true. To top it off, he was wearing a pair of plaid pants, an olive-green T-shirt that exposed his pierced navel, and a pair of silver *clogs*. We looked like twins.

'You looked so glum, I thought I'd come over here and cheer you up. Charlie Mate!' said Charlie, like we were old chums. He sounded like Tom Waits. He gave me an elbow to shake, as his large, manly hands were in the middle of attempting to peel an orange in one perfect tear. His knuckles looked like the knots in a hundred-year-old tree.

'America.' I said.

'That's a cool name,' said Charlie. 'Were your parents hippies?'

'My dad was an artist.'

Whenever I have a conversation with an intimidating guy it always feels like that scene in *Ordinary People* where he runs into the crazy girl who tells him everything is going great in her life. The next time he hears about her, however, she has committed suicide. I wonder if he can tell that he is saving my life by having eyes that green.

'Voila!' he said, and handed me half of the prize with his sticky, orange-scented paw. He reminded me of a cross between Winnie the Pooh and a golden retriever.

Suddenly an old guy in a gold Speedo and gold roller skates offered us Kim Chee Caesar salads in paper cones, which we ate with our fingers and ended up burping throughout the entire rest of our conversation because the dressing is made with rancid oil. At first I was embarrassed by the continual belching, but Charlie turned it into a game. Points for loudness, duration, smell and frequency. After discussing our favourite books, music, artists, and places to hike, along with therapy and yoga (we'd both been to Golden Bridge!) Charlie asked me 'Do you ever just feel *done?*' he said.

'Well, actually yes.'

''Cause I sure do. No more bullshit, excuse my French, that's what I'm about.'

'I hear ya. I am beyond done with about seventy three things including men, dating men, dealing with men, not dealing with men, oh, and did I mention men?' It felt so good not to care if I was impressing him or not.

'Taking care of other people's feelings is pretty overrated.'

'My new motto in life is, "Just make yourself happy".'

'My new motto is, "My other car is a broom".'

'That's a bumper sticker!' We both laughed.

'Hey, you have something in your teeth.'

'Do I?' I said, blushingly smitten.

Over by the speakers, I watched an oblivious-to-my-life Sadie get chatted up by a fat Spock.

Just then Lila appeared behind us. 'God, please tell me you two know each other and planned these outfits because you practically look like twins! I mean, except for his clogs.' His were silver. Then Lila turned towards the stage. 'Spoonie's on in, like, three minutes.' She pointed to her red g-shock. 'See you next year!' Then she darted off, but not before mouthing, 'He's cute' when Charlie wasn't looking.

The lights dimmed, but not enough for me to miss a glimpse

of my mother positioning herself next to Denzel Washington at the foot of the stage. The crowd began to throb, like a giant amoeba, in time with the industrial guitar, drums, and electric bagpipes. I spotted my mother going in for the kill by nudging Denzel to clap, which he half-heartedly does for a measure, before moving two people over. I smiled at Charlie. He smiled back.

At ten seconds to midnight, Spoonie stopped the music and for a moment everything was perfect. Then we all counted down: ten! I looked at Charlie. Nine! He wouldn't try to kiss me would he? Eight! Charlie looked at me with a devilish grin. Seven! In the corner I caught a gander of Sadie and a fat Spock already stuck together at the face. Six! I looked back at Charlie, smiled and blushed. Five! Maybe he had a girlfriend. Four! Maybe he didn't. Three! Anyway, it's too soon to kiss. I started to perspire. Two! No more guys. I closed my eyes 'ONE!!' we all screamed. Just then, Charlie reached over and grabbed my hand and licked it.

Later after chatting a bit more, as we exchanged numbers, Charlie with a curtsy, and me with a bow, we shook hands and parted ways by the valet. He looked fancy and humble as he waved goodbye in his blue flat-bed truck with the dent and the sticky starter.

'Did he get it all?' I said to Sadie drily, once we were a safe distance away from our new pals and the previous year. 'That larynx operation looked like it was taking a really long time.'

'Who, Spock?'

'Were there others?' I said, pretending to be shocked.

'Maybe!' She giggled wildly. 'Does Charlie have a girlfriend?' she asked.

'I don't know,' I said.

'What sign is he?'

'I don't know.'

'Well, does he live here?'

'Uh... I didn't really ask.'

She clicked her tongue and rolled her eyes. 'Well, what the hell did you talk about?'

'Everything else, I guess,' I said dreamily as Sadie missed my turn-off. 'It's like we're from the same tribe. We don't even know each other and we were already finishing each other's sentences. I swear, Sadie, every time he smiled at me I felt the presence of all the good things in the world that have ever existed since the beginning of time. And he's really funny, too.'

'New rules! Next time, find out some pertinent information so I can assess the outcome properly. Do you even know what he does? I mean, besides drive you completely mental.'

'I know this, I know this! He's an ice sculptor!'

'In California? A real rebel, huh?'

I swatted her. 'Hey, Sade, how come you never want to be in something deeper than temporary fun?'

'Because, because . . .' she slammed on her brakes and stopped the car in the middle of Sunset Boulevard. 'Oh, bother.' She turned on her blinker and waved people on to pass her. Someone honked so she flipped them off, then made a swift and illegal U-turn.

We drove on in a happy, familiar silence. When she dropped me off she turned to me and said, 'It's all gonna work out for both of us, isn't it.' I nodded, and we hugged and grinned at each other like Cheshire cats.

When I got home there was already a message on my answering machine from Charlie Mate. 'Are you around? Are you a square?'

'I say that!' I screamed out loud!

'I just want to say it was really nice meeting you tonight, and I hope we can get together when you have some free time.'

As I lay down on my bed and swathed myself in cosy layers of white flannel and down, pieces of myself came back to me like iron filings to a magnet.

TWENTY-THREE
A Month of Sundays

'Close your eyes and try to sleep, close your eyes and try to
dream. We belong to the night, we belong to each other, we
belong, we belong, we belong together.'
— Pat Benatar

Charlie and I met in Santa Monica at the mouth of an old fire
road, which wound round a massive mountain to an overlook for a
panoramic view of mountains, sky and sea. I had called Charlie up
the next morning and asked him to take a walk with me in nature.
It felt good to have a no-pressure outing with a nice guy. All the
same, I chewed three pieces of wintergreen gum. Poor hygiene is
just poor manners.

Charlie arrived dressed like a trendy forest ranger in olive khakis,
with a vintage Boy Scout shirt with a patch that said 420, mirror
police-officer sunglasses, and clunky, mustard-coloured lace-up
boots. I was brave enough to pour myself into a pair of shorts and
a long-sleeved, ribbed purple cotton T-shirt, even though my legs
were wintery white and unshaven. I figured I needed to be utterly
myself right away, that way I'd find out quick who stuck around.

'This is white sage,' he said as we made our way to the first of
several plateaus, and then told me its Latin name along with the
names of about sixteen other neighbouring green items. Of course
he knows about plants. It turned out Charlie had his own little

herb garden. Mint and chocolate geranium were his favourites. I was so nervous about my breath, and memorizing the plants and their corresponding names, that at no time did I notice the ingrown hair on my leg the size of a small dog until we began to dig into our ascent. I panicked, decided to hug the area closest to the fall so that he wouldn't see the red, inflamed boil side of my leg; but Charlie was wily and criss-crossed back and forth in front of me to point out some type of succulent ground cover and tiny yellow wild flowers. 'This is mustard!' He pulled the yellow blossoms of the slender green stalk for me to taste. I had to laugh inwardly because Mustard was Spoonie's and my codeword for Big Trouble.

Once in tenth grade I had made the mistake of telling Spoonie about a guy I liked who had never tried mustard before. I've always found it charming whenever people have a marker in time that delineates who they were before an event and who they are after, whereas Spoonie found it instantly pitiful. He couldn't believe the guy was so sheltered as never to have been exposed to mustard. 'It was practically used as a lubricant in our household!' Spoonie said, holding his sides. 'Or does he even know what a lubricant is?'

'I stayed low, kept my arms close to the ground like an ape, and pretended to scratch my leg so I could get a good look. It was at least a quarter wide and a stack of dimes deep. I wondered, did Charlie see it? We were only a third of the way up the mountain. I was panting and wheezing like an asthmatic cow. 'This is licorice, and this one is yucca.' I couldn't concentrate on a thing Charlie said because I was sweating so much *and* straining to hide the bump as it pushed up, up, up the mountain. Why me? Why can't something good work out in my life, just once? I tried my hardest to keep Charlie on my right side, but he kept darting hither and thither, pointing out plants and birds and creepy crawlers.

I touched *it* compulsively now, with every other step. I was all bump and minimal forward motion.

'Are you OK?', he asked suddenly.

'What? Why?'

'Because you're walking kind of funny.'

'Oh?' I said, a deer in the headlights.

'You're walking like this.' He demonstrated it for me, 'Like you have poopy trou or something,' he said grinning. I dropped to the ground and pulled my shirt over my bent knees, buried my face in my hands.

'Dude, did I say something wrong?'

'No,' I said to my belly, 'it's just that you're so honest, and I don't know you, and ... and ...'

He crouched beside me, put a hand on my back. 'Just say it.'

I pointed to my leg, ran my hand over the fabric that hid it. 'Bump!'

'Where?' He pulled at the end of my shirt, trying to get a look. 'NOOOOOOOO!'

'Let me look at it.' He bent down on all fours and leaned forward. Without lifting my face, I lifted up the shirt and revealed the lump.

'Eeuwwww! It's *huge*! Can I pop it?'

'Noooooo!' I screamed again. I pulled my shirt back down and began to rock myself back and forth. 'Go away!' I peered at him over my left kneecap. He was smiling devilishly.

'Let me pop it! Can I?' his intentions seemed so pure, I let him lift up my shirt once more. Upon closer examination he decided it wasn't ripe for picking and found some wild lavender, plucked a spring, crushed the blossom and the stem and applied it like a salve instead. Then we collected eucalyptus leaves and he told me to boil it with some gauze and apply it like a poultice. I had never heard the word 'poultice' used in real life before, certainly not by a handsome, heterosexual, twenty-six-year-old man.

The following Tuesday I asked Charlie if he wanted to hit the museum for the Cubist show that was still running. My dad's stuff had been up at LACMA for weeks and I kept promising myself I'd go. Charlie was dressed like a Salvador Dali painting complete with pocket watch. Before we piled into his giant dented blue flat-bed truck with the sticky starter, he climbed my tree. My tree! The one the feng-shui people told me prevented me from ever getting a man, that tree. Charlie climbed it. *Climbed* it. Climbed *it*. I was so shocked I dropped my purse.

Of course all the contents spilled out in the grass. As we scrambled to pick up flying lipsticks, receipts, loose change, hairbands, gum, an old band flyer that coffee guy had given (which now blew across the street and under my neighbour's parked car), and, of course, three o.b. tampons.

Blushingly, I told Charlie about the curse and the psychic. He just laughed and said it was all a bunch of superstitious nonsense, and that he wanted a photo with the two of us in front of my tree. I thought, if he isn't afraid of any old tree or any old curse, maybe there is a God after all.

Strolling through the great halls, I saw the look of awe on Charlie's face as we stopped to examine a piece of my father's. He looked at me. There was nothing to say. Then I had an epiphany about cubism. I had always despised cubist art, but now I understood that it wanted us all to comprehend the full scope of things, to be able to see and *know* everything in front of you from exactly where you stood. To see the *back* of the head of the one you love, and the inside of their heart at the same time as looking them directly in the eye. Because I wanted to see all of Charlie, truth could not help but reveal itself.

When I got home I decided to spruce the place up a little, so I snuck out and picked wild flowers from all my neighbour's yards and hillsides. Daffodils in an old tea tin in my kitchen window near the sink, iris in a jelly jar by my computer, and a single white camellia in a mint-green and white chipped finger bowl by my bed.

The next day I was still feeling so inspired from our museum visit, that I called Charlie and asked him if he wanted to paint pottery. In the clean little terracotta-tiled shop on Main Street I was suddenly nervous. I felt the pressure of my father's artistic legacy, and picked out an inconspicuous unfinished soap dish, but Charlie wouldn't have it. He picked out a large white unfinished salad bowl, because he wanted something large he could paint with me. My courage surfaced. I wondered if it would stay at his place or mine, or if we should just move in together to avoid an argument.

I let Charlie choose the colours. A girl in a navy apron squirted them on to a single square of glazed white tile, orange and ice blue and magenta, dark green and brown, pink and plum. I looked around the room. It was hard not to notice things differently with Charlie around. For example, the relationship between things in pairs, the edge of the table we sat at and the corner of his chair, the bottom of the clock and the door frame overhead, the way the viny plants in the window leaned in towards each other, and of course the people outside and their quarter-starved parking meters.

'What are you thinking about?' asked Charlie.

'Uh!' I said, blushing, twirling my paintbrush in the water, watching it turn to a milky blue. 'Um, things in pairs, actually.' Charlie jolted straight up in his seat, turned his side of the bowl around for me to see: a big fat *pear* next to a bunch of dancing bananas with top hats and faces, and a scruffy-looking creature with four legs and antlers that looked like it had started out as a dog and then turned into a goat, maybe.

'OK, I know that's a pear and those are dancing bananas, but what in the hell is that?'

He contorted his body to my side of the table to examine it again, and then sat up triumphantly. 'It's a goatbear!' Then we erupted into peals of laughter. 'What did you make?' He sat straight-spined in his seat now. His whole face softened. 'Wow!'

I lightly smacked his arm. 'Shut up!'

'I'm serious. It's really nice. Really . . . feminine.' I crinkled my nose up. 'You're like a real artist. I love the colours.'

'Nah.' I pulled a face.

'Really.' He looked sad now. 'Don't close off. See?' He turned the bowl back around for me to see. I looked at what I had done, trying to see it through Charlie's eyes: intertwining vines and roses and two birds and two dancing fairy ladies and some snakes with mosaic, multicoloured backs.

'Not *so* bad,' I said, brushing my hair behind my ear. Affection-ately he conked me on the head.

★ ★ ★

Later that night we ended up in a carpeted piano bar at some divy hotel in West Hollywood. Charlie knew that no one was ever there, so we sat and played the piano even though I can't. We ended up singing all the Pat Benatar songs we knew at the top of our lungs, to the dead-drunk amusement of a few lingering lonely hearts and some random staffers. Soon the man with the industrial-strength vacuum cleaner and the too-shiny skin was using the end of the nozzle as a microphone for a duet with Charlie. 'Hell Is For Children' never sounded so good.

'Did he try to kiss you?' Sadie asked when I called her from my cosy bed. I had Tulie curled up beside me, and I watched her dream with her eyes open.

'No,' I said, softly poking at Tulie's pink belly.

'Ooh, that's a bad sign.'

'Sadie . . .'

'He's either gay or he has a girlfriend.'

'Maybe he's just being respectful?'

'You see each other all the time and talk five hundred times a day and have all this synchronicity and he hasn't tried to jump you? Something's fishy in Denmark.'

'Or maybe he's a grown-up, Sadie, and what's the rush if it's forever? It's like he lives his life like in The Book! Every day he shows me something else! Every day he has a passion for some *new* thing!'

'Where's the rose connection? If he's the one, where's the rose, huh?'

I twisted my hair around my index finger. 'Maybe she got it all wrong. Maybe that's all superstitious nonsense.'

'Just do me a favour and go out with this guy I met in my spinning class. You might like him.'

'What guy?'

'He's a maths teacher. He's from *Roseville*.'

'Sadie, my plate is full.'

'Well at least add a side dish, or for Godsakes, at least find out if

204

he has a girlfriend before you go all gaga on me.'

'Goodnight, Mom.'

'Goodnight, *Mission Impossible* to deal with.'

On Wednesday night I asked Charlie if he felt like dancing. He suggested that I meet him at The Temple, a dance studio tucked deep in the valley, Sun Valley far, Ikea far. At a warehouse with a little parking area surrounded by barbed wire. He told me to look for a single red light, that's how I could tell the difference this late at night between the dance studio and the sheet-metal supply house, the wax supply house, the paint warehouses, the marble supply house and the terracotta pot and garden outlet.

Passing through the entryway with the cement floors and stark, white walls, I was ill prepared for the calming beauty assault of the large room with wood floors, and high airplane-hangarish ceilings. It had three humungous white ceiling fans, mirror and ballet beam that ran the length of the room, and in the corner, a bench had been decorated like an altar and lay littered with fragrant magnolias and a row of lit white candles. Industrial music with African and Brazilian samples blared. Barefooted, people in every size, shape and colour had their eyes closed and were just dancing wildly. It looked like a scene out of the Woodstock movie, like one of my dad's sittings, only holy. As reckless as their movements were, and as loud as the music was, there was a quiet library feeling in the room.

'It's a moving meditation,' Charlie said as I slipped off my shoes and waited for my eyes to adjust. He smelled like sandalwood and honeydew. 'Just let your body move the way it wants to. This is like the opposite of yoga. Just totally free your mind. Over there on the altar you can offer up your intention. Tonight I am going to dance the purity of connection along with a little don't-make-me-pay-Visa-late-charge on the side.'

At first, I was shy about letting Charlie see the way the music moved me, but he started hopping around like a Mexican jumping bean, so I felt a little more free. After an hour of swaying and jumping and bumping and weaving in and out of sweaty backs and damp pits and fingers outstretched like sea-anemone feelers, it felt good to be in my own skin. To be myself completely, opposite Charlie who was also himself, and not lose *me*. I felt a radiance in my belly, like we were all walking around with little pot-belly stoves full of light beaming it back and forth at one another. Everyone was just a light being on a path, dancing through life.

I wiped my eyes with the back of my hand for the realization. Maybe this is what Jasper meant in his letter. I looked over at Charlie. His eyes were closed. He was giving himself a luxurious hug.

Later, over cheap Mexican food in a divy orange and yellow stuccoed hutch in Glendale, sitting on plastic patio furniture, I broke down and told Charlie about Jasper and Jym, mainly to get things off my chest, but secretly to initiate a dialogue about our possible future together, without scaring him off by talking about myself. I figured he'd just naturally bring up this whole relationship deal if I just broke the ice.

When I got to the part about how I didn't understand why all the people I have ever loved never loved me back, including my dad, and that I had never actually seen a relationship that actually worked, it started to sound like a story about a girl I knew once or had heard about a million years ago. Charlie must have felt this too, because in the middle of building his guacamole fortress, like that scene in *Close Encounters*, he looked at me and said point-blank, 'Dude, you didn't do anything wrong. No one did.'

'What do you mean?' My chest tightened and vibrated like a paper drum. Like a revelation was about to blast on through.

'Maybe they weren't able to receive what you had to offer, and vice versa. I mean, relationships are all about flow, and finding someone who makes you feel good because they are just flowing right along side of you, doing their own flowing thing. A lot of it just comes down to plain old timing and luck...' He leaned in closer, smelling of onion salsa, dried sweat and denim, and popped a tortilla drenched in guacamole in my mouth. The candles on the table in clay pots made his face light up like a sun. 'When something's right, it's just... right. Dude, you're totally great, so don't even sweat it.' I felt so seen, I ached.

I stared at the pile of food on my plate to avoid being incinerated entirely. The cheese had formed a hard crust that looked like a smiley face. 'I feel so lucky to have met you.'

'Me too,' he said, taking my hand. I looked up at him. Tears of joy were in my eyes. He handed me a hankie from his jacket pocket, embroidered with tiny hand-stitched roses. I could not help but laugh. Of course you carry real old-fashioned handkerchiefs with roses on them, you're a miracle.

On my drive home, alone, speeding along Mulholland under a canopy of stars, I thought, let me get this straight: men *can* do nice things for you? Men can show up when they say they are going to, *and* do their own laundry, *and* drive, *and* let you express your feelings, *and* hug you when you cry, and give you *good* advice? Is this some kind of a gag? Where the hell have I been? What have I been hanging out with?

Then I had a conversation with the moon. When I was little, on the long drive back from picking up my father from his old studio, I would lie in the back seat while my mother drove him home along this very same road. As we winded along, I would alternate between watching my exhausted father's profile as he reclined in the front passenger seat, and making sure the moon was still following us. Sometimes it seemed she was leading the way, ducking behind great dark pines every now and then, but mostly it seemed like she was making sure we got home safe. Now I'm checking to see if she's watching over Charlie tonight. Leaning my head out my window, I was sure her benevolent face was saying yes.

At that moment, Angelyne pulled up beside me in her pink Corvette. She looked spun-sugar fragile, tired. I thought, underneath all that hair and make-up and baby-doll sexuality is someone just like me, someone who wants love, someone who wants to leave their mark on the world, to say I existed in this moment of time. I wondered what love she had lost, and hoped she had found someone who truly saw her beauty like I saw hers, like Charlie saw mine. When the light turned green she sped past like a pink human comet. Don't we all want the same things?

When I got home, in my journal I wrote:

Things I will not miss about being in a relationship with Jasper Husch and Jym Court that I have discovered as a result of knowing Charlie Mate:

1   That panicky feeling that I couldn't be myself.
2   That jealous feeling whenever we were apart.
3   That anxious feeling when they didn't call me when I was so desperate to hear from them and they were too busy to call.
4   That frustrated feeling when we talked things through and neither one of us felt resolved.
5   That lonely feeling when they didn't compliment me enough or hold me enough or ravage me enough.
6   That painful feeling when we'd have sex and they'd just grind away and only he'd orgasm and I'd feel empty inside and physically uncomfortable, if not in actual pain.
7   That embarrassed feeling when people saw that they were nowhere near enough for me emotionally and intellectually, and were only being polite to us because they didn't want to hurt my feelings.
8   That angry feeling when they didn't care enough to see a couples counsellor and to work through things, even though they said they loved me.
9   That less-than feeling when they'd hang out with losers and treat them like they were so much more interesting than me, just because their egos were much more comfortable feeling inflated, which gave them the illusion of being free; instead of being real.
10   That empty feeling when I would bare my soul and they couldn't find the words in the moment or even much

much later to acknowledge anything I had said, factor in anything that was different, or accept responsibility or accountability or possibly even apologize for.

PS God, if it's not too much to ask, could you make Charlie love me forever, and send me a little job or a sign as to my purpose, just so I know you're real? Thanks.

The rest of the month went like this:

Tuesday: Picnic in Griffith Park. Drink virgin sangrias, take pictures with real camera and read poetry aloud in the sun. Rumi, Hafiz, Mary Oliver... Discuss importance of classical music. So swoony, accidentally leave wallet in Charlie's truck.

Come home to three annoying messages from my mother saying she misses me, and when can I come help her clean out the office, and to remind me that she is thinking about selling our childhood home or at least remodelling the kitchen (again), and to say the real estate person is coming on Friday, so, again, could I please, please, please come help her clean out the 'office'.

Wednesday: Meet Charlie at Starbucks for wallet and surprise pix. Sit in car and talk for hours. Smell and covet jean jacket he accidentally leaves in back of car. Drive home holding it to face. Get home and pin photo of us looking like the Twin Stars on bulletin board above computer I never use.

Friday: Go on voice-over audition for BBQ sauce wearing lucky jean jacket. Meet at Starbucks to return jacket. Receive gift of old T-shirts and patches Charlie thought I might like.

Spend rest of rainy afternoon alone, whimsically darning socks and jeans with home-made patches and embroidery thread. Have massive crush on Self. Listen to only Bach (Glen Gould on piano, Heinrich Schiff on upright bass). Avoid picking up phone when my mother calls again about today being the perfect day to clean out 'office'.

Later, go with Charlie to see Spoonie open for Repeat Offenders and Squeezebox.

Tuesday: Receive annoying phone call on car phone from my mother about making time to talk to annoying journalist for *Vanity Fair* piece on her to run in conjunction with my father's birthday and retrospective in Frankfurt, in the middle of drive to beach with Charlie for guitar singalong and lesson on how to build fire in sand.

Thursday: Talk about luck and flow, book a commercial for BBQ sauce called Luv 'n' Fun. Call Charlie. Make a plan to go to Big Bear to see snow to celebrate. Make perfect cup of Earl Grey tea with half-and-half and two sugars. Thank God up and down, mostly for getting out of cleaning out 'office' with mother. For first time ever, feel like things are turning around for the better. Think all suffering was meant to lead me to bliss as result of Charlie.

Know beyond a shadow of doubt consummation of Charlie's love for me is only matter of time.

TWENTY-FOUR
Baby's Breath

'You keep this love, thing, child, toy. You keep this love fist,
scar, break. You keep this love.'

— Panterra

You learn a lot about a man from his toothbrush. Charlie had two.

He had finally invited me over to his tiny, Silverlake one-
bedroom house for a home-cooked dinner. While he checked on
the parchment paper salmon and cockle rapini he was cooking in
his dishwasher, I snooped around. Out on his tiny wooden deck
decorated with small white hanging lights, I met his various herbs
in tiny terracotta pots neatly arranged on a low picnic-table bench.
Lavender and tarragon and basil, only they had names like Lola
and Sweetums and Nettie-Arlene. Near a spotted dish with a
generous portion of old scrambled eggs for the neighbour's cat, I
spun the tyre of a bicycle that hung from a hook under a
yellow-striped awning and went inside the humble cottage.

Near a large window there was a small metal card table from the
fifties with a white enamel top and three mismatched metal chairs
with diamond-patterned velvet cushions in sumptuous gold and
purples. A patchwork quilt covered one wall, while exactly opposite
hung an Israeli poster of Sammy Davis Jr in a pair of sunglasses
giving the 'smokin' guns'. Above a fold-out futon couch, there were
hats with buckles, buttons, plumes and silk flowers for nearly every

occasion. Even though the digs were small, it was cosy and magical. It looked as though a secretly rich jester lived there.

While we waited for the wild rice, we decorated devil's food cupcakes. Charlie put a big wipe of blue frosting on my nose. I let it dry there, almost wishing it was a tattoo. I thought of how my father would affectionately draw things on my nose with a thick, black felt-tipped pen when I would bring him cups of coffee, and how much it annoyed me. But now, with Charlie, I saw the sweetness in it.

Then I made the mistake of excusing myself to use his restroom to pee (and secretly see how I looked with blue frosting on my nose), only to discover excitedly that we had the same Queen Amidala toothbrush.

When I emerged, waving the toothbrush wildly in my hand, he froze, and before he could utter a word, his body gave him away. 'That's my fiancée's. Mine is the other one, the plain blue one.'

'Oh,' I said, trying to play it off like I already knew he had a fiancée, 'Well, I have the same one as her.'

Her sounded funny and separated itself from my sentence, hung suspended in the air like that staticky transmission of Princess Leia when she appears and begs for Obi Wan's help. Of course he had a fiancée. As I looked around his house now, it became crystal clear.

There were little feminine touches everywhere: Chinese rain-scented candles, a pink paper lantern in the window, a framed poem written on a stained cookie doily, and a fucking right-out-in-the-open Goddamned Lilith Fair CD. At that point Charlie began to pace, and I couldn't shut him up. He looked silly with a stripy pot holder in one hand and a pair of tongs in the other. All the facts came rushing out in a steady, soul-crushing barrage of machine-gun fire.

'Her name's Arielle, she's a part-time model who works with the blind training guide dogs and she's away right now on a bathing-suit assignment in Jamaica, but she hates it because the modelling world is so fake and what we really want to do is open up a little restaurant and have a full-service catering business, complete with flowers and ice sculptures and hors d'oeuvres and stuff because, I mean, people love parties, and with the whole Internet deal I think people are really gonna want to get back to basics like good, clean eating and artistry in general and dinner's almost ready, so why don't you take a seat?'

I thought about all the men I had ever loved in terms of their toothbrushes. Jasper's had bristles made from hemp and he was obsessed with porn; Jym's was electric and he wasn't so great at head; my first boyfriend used a Water Pik and he never wanted sex. I wondered what horror I was being spared by seeing Charlie's plain blue toothbrush – impotence? Infidelity? Schizophrenia? Nymphomania? *Was he a woman?* Suddenly I was furious.

'Did you think we'd have an affair?'

'No,' he said sweetly, 'I thought we'd become awesome friends.'

'Oh, so I'm not good enough, is that it? I'm not attractive enough for you?'

'No ... I ...'

I brushed my tears away with my fingers. 'Why didn't you tell me?'

'It never came up. I really wanted to, but I didn't know how. I was actually gonna tell you tonight, and I'm really glad we are talking about this now.' Then he calmly said, 'Phew! I feel a lot better.'

God, he was worse than Karl, so thorough and even-tempered. I felt like the Tasmanian Devil spinning out of control next to him. Then Charlie began to cry too. 'I'm sorry for not telling you sooner. I had no idea I would like you this much. I never meant to hurt you.' He wiped his nose on his arm. I noticed how golden-blond and hairy his arm hair was. The snot made a silvery trail as it dried on his skin.

Click click click click click: my mind was a busy train-station sign updating its schedule again. That would explain why he never tried to kiss me, why he never walked me to my door and never even came in my house, ever. I thought, oh, Jesus, did I make all the overtures? Had I filled in the empty spaces with my own explanations and deductions *again?* What did I do *this* time? I wanted to run out to my car and drive away and never see him again, but even standing here arguing and being sad with him was more fun than anything else in the world, so I stared out his big bay window instead.

The sun was setting now.

Down the street, in the distance, I watched a young boy lose his balance and wipe out on a skateboard. *She's a part-time model and works with the blind* repeated in my head. I thought, Part-time. Oh, she's beautiful *all* the time, but she just models part of the time, making a fortune when it's convenient for *her*. But her real passion? That's donating her time training dogs for the blind.

I looked at Charlie now, watched him light three blue candles. His eyes were damp and shone wet in the candles he was lighting now. Guide dogs and a model? This guy is never going to leave her. I'd have to be modelling for Amnesty International on a full-time basis to turn his head and even make a dent.

'She's coming back in two weeks' and I'd love for you two to meet. I think you'll really like each other.'

'Yeah, sure, whatever.' I tried to laugh it all off, but I snorted snot out of my nose and had to excuse myself. In the safety of their bathroom, hugging my knees in close. I said her name out loud, 'Arielle'. Then I rested my head on the toilet with the clear undersea-themed plexiglas lid. Seeing the seaweed and tiny opalescent seashells and a sea horse trapped-forever-in-polyurethane made me feel even sadder. Charlie knocked on the door.

'Everything OK in there?'

I wondered if I would ever have real love all to myself with someone real, forever.

'Mer, please come out here and have dinner with me.'

I opened the door. 'Charlie?'

'Yeah.'

'Does she know about me? I mean, what did you tell her about me?' But their phone rang.

The machine picked up and a girl's voice, soft and nervous, pleaded 'Baby, are you there? It's an emergency.' He ran for it. I moved outside to give him some privacy. Under a million twinkling galaxies I wondered how many other people were sitting down to

214

awkward heartbreaking dinners this minute. I could see him pacing from the warm yellow light of the kitchen to the dark of the den. Then I heard him say, 'OK. I'll be on the next flight out.'

With heavy steps Charlie came outside to tell me the news. 'Arielle's father had a heart attack.' The news hit me like a bowling-ball punch in the teeth. 'They don't know how serious it is, but . . .'

'Of course. Yeah. My God. Is there anything I can do?'

'No,' he said. 'Just leave it.'

The air felt cool against my face. Suddenly I'm three, my father is stroking my cheek. I am sitting in my father's lap in a dark room. I am holding my stillborn baby sister. I'm trying not to spill her off my lap. My mom is mad at me and won't let me hold her all by myself, even though she is not heavy at all. My mom holds the head. The baby girl is blue-grey. I like how tiny her fingers are. My mom says her name over and over again, 'Shiva Plum, Shiva Plum.' My daddy is crying. I think he is mad at my mom because she won't let the men put her in the tiny coffin my daddy made for the baby. My mom just keeps kissing her. I kiss her too. Then my daddy pulls her away gently and my mom's fingers are stiff and she is crying and won't look at us. Thinking of it now, I must have felt something of me go with her in that dark place in the earth, a seed mixture of grief and love. I wondered why our capacity for grief had to grow roots too. Guide dogs and sick fathers? All hopes of me and Charlie ever being together vanished as I blew out the candles in front of me.

Gathering up their dishes I looked up in time to see a shooting star streak across the night sky. I made a healing wish for her, for them, then wiped the blue frosting off my nose.

TWENTY-FIVE

Abominable Snowman

'Ooh, ooh, little earthquakes, here we go again.'
— Tori Amos

'Meet me at Liquid Kitty, and don't even think about saying no!'
Sadie wasn't fucking around, and neither was I.

I grabbed my car keys and checked my reflection in the
bathroom. It had the worst light in the house. I knew if I could
pass the bathroom lighting test, I'd look good anywhere. But
something ghastly caught my eye.

As I stood before the white wicker garage-sale mirror in my
small black-and-white tiled bathroom and dived deeply into something that was not quite a cyst and not quite an ingrown hair at the
base of my throat, I wondered if I was indeed cursed. My phone
rang again. I hit speakerphone so I could keep up with my surgery.

'And look gorgeous!'

'Bye!' I said angrily.

The more I dug into *it*, the more it let me know that it was *not*
ready. A bubble of blood had pooled beneath the surface now. As
the skin grew thicker and more inflamed with every pass, I thought,
I am more boil than human. Is this what you want for me, oh,
Lord? Suddenly, the Thing next to my clavicle bone exploded and
made a perfect splatter image of the Abominable Snowman. Like
Charlie, Jym and Jasper before him, it mocked me and left a smelly,

217

oily smear as it attempted to streak past me and disappear.

My phone rang again. I picked it up, held it between my shoulder and my ear, and tried to put concealer over the oozing bulb. 'I'm coming! I'm coming!'

It was Spoonie and Lila on three-way. 'We were going to go and see Rows Five Through Seven at Largo, and just wanted to know if you wanted to come with us!'

'Oh, no, I'm sorry, I already have plans.' I held a tissue up to my bleeding bulbous knot. My other line rang. 'I gotta go, there's my other line.'

'OK, bye,' they said in unison. Ick! I clicked over. 'I'm coming! I'm coming!'

'I'm already here, hurry!'

'OK,' I said, and hung up. I checked the tissue to see if I had successfully stopped the bleeding where my neck met my torso, then applied a sparkly Band-Aid. I cocked my head, thought, it almost looks like jewellery. I went for my car keys. Tulie made her famous licking sound.

'*No*, Tallulah, no!' I marched towards her, imitating her awful windshield-wiper tongue as it swung up and over her piggy nose, to show her how positively annoying she was being. She looked up at me with those big, soft eyes so sweetly I had to lean in and kiss her warm belly. She needed a bath.

'What do you think, Tulie?' I showed off my outfit: baggy jeans with too many pockets, a low-cut, navy-blue sheerish top and a sparkly star to cover my weird scab brooch. She let out an enormous yawn.

The phone rang again.

'*Shit!*' OK, Tulie,' I said, giving her foot a little squeeze, 'back in your crate. Back, back, back.' Back to the drawing board.

'Yoo-hoo! Over here!' The place was dark, with black built-in booths and high tables resting on glass brick. Very eighties coke-dealer-esque. I headed towards a booth in a corner near the bar. 'Come meet my friends,' Sadie said, pointing to a chubby version of Tom Hanks and three empty martini glasses.

She was sitting on his lap, even though there was plenty of room in the booth. She turned to him. 'This is the girl I was telling you about. The one with all the wrong roses.' He raised his beer to me in a toast. She patted his fat cheeks, then goonishly looked back at me, smiling. I glared at her.

'He's not the wrong rose,' I said defiantly.

'He just already has a fiancée.' She turned to him. 'It's all very *Bridges of Madison County*, don't you think?' He took a swig of beer and nodded. She pressed her cheek to his. 'Another mudslide, Mer?'

'I haven't even had my first.' I sat down, and glared at the stranger. 'I thought we were having a girls' night out? Now that we are both finally single, I thought we could celebrate.'

He stuck his hand out. 'Swane. Swane Swanee.'

'He's a puppeteer and a fire-eater! Isn't that marvellous!' I thought, who is this person, and what has he done with Sadie?

'Is that your real name?' I said icily.

'Would I make something like that up? I'm a huge fan of your dad's. I had a poster of his in my dorm room in college. Have another mudslide!' He tried to get the waitress's attention. I exhaled loudly.

'They have dorm rooms at circus school?'

He laughed louder than necessary and thwacked me on the back, then turned to Sadie. 'She's a funny one, all right, just like you said she'd be!' He toasted me again. I pulled on Sadie's sweater sleeve. She turned and I saw it was cropped and exposed her belly-button ring. I leaned in and whispered, 'Sadie, I mean it. I thought it was going to be a girls' night out.'

She pulled her head away from mine and announced, 'It is!' and kissed Swane on the ear.

My drinks arrived and I pounded down the hot-fudge-sundae equivalent of booze until I was bleary-eyed. While Sadie and Swane sloppily began to make out, I noticed the napkins had little white snowflakes on them, and was suddenly deeply moved by the bar's little touches. The alcohol-induced train of thought went something like this: 1) Snowflakes are sooo beautiful; 2) The last time I was in snow I was with Jasper, who is as individual as a snowflake; 3) So is Charlie; 4) Charlie and I were gonna see snow; 5) Charlie is an asshole. I rested my face on the flat of my palm then I noticed that the snowflake pattern repeated itself. I felt I might be sick, so I moved closer to the bartender and tried to concentrate on all his tattoos.

He was a very confident bartender. He left his tips on the counter for a really long time. He held up his fingers to let the customers know the prices of drinks. I noticed another pattern. Four fingers on one hand and two on the other meant the drink was six bucks. (That seemed to be for the ladies.) Five fingers on one hand and four on the other meant nine. (That was for the men.) But he kept holding up two fingers every time Sadie ordered.

To me, he was a rock star behind his little stage with all the pretty bottles and their pretty, multicoloured liquids. In my 100-proof stupor I got an instant crush on him because, he too, looked vaguely like a chubby Tom Hanks. In fact, most of the men in the bar did that night. Except for a guy in the corner with a Lincoln beard who sang sad folk songs that the crowd did not want to hear. Songs about racoons and preserving wildlife and composting, all sung poorly to an even more poorly tuned, beat-up acoustic guitar. I nicknamed Sadie's crush Tom One and mine Tom Two, while I twirled the clear plastic drink-spinner in my glass. Then I thought about how the real Tom Hanks loves his wife so much, and always makes mention of how she is the most important person in his world every time they are on camera in public together. I bet Tom Two would be faithful too.

'Gee, you have a lot of tattoos,' I blurted.

He turned and washed down my corner of the bar with a beer-soaked rag. 'What'll you have?'

I leaned on my elbow. It slid a little on the slick surface. I bit my tongue. 'I'm really lonely.'

Sadie pulled her face away from Tom One and burst into hysterical laughter. 'She'll have another mudslide.' I glared at her. I was drunk.

I turned back to face the barkeep. 'Gee, you have a lot of tattoos.' He proceeded to ignore me and focus entirely on my drink order, so I swivelled around on my bar stool to watch the crap singer sing about a recent trip to Tibet. I yawned. He was looking right at me. I elbowed Sadie. 'Why is that guy staring at me, huh, Sade?' Sadie was giving the guy next to her a Goddamned tonsillectomy. I elbowed her again, this time a little harder.

Sadie leaned in too close, smelling of olives and gin, and whispered, 'I'm kinda in the middle of something, Mer. Do ya mind?'

I looked over at her date. 'Yeah, I mind. I'm fucking ready to be fucking single together, and you're fucking giving this loser the tongue.' I looked over at her date again. He looked annoyed. I stuck my tongue out at him.

'Hey, I'm trying to have a little fun here! I already did my time back at your *Green Mile*.'

'But *him*, the one with the Lincoln beard and gold tooth.' I pointed to the guy on the stage. 'He keeps staring at me.' I made a pouty, booboo face.

Tom One leaned across Sadie. 'He's cute, go for him.'

Sadie stared at Tom One. 'Do you mind?' She turned back to me. 'He's cute, go for him.' They squealed with cross-eyed glee.

I leaned over Sadie and shouted to Tom One, 'I'm off men thank you very much.' I said it with real venom. 'Plus, I'm not attracted to that guy.' I took another sip of my drink.

'So what, I hate the personality of the guy I'm making out with, but he's hot.' Tom One belched loudly, as if on cue, then toasted us, and did another ouzo shot. Sadie aimed for my ear, but shouted in my mouth, 'I mean, you've tried it with the guys that do it for you, and look where it's gotten you.'

'Fuck off!' I swatted the information away like a cloud of gnats.

Tom One's hand was under her sweater now, so she swung back around and docked her mouth back into his face. I rested my elbows on the table and cupped my chin in my hands. Suddenly my scalp felt like a heated wig. Then I stared down the loser musician and mouthed, 'You're on, guy.' But the room began to spin. I steadied myself with the edge of the bar. 'It's hot in here.' I bit Sadie on the shoulder. 'Is it hot in here?'

221

'Ow! Jesus, you are wasted.' She started laughing. 'You sound just like . . . What's his name . . .'

'Dudley Moore,' Swane said.

'Yeah, like in *Arthur!*' They giggled and tried to suck each other's tongue out of each other's head. I got the sweats again, followed by a batch of shivers. I knew I'd vomit soon enough.

I draped my coat over a nearby bar stool and zigzagged my way through the obstacle course of Tom Hankses to the restroom.

Once inside the maroon and marigold bathroom, I wedged myself between the phone and the metal condom dispenser for support, then sprang for the sink and hung my head over the smooth white porcelain.

To my left, a crying lady in a white lace minidress held a Furby with its eyes half closed in the palm of her hand. 'It's not fucking breathing. I fucking missed its fucking feeding time and now its not even making a fucking sound.' A rush of hot liquid burbled up and slipped back down.

The lady to my right was *also* crying at the other sink and had make-up running down her face. She wore a lime-green crop top and an acid-wash miniskirt and a diamond stud in her protruding two-inch navel. Her voice was shrill *and* nasally. 'That's nothing. I mean, we had this totally amazing time in NY and then he's all, I just want to be alone. And I'm all, fine. And he's all, I'll call you tomorrow.' I started to push my way past them towards a stall. 'Someone's in there.'

'Wait, is this Bill, or that plastic surgeon guy?' said the lady with the dead Furbee. I headed for the other stall. 'Someone's in there, too.'

Limey applied coffee-coloured lipliner to the outside of her lips, then filled the centre in with cream. 'No, Jim, the divorced guy with the girlfriend. The pro*ducer*.' I swung my head around to get a better look at her. She was either seventeen or a hundred and seventeen, I was too drunk to be sure. 'I'll bet he's fucking her this minute.' My jaw dropped open. I could only stare.

'Can I help you?' said Shrillietta snottily. I don't know how long I continued to study her. It could have been a few hours or a few days. Her lips looked enormous, like two big Boston cream-filled donuts. 'Take a photo, it lasts longer,' she said snottily, and the two of them trotted off past me, laughing.

I smiled to the door closing behind them and threw my head back. Since my motor skills were so far off, my fake-smiling face recoiled in slo-mo, like I was in a movie and I'd been shot in the head and this was my big death scene close-up. Could it be the same Jym? Even if it was, what did it matter now? All I wanted to do was pee, vomit, find Sadie, go home and kill myself, in that order.

Instead I made a phone call to Charlie. Luckily I got his machine. Not so luckily I left a message.

'Pick up the phone. Pick up, pick up, pick up, I know you are there. No? Out saving the world? Well, Jasper, I mean Jym, I mean, fucking...' I tapped my head with my hand, trying to remember, 'Fuckin'... ohmyGod, with the... magical place in Silverlake and all the... cold stuff, whatdyacallit, ice.'

I pressed the phone into my chest and started to pace as far as the metal cord would stretch, stared at the corrugated ceiling. 'Jesus, I don't fuckin' believe this. I'm supposedly fucking in love with you, and I can't remember your Goddamned name!'

I hit the stall with the heel of my hand. 'Hey, get the hell out of the fucking stall, already!' I put the phone back to my ear. 'It doesn't fuckin' matter. Fuck you, *you*. You know who you are, with the long looks and the long walks and all that *icing*. Fuck you and goodbye!' I started to hang up, then I bent down and leaned in close to the shiny silver numbers. 'OK, bye. I love you.' I petted the mouthpiece. 'OK bye, I love you.' Then I placed the phone down gently in its cradle. Another wave of nausea erupted. I hung my head between my legs. From this angle I could see that no one was in the stalls.

Back at my bar stool, I ask Tom Two if he'd missed me. He looked at me with what I perceived as pity, so I ordered a fuzzy navel and waited for Sadie's return. I kept craning my neck around every half-second or so, scanning the crowd for any sign of Sadie, but she was nowhere to be seen. That's when I felt the tap on my shoulder.

'You shouldn't mix your drinks,' said Lincoln the loser musician as he handed me a note from Sadie. 'Your friend wanted me to give you this.' In sloping blue ink on a damp napkin, it said, 'Mer, pleeeease don't be mad but Mama just got lucky! Call me mañana, Sadie.'

The bearded tree-hugger sat cross-legged on the bar stool next to me. 'I know you.'

'Pardon?'

'We went to school together. I kissed your neck in third grade and you screamed and went running to the principal's office. I had the biggest crush on you all through elementary school.' He extended his hand, and when I reached mine out to shake his he kissed it. He kept his eyes missile-locked on mine. I was so shocked by his inappropriate confidence that I stared back. 'Steven,' he said seductively.

'Jesus, I think I remember you. Are you Steven K. or Steven W.?'

'Steven W. Actually Steven Z. now, but I'm thinking of going back.' I tried to look busy by hunting for my car keys. 'Sorry about your father.'

'Oh, uh, thanks.' I said awkwardly. 'Look, I'd love to stay and chat but I really have to get home.'

'What's the rush? Tell me what you've been doing with yourself for the last ten years.'

I scowled at him. 'Nothing much. Just looking for my car keys really.'

'I've just been travelling around the world, really connecting to the mother, yunno? I just got back from Tibet, and now I'm here spreading some joy to the City of Angels.'

Tom Two leaned in and pointed at me. 'Anything else?' Yes, I thought, please take me away from all of this! Instead I politely mumbled, 'No, thank you.'

Steven Z. flashed him the peace sign with one hand and held up a silver chain around his neck with dog tags and an Alcoholics Anonymous three-year chip. Now I really decided to blow the joint.

I reached into my purse again and dug around for my keys,

retrieving only foil gum wrappers and stray pennies. I stood up and headed for the door, head buried in my bag, fingers frantically feeling around.

'So that's it? No goodbye?' Steven Z. shouted over the din as he followed me to the door.

'Looking for something?' he said.

'Yeah, my keys,' I said, slightly panicking. I checked my jeans and coat pockets before rummaging through my bag once more.

'I could drive you someplace.' I looked past him over at Tom Two, to give him one more chance to save my life, but he was holding up one finger to a redhead with gigantor breasts.

We stepped outside. A smack of cold air hit my face and arms. The fog was rolling in. I dumped the contents of my purse on the ground, spotted a blue valet ticket.

'Maybe you valeted it.'

I looked up at Steven Z. and half smiled. 'I guess I'm pretty drunk.'

I stood up and handed the valet guy my ticket. I wrapped my arms around myself and stomped my feet. I could see my breath. A cluster of people were smoking near the valet stand. The smoke blew in my direction. I brushed it away and turned my head. Steven Z. pulled the collar of his jean jacket up and stuck his hands in his pockets. I walked to the corner to stay warm. Steven Z. followed. My legs felt like I had casts on them. At the corner I saw a mustard-coloured van with rust patches drive past. The guy in the passenger seat looked like that coffee guy. I waved, but he didn't see me.

'You wanna get some coffee somewhere? I had the biggest crush on you in school.'

'Yeah, you already said that.' I clicked my teeth with my tongue. Another wave of nausea washed over me. I felt I might hurl for sure this time. I hit my funny bone trying to lean my elbow against a parking meter to steady myself. 'Ooh! Ooh!' I said. I rubbed my elbow with my frozen fingers to dull the pain.

'I'm just parked right over there. We could leave your car here, just until you sober up. I really don't think you should be driving.'

The valet guy honked my horn. Steven Z. wagged a just-a-minute finger at him, then looked back at me. I burped. It tasted like puke. The valet guy honked again.

'Where are you parked?'

'Over there,' said Steven Z., pointing to a magenta 2002 BMW. 'It's the one with the Guns 'n' Roses sticker on the back.' I thought, of course it is.

'I'll be right back,' he said. 'I'm just gonna re-park your car and come right back.' He ran towards the valet guy, pulling bills out of his back pocket.

Steven Z.'s mouth formed a suction cup over my own as we made out on his tattered brown Indian-food-smelling couch. His tongue was small and hard and pointy. It poked. Not only that, it did it with a kind of force that reminded me of movies about break-ins that turn ugly very quickly. I had a couple of cops posted at various stake-out points in my mind, and they were radioing for back-up.

As he slid his hand under my blouse, and then under my bra, I noticed the topside of his tongue had a sandpapery surface like a cat's, while the underside had wet flaps of skin, like a car wash. Along with the hot poking and the flap-slapping, there was the deposit of a dump-truck-size portion of saliva followed closely by a 'yummm', a sharp inhalation of air and then the sucking again. Somebody was enjoying himself so much he didn't notice I had stopped breathing.

But, and this is the important part, I did not stop kissing him. I don't know if it was pity or a morbid fascination with the details of the worst kiss I have ever had in my life bar none, but I didn't stop. In fact, I couldn't. The kiss and the tongue had their own gravitational pull that kept me in a kind of suspended animation, like a sexy version of that Munch painting, *The Scream*.

Mer, *run!* My inner voice pleaded. I thought, but I don't want to hurt his feeeeeelings. I knew what it was like to want and not get, so why not make someone's day?

Steven squirmed out of his filthy jeans and boxers. My hand

went on autopilot, stroking his uncircumcized bulge with zero enthusiasm while it went in and out of being erect, like an accordion. I thought, why is it when I choose the guy he has a huge cock, but when the guy chooses me it's small or weird or both?

Soft, it looked like a sea cucumber; hard, like a loaf of Home-pride bread. The tip, anyway. My tongue traced the large vein that ran the length of it all the way down to its skinny little base. He kept saying, 'Check out the girth.' I alternated between sucking him off and giving him a hand-job, shaking his blood-filled sausage like an enthusiastic diplomat on a peace mission. In my head I could hear Karl's voice. I thought, where are your boundaries, America? At least I kept my clothes on, I argued back (but that was mainly because of my fear of bare skin against the couch). Then suddenly came the sweats again, the hot geyser at the back of my throat.

While Steven Z. thrust his penis in and out of my mouth in time to Bob Marley belting out, 'Where is the love to be found?' hot vomit rose from my murky depths like an epiphany. I threw up on his cock *and* the chana masala couch.

In the bathroom, I thought, the last time I heard Bob Marley was in that nice coffee place with that nice guy. Why can't I like nice guys like that, huh, God? I pried open a window and contemplated escaping through its three splintery inches. I closed my eyes and took in the cool February air. It would be spring soon. I prayed, dear God, please let me be different then, please let me have boundaries and self-esteem.

I returned to the living room just in time to see Steven Z.'s hips moving jackrabbit quick. He pulled at his cock herky-jerky, like a speed bag, as if pulling taffy, as if he were a junkie trying to get the top off a jelly jar filled with cocaine, PCP *and* the solution to world peace.

Without warning, the anteater nose exploded with something as thick as frosting. I watched it arc and land on a kitchen table covered with ecology pamphlets, watched him lean back and spread the remainder on his hairless stomach.

'Can I get a ride back to my car?' I said politely.

Steven Z. whistled and pounded his steering wheel like a drum as we headed up Main Street and turned right on Pico, taking breaks to talk incessantly. 'Do you know about the buffalo up in Yellowstone, and their whole feeding migration deal in Montana? The farmers kill the buffalo on sight, while my activist brothers and sisters get in the line of fire in the deep snow. I'm thinking about heading up there. I mean, the last pure-strain lineage of our animal ancestry mowed down for what. Money? Yunno?' As we careened past a billboard for dandruff shampoo on two tyres, I was thinking about how much I hated my life and Jasper and Jym, Charlie and this guy, but mostly my father.

Then I caught a glimpse of an old black homeless man with a mop of matted salt-and-pepper hair. His arms were outstretched and he stood perfectly still, smiling up at the night sky, frozen. He looked like a dirty statue of a saint, Buddha in a sacred *mudra*, the Blessed Virgin Mary watching over Medjegore, and I felt humility catch in my throat like an endangered animal.

I came home to two messages. One was Charlie, calling to tell me that everything was fine with Arielle's dad, and he was just thinking about me and wanted to make sure I was all right, and please not to leave messages like that in the future, and that he wondered if I wanted to have coffee on Thursday when he got back to town. 'No thank you,' I said out loud.

The second, from, my mother: 'Mer, darling, it's Camilla calling. Listen, Larry Flynt saw the piece they ran on me in Vanity Fair, the one with the family photo, anyway like I said, his office called and wanted to know if you and Grandma and I would be interested in doing a photo spread entitled "Three Generations of Pussy" for *Hustler*. I told them I didn't think you would be interested, but just call me so I can let them know for sure. Grandma said whatever you decide is fine. It would be a free trip to Capri or the Bahamas, but I'm fine either way. Love you! Mchwa!'

TWENTY-SIX

Radioactivate (Reprise)

'You are a free moth, go chase the light'
— Innocence Mission

'Jasper, are you there? It's me. America. Of course you're not there, it's voice-mail. I . . . I just wanted to tell you . . . I'm thinking about you . . . and that I love you. Bye.'

Fuck.

TWENTY-SEVEN
Crack-Baby Petey

'She did it all for the nookie . . . so you can take that cookie
and stick it up your ass.'
— Limp Bizkit

'You *do* know it's not OK to give blow-jobs to people just because
they've travelled to exotic places?' asked Dr Karl sternly.

It made me blush to hear him say 'blow-jobs' as though this was a
perfectly natural thing to be discussing with a client twice his junior in
a situation where money would be exchanged. In a different outfit on a
different street we might be arrested. 'As far as calling Jasper goes, a
year ago, *six* months ago even, you would have driven up there, so
although it's a minor backslide, calling and *not* engaging is actually a
tremendous progress. And Charlie, well America . . .' Karl said as
patient as always, 'It's a hard lesson to learn that you can have it all and
it still might not work out, that nice guys can sometimes just be boy
friends.' I sank a little deeper into the folds of the couch. 'He obviously
cares for you or he wouldn't have spent so much time with you. And he
surely wouldn't have told you the *truth*. All right now, shall we work on
Mom today?'

I trained my eye on the airplane that kept disappearing into
patches of grey, looming clouds outside. 'For what? Look at me.
I'm a loser. Nobody wants me.'

'That's not true.'

231

I looked at him, rolled my eyes. 'You're right. Nobody wants me, *except* losers. Oh, and *you*. The fact that I am here in this room with Elmo and Beary and Kanga and Froof-Bunny is total proof.' I looked at the stuffed animals all lined up in a row now, their blank, black, googly eyes staring back at me from the tantrum couch. I faked a gag reflex. I disgusted myself.

Karl smiled. 'That's not what I'm seeing. I'm seeing break-throughs. I'm seeing someone who has come a long way in a very short time, a person who attracts "loving someones" she can express her vulnerability and anger and disappointment to without fear of being rejected. You are rewiring your nurturing matrix, your receivability.'

'Well, I want the rest of it, Goddamnit!'

'I hear your anger, but maybe Charlie can be a friend to you.' The way he said 'friend' made me think of movies about cavemen. Me friend, this fire, fire bad.

'No,' I screamed. 'Anyway, it doesn't matter now because I am thinking about adoption, either a little Chinese girl or a crack baby. I am thinking of naming him Petey. Crack-baby Petey. Or Crack-baby Doris, if it's a boy.' A muscle in my right foot twitched. 'I mean, if I'm just gonna give love away, for free, why not give it to someone who really needs it, right? Give it to a fat little stiff-as-a-board gingerbread, plank-backed, crack-loving chubster with zero mobility. Not even the power to turn itself over; just some stiff, hopeless, kicking pile of drool that, if left unattended, could choke himself to death.' I was throttling a pillow with both hands now.

'How are you doing, America?'

'It's not fair. It's just not fair. I'm healthy, educated, I can vote, I can wear whatever I like, I have no *real* money worries, my car is paid for, I have a beautiful home, I'm white...' I looked at Karl pleadingly. 'What kind of happiness can I really expect to have?'

He coughed into his hand, adjusted his ass in his seat. 'Well...'

'Why isn't that enough? Why do I want a boyfriend so much?' I pounded my fist into my thigh. 'What kind of a person *am* I to be this blessed and this unmotivated?'

'Don't beat yourself up, America. I think we are doing real work

232

here to make sure you are whole in *you* first. The true desire to reach out to Other naturally arises when it stems from a real satisfaction with Self.' He traced an invisible capital S in thin air.

'I'm bored of being sad. I'm bored of being miserable. I'm bored of wanting, bored of not appreciating what I have. I have exhaustion fatigue, compassion fatigue, depression fatigue, family fatigue, Jasper fatigue, fury fatigue, boredom fatigue, me fatigue. I'm soooo fucking *bored*!'

'How bored?'

'What?'

'How bored?' he said again.

'What do you mean?'

He faced his desk, unlocked his file cabinet, pulled a piece of paper free from a tan folder and handed it to me. It was a flyer, black ink on glossy white paper in calligraphy font next to a dark-haired woman's smiling face and shining eyes. It read:

There can be no suffering in True Freedom. Join Luna Forrest at The Thistlewood Community Retreat Center for eleven days of silence in the beauty of an old-growth forest for an opportunity to remember your true nature.

I looked over at Karl's smiling face. *Eleven* days of silence? The worst cases in his practice only needed nine. Was I *worse* than the worst case? Karl must have seen my panic because he said, 'Mer, she's a wonderful teacher, she cuts right to the heart of things, well actually *you* do . . .' he trailed off, as if remembering a wonderful vacation. Outside the sun was beginning its descent. I traced a slat of light and dark across the deep sea carpet. It cast a shadow across Karl's face and made him appear as though he were wearing an executioner's hood. Then he looked at me. 'I think you're ready.'

I swallowed. 'Can I think about it?'

'You mean postpone?' he asked patiently.

I forgot how annoying he could be. I promised myself never to come back ever. If I accomplished one thing in my life, it would be never to return to that office.

Dr Karl leaned in and rested his elbow on his tweed leg. 'If you do decide to go, I guarantee you will be a different person.' A fire truck roared by, sirens blaring. I felt like that truck.

'I want a good life.'

'You have a good life now. You are just playing some old tapes that you need to unlearn.' He sounded like one now. 'All right now, I think we are done for today. This one's on me.'

He stood and moved towards the door. 'What I want you to do is go home, eat something healthy, make a list of all your talents, so you know how wonderful you are, and get a good night's sleep to really think things over.' He unlocked the door, held it open for me. 'You did great work today.'

'Thanks,' I said, smiling weakly.

When I move towards the open door to go, Dr Karl held his arms out and offered me a hug, smelling of almond massage oil and tobacco. I leaned forward and stuck my butt out so our hips wouldn't touch. He patted me on my back behind my heart, like he was trying to burp me. 'How 'bout letting future-you start to make some of your decisions from here on out? And remember, the treasure doesn't do the hunting. All right now!'

My stomach growled, but the thought of going home to the fridge with the baking soda, expired mayonnaise and the home made guava jam my grandmother had sent from Hawaii frightened me, so I stopped at Wild Oats on the way because Future Me said I should.

I grabbed a red, plastic basket and wandered around in a stupor, Little Red Riding Hood on downers, down the various aisles, past soy butter and goat's yoghurt, and eleven kinds of miso, past rainbow kale and Fuji pears and burdock, past the clear plastic dried-grain bins and Jasper's healthy dandruff shampoo, all the while knowing that a quack thought I was a basket case.

Nothing looked good except some health-food organic tampons, which I grabbed and put in my basket, and maybe a strawberry/banana smoothie.

I took a number at the display case, where I waited patiently for

234

the guy with the fuschia hair in the white apron to call out lucky number thirteen. When the guy in wife-beater, grey sweats and flowered flip-flops got his flax seed tamale, the red, digital display switched over to twelve.

'Twelve!' shouted the fuschia-haired guy. 'Twelve?' He hit the number again, this time it went to thirteen. 'Thirteen?'

'Hi.' I pressed my belly against the slant of the glass. 'I'll have—'

'Here I am . . . here, here!' I heard a familiar breathless voice call out from behind me. 'Twelve.' It was the guy from the coffee place in a bowler hat, high-waisted pants and black kohl eye make-up. 'Strawberry/banana smoothie with protein, please.' I pulled the hood of my sweatshirt up over my head, hoping I hadn't been spotted, and tilted my basket so he couldn't see the lone tampon box. He turned to me. 'Hey, Fat City! How's my cup?'

'Ho, hey,' I said, lowering my hood back down. 'It's fine, but it is *my* cup.' Why did I have to look so awful?

He laughed. 'Why don't you bring it back in to visit sometime?'

'Can I get free refills?'

'For outlaws?' he exaggeratedly scratched his chin. 'Sure, I mean, if it's for you.'

'Here you go, sir,' said the lit match.

'Thanks.'

'Thirteen?'

'The same as him, please.'

'Copycat,' said the coffee guy.

'Isn't it a bit early for Hallowe'en?' Idiot! He looked at his shoes, then tapped the toe of his clunky, black boot behind him two times.

'Aw, come on now,' he said, sounding defeated. Just then the muzak version of 'You Are The Wind Beneath My Wings' came on the speakers overhead, and it was more than I could bear. I pulled the string of my neckline until my hood tightened like a noose.

'Well, I gotta go. See you around. I'd give you a flyer to come see my band, but you never show.'

I smiled meekly, then watched the nice guy walk towards the checkout stand. I watched him pay for his smoothie in only change, watched him make the dark-skinned checkout girl with the yellow daisy behind her ear smile, then the fuschia-haired guy handed me my Powerfruity; I felt like shit.

As I turned left on to 26th heading towards San Vicente, past shops and homes with neatly clipped hedges, my car phone rang. It was Sadie.

'There you are! He fucks like a Goddamned criminal, Mer. I'm serious. I'm totally in love.'

I stopped at a red light and watched a blonde woman in an all-white g-string yoga get-up drop her purple rubber yoga mat, only to be helped by some dreamy yoga hunk with long flowing brown hair.

'That's great,' I said, forcing enthusiasm.

'What's the matter? You sound sad.'

'I'm just a little depressed. I just came from—'

She cut me off. 'Listen, come and meet me and Swane tonight down at Spaceland. Swane wants us to go see this band Rows Five Through Seven. Supposedly they do an insane version of "You Are The Wind Beneath My Wings".' I squinted. The light turned green.

'You mean, like a chaperone?'

'Oooh!' she squealed. 'No, but that is so funny . . .'

'I'm just feeling—'

'Oh, boo, never mind then.' She whispered now, 'Mer, he's huge, I'm serious. Hung like a horse. I have to whisper 'cause I'm at his house, and . . .' I heard a male voice now, shouting something from another room. She called out to him, 'What, honey? I can't hear you. Yeah, OK, in a minute. Mer, he wants me to join him in the fucking shower. Can you fucking believe this? I wish you got a chance to get to know him better the other night. I totally get what you mean by "you just know"! I gotta go. If you change your mind, meet us down there at eleven!'

'Yeah, OK,' I said. I hung up and thought, this is so my life. Just when I'm single and miserable, Sadie gets a boyfriend.

As I sped up the tree-lined street, past joggers on cellphones with miniature headsets in the centre divider, a flock of migratory birds caught my eye. I leaned against my car door, craning to see the birds rise and fall, rise and fall, felt the cool of the glass against my skin.

'I'm coming, I'm coming!' I shouted to my ringing phone as I turned the key in the lock of my front door, that I had only recently painted cranberry to attract love. 'Hello?'

'Mer, it's Camilla calling.'

'Yes, Mother, I recognize your voice.' I dropped my keys on my kitchen table, thumbed through mail, bills, coupons, a postcard from my dentist reminding me to come in for a cleaning, and a menu from Totally Thai!.

'Listen, darling, I really need you to help me clean out the office. Those documentary people are coming and I need you to help me pull slides, and—'

'What documentary people? When?' Tulie scratched on the back door, asking to be let out.

'The people from Belgium radio.' She made a crunching, chewing sound. 'For the show in April to coincide with the show at the Kunst Museum in Frankfurt.' She was slurring some of the words. Trying to talk and swallow at the same time. 'Yunno, the one I asked Jasper to do the programme cover for.' My hair stood on end. Hearing Jasper's name plunged me into a frozen lake. My mother took another bite of something loud. 'Now I need you to be available to be interviewed, and I need the house to look—'

'Radio, Belgium, Frankfurt, wait, what? Why did you call Jasper? When did you talk to him? What the fuck are you eating?' Tulie scratched the back door again, please let me out.

'Potato Chips. I didn't, he called me.' I was pacing now. 'America, I told you all this, we are all going over there in the spring and Jasper expressed interest in doing the programme guide and I don't think he can be there at the show, but—'

Deep creases formed along my brow. 'No, Mother, no you didn't tell me, because if you did I would have told you then what I'm telling you now, *do not fucking talk to him.* And I certainly would have told you not to ask him to do the programme. When did you talk to him?' I absent-mindedly rapid-fire flexed and released the muscles in my calf.

'Oh, I don't know, right around your birthday. He said he has the time even though he's right in the middle of about seventeen things . . .' Tulie scratched at the door again.

'Please don't chew in my ear, Mother.' I grabbed a clump of hair on the top of my head, began to pace again, stretching as far as the cord would allow. 'I cannot fucking believe this. Jasper and I aren't even speaking, and—'

'I can't talk to you when you're like this. Goodbye, Mer.'

'He broke my fucking *heart*, Mother! Do you understand that?' Tulie made a whimpering sound. I watched her squat, then heard the sound of liquid against wood. 'Nooooo!' I screamed, as I watched a fine, clear stream make a puddle on the floor between her legs.

'Shall I tell them Tuesday? You and I can get the room done quickly at the weekend, and—'

'I really have to go Mother.'

'Well, what about Jasper?'

'I have to go!' I slammed the phone down so hard I startled myself.

After I damp-mopped with a lemon-scented ammonia, I smoothed the blank page of my journal with my hand and at the top of the page wrote:

THINGS I AM GOOD AT:
Being annoyed by my mother
Being single when Sadie has a man and vice versa
Choosing bad men
And, later, hating them
Looking ugly and saying stupid things when cute nice guys are near
Being jealous of Spoonie and Lila
Getting dumped
Getting mad

Staying mad
Not believing in God
Breaking out
Having continuous thoughts about dying or killing myself,
alternating with guilt about having those thoughts in the first
place
Missing my dad
Hating Tulie
Hating myself
Secretly staying in love with Jasper, no matter how much he
has hurt me or how awful he is.

That night, I dreamed I was a long-distance runner. I am running
along a sidewalk in a suburban neighbourhood with neatly
trimmed hedges, pacing myself in even measures, my breathing
perfectly in sync with my body and the scenery I pass. I run past
aspens with shimmery leaves and houses with picket fences and
dogs and parked cars in clean driveways. Past Spoonie and Lila
smiling and waving. Past my mother gardening. Charlie is there,
trying to hit Star Wars *piñatas* out of my tree with the end of a
broom. I jog in place now, and the sky grows suddenly dark. Then
I see a woman with a large-brimmed hat drive by in a red pick-up
truck. In the flat-bed part I see Jasper in a naked half-backbend.
He has an enormous erection. He massages it in long strokes in
time to my breathing. He looks at me and smiles. Then I see that
the woman driving the truck is my father. He is smiling at me too.

I woke up to a ringing phone. I looked at the clock. Two-
seventeen a.m.

'Hello?' I said, clutching at the bosom of my cotton nightie. It
was Sadie on her cell. I could hear a mixture of loud, garbled voices
and then bustling street sounds.

'I have to walk outside so he can't hear me. I think I have found
your dream man. As I am speaking to you I can see the outline of
his penis in his jeans, he's *huge!*'

'Do you even hear yourself?'

'Listen, we're down here at Canter's. The guy doesn't drink. He doesn't smoke. I'm looking at him through the window this minute. He writes *poetry*, Mer, published poetry. He only subscribes to *The New Yorker* and *Harpers* and he does crossword puzzles. With a *pen*. Come down and meet us!'

'Sadie! Jesus . . .'

'The only bad thing about him is that he doesn't like to be touched.'

'Sadie!'

'In public, in public! Now I know what you're thinking. You're thinking, why would you want to go out with someone who doesn't like to be touched, right? Because his last name is *Rose*.' I rolled onto my side, tucked my knees in towards my chest and adjusted the comforter around me. 'Chuck *Rosenzweig*.'

'Goodnight, Sadie.'

'No no no, don't hang up, OK, OK. What about Swane's friend, Danny? He had a small part on that show *Roswell*. Does that count?'

'Bye, Sadie.' Even in the dark I easily put the phone back down in its cradle. No more roses, no more Jasper, no more therapy, no more *men*. The phone rang again, but I didn't pick up.

I knew what I had to do.

PART THREE

Awake at Last

TWENTY-EIGHT

Om Sweet Om

'Hold on, hold on to yourself, this is going to hurt like hell.'
— Sarah McLachlan

I arrived at Thistlewood in a light drizzle in the dark. At a badly constructed rickety wood and glass kiosk I was given directions by a heavy-set, highly distracted bearded mountain man as to where I could park my white, cigarette-smelling rental car. The flight to Portland had been unremarkable, save a certain chicken dish coated in a pineapple-flavoured cough-syrup glaze and served on a baby-size dish to be eaten with a spork. Even after tasting it I could not detect which president was in office when the chicken was last alive.

I noisily made my way back to not-so-gentle-Ben, dragging my enormous rolling Tumi luggage across the gravel parking lot, led mostly by the slender glow of a small red pocket flashlight on the end of my keyring.

The mountain man then proceeded to give me still more spaced-out directions to a certain cabin, pointing it out, in the pitch-black, on a handout about the place which he gave me, along with a wheelbarrow for my gear. 'It needs to be promptly returned for others to use.' Little brown teeth appeared under the moustache now.

When I asked him the reason why there were absolutely no

lights on anywhere he said it was because they make their own energy here at the Thistlewood Community Retreat Center, using a generator and rushing river water. 'It gets recharged overnight, so we use electricity sparingly if at all, dude.' Then he added, 'But hey, isn't it fun to learn to see in the dark like our owl brothers and sisters?' I thanked him and he bade me farewell with a final, 'Make yourself at home!' The little brown teeth shone again in the dark.

Oh, he's smiling, I thought, as I felt my way along a sloping garden path under a moonless sky.

After several minutes and zeroluck in locating *my* thatch-roofed shelter, but finding several others, the drizzle turned to rain. Then, into an actual full-blown storm.

As I pulled my sweater on over my head and turned my flashlight towards the handout for a clue as to the whereabouts of cabin eight, I thought very seriously about going back to kick the living shit out of the stupid overweight vegetarian, but I didn't even know what direction he was in.

It was muddy and I was frightened to the point of temporary blindness, though I did manage to notice how good it smelled there. Wet and woodsy. Air so clean it stung my lungs to inhale. I thought, this is *so* my life. Being angry and frightened and alone in the unknown; I could die here and no one would ever find me.

Marching over leaf-covered terrain, I finally found cabin eight – the one with the infinity sign – the one I had been circling for nearly an hour because I had not realized that they used no numbers here, only symbols (a simple fact that I felt I should have been explained right up front), I opened the squeaky screen door and went inside to make myself 'at home', resolving to get a certain stoner's resignation by lunch.

When I turned on the light, it dimmed and hummed. Still, I saw that the two or three 'beds' were already taken. The room looked like a kidnap crime scene *after* the police bust; stained mattresses and sleeping bags rolled tightly on the floor near an old dirty sink. What was left was a faded, drooping army cot by a draughty

window, the glass of which was cracked and sort of whistled when
the wind whipped by.

'It's rustic all right, but I'm not so sure about the charming part,'
I said aloud to the silence as I began to unpack my toiletries using
my pocket light, placing them on half of a little home-made shelf
near one of my room-mate's stash of granola and a fluffy purple
washcloth.

Getting settled can be one of my favourite things about
travelling, unpacking tiny containers of your home-away-from
home items, but here, my expensive imported creams in black and
gold containers looked garishly out of place against the backdrop
of shabbiness; I suddenly saw myself as a spoiled, overpacked
Empress of Good Taste. Then the light flickered itself out.

I was so distraught about how far I had come only to pay seven
hundred dollars to be alone, in the dark, in an abandoned garden
shed, that I decided to punish the entire Thistlewood community
by not returning the wheelbarrow.

I sat on my cot, and after a few minutes of extremely shocking
dark and quietude, decided I did not want to be alone. So, against
my will, I fished through my luggage for my rain slicker, Banana
Republic pink and blue cashmere scarf and matching cap. Led by
intuition, the smell of burning wood and a bit of light I could
make out in the distance, I headed to the main room of the big log
cabin; but not before kicking the captive wheelbarrow over on to its
side in a further act of mutiny.

Once inside the main cabin, I spied a carved wooden placard above
two double doors that read: 'Om Sweet Om', and another one that
said: 'Namaste'. Ugh. Namastay-away was more like it.

I looked around past two couches and two tables with lamps
flickering dimly. I identified a desk, a darkened room with tables
and chairs I assumed to be our mess hall, according to the tattered,
rain-soaked treasure map. Beige couches. Beige chairs. Plank floors
that warped. And several braided rugs in royal blue, rust and Robin
Hood green. How homey.

Near an old-fashioned radiator I noticed about thirty pairs of muddy shoes. Did they expect me to remove mine? Ha. On the wall above them were pictures of the Thistlewood staff in headbands and brightly coloured garb, barefooted or in mismatched socks, smiling and hugging trees, and smiling down by the river building rock sculptures or holding hands in sacred circles. Some were candid photos of the staff at work in their various practices: Mystical Theatre, Creative Movement, Massage (Watsu, Swedish, Deep Tissue, Thai, Reiki or Esalen-style), or Continuum Faerie Dancing. When I saw the 'e' in faerie, I began to feel my depression turn from sadness to horror and devastation as I began to realize what loving Jasper Husch had amounted to.

I was about to turn into Jack Nicholson from *The Shining*, when squeaking hinges bade me turn my head to see someone coming out of the big hall where all the shoeless feet were hiding. The frumpy elderly lady with the matted hair and stretch pants smiled at me so sweetly, I removed my rain slicker and my shoes and went inside.

I chewed on my pinkie fingernail as I entered the room, where fifty or so people in mismatched mountain attire and wool socks were sitting quietly upright, meditating cross-legged on the being carpeted floor or in folding metal chairs in front of a big roaring fire. At the front of the room I recognised a radiant, dark-haired woman, roughly fortyish, in a taupe sweater set and long white skirt sitting in the lotus position. I thought, am I as crazy as these people? Do I look like these people to them? Like these sad women with the braided hair and these lonely, balding guys, all gathered together in miserable quietude? I thought not. Still, I guessed we had all been through something pretty awful to end up here.

I scanned their pathetic faces – not a cute guy in the bunch to distract me. I sighed, then took a seat in the back next to a woman swathed in a tie-dyed blanket thrown over her shoulder like a cape.

My chair made a loud squeak when I sat down, but no one acknowledged it. I sat upright, crossed my stripy-sock-covered feet and folded my palms in my lap, mostly taking my cues from a large man in an even larger poncho, to my right. With my eyes closed I was more aware than ever of the night sounds and my exhaustion and relief just to be still and dry. I listened to the sound of rain beating down on a tinny-sounding roof, to the crackling fire, the modest coughs and blowing of noses, the rustling of fabric, the syrupy yawns and deviated-septum breathing, the whistling of the wind. I was just settling into a quiet moment in my busy head when I heard the ding of a tiny bell and looked to its source; Luna clutched a little copper bowl and a small wooden wand and she let its sound resonate and dissipate completely before resting it back on the small wooden table with the burning candle and the photo of a smiling old man with dark skin and a long beard.

She said nothing, just set the bowl back down, folded her hands in prayer, held them to her forehead and turned her head to everyone, smiling, until she had blessed every last one of us.

As she stood and moved towards the door, some people stayed seated, some gathered belongings or folded up portable seats and lined them up in a tidy row. More people stood now, and either stretched or wandered out of the room towards their shoes. Some headed towards Luna's empty chair and pressed their foreheads to the floor in respect, or bowed their heads at her as she passed them. When Luna got close enough to my chair for me to notice that she smelled like sterling roses, I was so stunned by her radiance, I bowed my head too. When I looked back up at her, she was bowing back at me. Then she leaned in close and whispered, 'Welcome,' in a thick Scottish accent, her voice as sweet as bananas and cream. 'We are now in the silent portion of the retreat, but there is a handout for latecomers at the front desk which lets you know what times to gather together. Are you America?'

I wanted to speak, but I made the mistake of looking directly into her eyes, which contained a certain vastness that made me feel both instantly at home and homesick to my core; my knees buckled.

I rested my hand on the back of a nearby chair to steady myself. I wanted to collapse at her hem and beg her never to let me return to my little pit of despair back in dumb old Hollywood, California. I thought, oh, my God, is she for real? 'Are you America Throne?' she said again.

I wiggled my toes inside my socks and managed to find my way back into my body and nodded yes. She smiled at me even more radiantly than before, obliterating any of the irritation from my arrival. And something else . . .

In silence she guided me to the desk where the handouts were resting on a knotty wooden shelf next to a bowl of floating flowers and a small tea light glowing inside a blue jar. I read the schedule:

Namaste and Welcome to Your Self! Three bells will ring indicating the following:

6.30 a.m.: rise and shine! (stick figure of a guy yawning with his arms in the air)

7.30 a.m.: breakfast (stick figure of a guy holding a steaming bowl and a spoon)

9 a.m.: group meditation (stick figure in the lotus position)

11 a.m.: silent yoga (stick figure with his hands folded at his heart)

12 p.m.: lunch (stick figure of a guy patting his stomach with his eyes closed and tongue sticking out upwards and the word *yum*)

2–5 p.m.: volunteer chores (Sticky with a bandanna on his head, hoeing)

5 p.m.: river-gazing (Sticky in profile next to squiggly lines for water)

6 p.m.: dinner (Sticky with a fork and knife and a bib around his neck)

7.30 p.m.: Satsang (Sticky with an open mouth)

9.30 p.m.: sky-gazing (Sticky with his head tilted back)

10 p.m.: lights out (Sticky horizontal with his eyes closed, and a bunch of zzzzzs)

At the bottom of the page, Sticky bids a farewell with a final finger to his mouth and *shhh* next to him, and the words 'No reading, no music, no writing, no talking. Just being.'

'In the meantime, just enjoy the silence and reeeelOXshh,' Luna whispered, before heading off into the darkness towards her shitty cabin.

I thought, in the meantime, in the meantime – what a funny saying! What a funny concept, 'the meantime'. Then my roving eye landed on a quote written on a little white board in blue erasable marker near the water fountain, underneath the heading FOR CONTEMPLATION:

> 'The real never dies and the unreal never lived.'
> — Sri Nisargadatt Maharaj

Suddenly I didn't know how long I had been standing there. My feet were both cement and jelly with little tingles of electricity rushing up and down my legs. I decided to find my way back to my cabin in the dark, by following the last of the herd and their pocket flashlights. I figured out which one was mine because my wheel-barrow was still there, turned on its side.

One of my room-mates had lit a candle, and was washing her face in a little sink by my cot, while the other was already in her sleeping bag in the back of the room. I prepared my toothbrush, running icy-cold water on chewed bristles alongside roomie number one, while roomie number two kicked her snoring into high gear in the back corner of the tiny room. When I needed to spit, roomie number one was still hunched over the sink, with soap all over her face, so I flung the cabin door open and hocked it on the forest floor. The door accidentally closed with a slam, and when I turned around, I got what I perceived as an evil look from the fresh-faced roomie clutching a towel at her cheek and neck. Roomie number two only changed positions and snored into the wall.

As I wrestled myself into my nightie inside my sleeping bag I thought, fuck her for not making eye contact. Fuck her for judging me when *she* was the one hogging the sink. If she weren't hoarding the basin, I wouldn't have *had* to startle her. Fuck the snorer, too. Fuck this whole place. Why do we even have to have room-mates, anyway? This facility is completely ill-equipped to even *deal*. I don't need a retreat, I need a fucking *vacation*.

I told myself, first thing in the morning I'm outta here. I will fly home and drive down to Twenty-nine Palms, or stay at a spa somewhere; fuck this.

I lay still now, staring at a small white spider's cocoon, wondered if it had already escaped or if it would happen while I was sleeping. Then roomie one blew out the candle and the room went dark. As I lay there with my eyes open, I thought, how clinically depressed was I to pay money to not speak, to share a room with two strangers in the middle of hippy nowhere, and to sleep on an army cot? No room service, no porter, no nothing even remotely vacation-like or nurturing. There and then I vowed to have Karl's licence revoked. I was suddenly startled into outrage as I listened to roomie two bark through her nose. That's when I named them, Snorey and Hoardie.

As I began to drift off, I could hear Hoardie shaking several pill bottles like maracas. She probably thought she was being polite by not turning the lights back on. She was wrong.

Day two: In the daylight of the next morn, just as I had been warned, three loud gongs sounded in the camp and let anyone within a thirty-mile radius know we had beaten the sun by a hair. Ugh.

My roomies were beginning to stir, but I was unconvinced this was even happening. I tested the air with my finger – too cold. I snuggled down a little deeper into my squishy tomb, pressed my face into the downy nylon, trying to warm my cheeks and nose, and decided to remain in bed. Forever. But my bladder had different plans for me.

Heckle and Jeckle were well into their little morning rituals now: one assumed various yogic postures while still remaining horizontal, while the other covered her yellow hair with a reusable yellow shower cap and walked out the door. I thought, Jesus, where is she going, then panicked, bolted upright, and looked around for something to blow my head off with.

Outside the window I saw several modest but scantily clad men and women trudging off towards a coed bathhouse.

This realization was bad, but not awful because in the light of day, it came to my attention that I happened to be in the middle of the most gorgeous old-growth forest I have ever seen! I mean, rainforest documentary, *National Geographic* gorgeous. Trees, trees everywhere. I thought, maybe this isn't so bad. Maybe there is a God. And maybe, during the night, I died and went to heaven.

I unzipped my sleeping bag, felt the sting of cold against my arms and legs, slipped my feet into a waiting pair of rubber and canvas flip-flops. That's when I heard the first clap of thunder. No, not heaven, I sighed.

I dropped my things on my bed, tied my hair into a knot on my head and waited for my roomie to leave so I could change my clothes in peace.

At breakfast, people with wet hair moved slowly, pretentiously I thought, as they made their way towards the choice of tofu scramble with scallions, bell peppers and sweet potatoes, or ass-blaster special number two, oatmeal with stewed prunes. Hot licorice tea and sliced oranges all around. I thought, sweet monkey Christ, I'll starve.

I stared at my meal with the courage of a mountain climber on a slippery rock face. Some people hung their head in prayer, blessing their food, or perhaps like me, wishing it would turn into sausage and eggs.

After the meal was done, everyone made their way to three grey buckets, one for dishes, one for silverware and one for food and napkins, because this was the land of composting. Suddenly, even in the downpour, returning the wheelbarrow was starting to sound like a real party.

I checked the clock on the wall: only an hour until meditation. And only another ten and three-quarter days until I could leave.

At morning meditation, I politely battled for a seat very close to the foot of Luna's chair. Even in silence people competed for a chance to be next to her. The rest took chairs, or sat on cushions with their backs pressed against the wall of the main hall. She was already meditating. I watched her eyeballs travel from left to right under the soft canopy of her moisturized lids. I looked around at everyone else as they adjusted their spines and sat up too straight. They all seemed a little too anxious to go 'inside', if you asked me.

I crossed my legs, closed my eyes and folded my palms over my knees. Softly, Luna said, 'See your mind as a flowing river, and let your thoughts effortlessly drift downstream.' Instantly my mind became a flowing river I tried to cross, but my thoughts were slippery stones. I leaped from one to another, trying to cross over to sanity. When my thoughts were at an ear-splitting decibel level I opened my eyes and came up for air, deciding instead to study the room. I noticed things like water damage along one wall or a place in the carpet where the corner turned up and revealed a carpet tack, and how I still held my stomach in, even though the men there were strangers (unattractive strangers to boot), and how five big asses could easily sit on the brick hearth comfortably. Then I thought about my mother and how if she were here I bet she wouldn't be able to keep her mouth shut.

Then came the demonic open-eye imagery: me dying, my dog dying, my mother dying, my grandmother dying, Spoonie dying, Charlie and Jasper dying, everyone else dying and me left alone to grieve their loss and then die myself. Then came the living-horror fantasies: me homeless, my family homeless, my family rich and me homeless and they won't help, me rich and my family homeless and I won't help, me rich and my family homeless and coming to live with me, me rich and Jasper homeless coming back to live with me, and so on.

After almost an hour of fending off additional grotesque images of Charlie fucking a model, Jym fucking a model, and Jasper fucking a model and them moving in together, Luna finally rang her little bell, and I was the first one out the door.

I thought, how can people live like this? Setting time aside for the mental onslaught. How come *they* all came out smiling? I decided to take a walk. As I put on my rain slicker, I noticed the little posted quote of the day: 'Marry the one that never leaves', it said. Whatever that means.

While people stared at the fire or foolishly grinned at thin air, I wrapped my scarf around tight. My head was a warzone; my brain would not shut up.

I wondered if Tulie was having fun without me while Sadie house-sat. I wondered if my house had burned down, if I had missed any auditions, if Jasper had come to his senses and finally called me. If, if, if.

Jasper used to call me Guava. He used to say, 'Guava!' when I would answer the phone. He would say it like I was his favourite pet. Whenever I would screen, he would say it loudly and I would run to pick up the phone. It meant he was in a good mood. It meant that he missed me. It meant that he loved me. It was the best when he would say it in person, because it meant that he wanted to be as close to me as possible. At least, that is how I had taken it, since I always wanted to be as close to him as possible. I loved him so much that I felt I missed him, even when he was deep inside of me. What makes a person mean Guava one day and then never again? What makes a person shake vitamins so in the dark? I could feel my hot tears intermingle with the raindrops.

Was I the only one who was not grateful to be here? How come we were experiencing the same silence and they were happy zombies and I was a theatre of pain, a live action cartoon of terror. I thought, I don't need a fucking *retreat*, I need a *fucking* retreat. I stopped to examine a tree entirely taken over by moss and thought, I am lost, Daddy, I am utterly lost. A short time later, the morning yoga bell rang. I decided to nap instead.

Day three: Lunch was served with chopsticks, in spite of the fact that the meal was in no way Oriental. As I looked around the room, everyone else seemed quite genuinely content, while my brain just raced on and on: images of me attempting a nocturnal escape while hippies hid in the trees, using them as makeshift sniper towers to either stop or bathe me. Me in Luna's chair suggesting group suicide as a remedy to everybody's cluelessness. Me escaping to a nearby café for a cappuccino.

I scraped my dish, put it in the grey bin and headed to the lobby area, deciding to spend the remainder of the afternoon dodging all humans, especially my room-mates and the golf-ball size raindrops, by way of more napping.

Then, in the safety of my sleeping bag, without warning, the sentence 'I am going to die' began to repeat itself in my head over and over until beads of sweat formed on my brow. I couldn't breathe properly. I was freezing and sweating at the same time. I didn't know if I had been alone for a second or for an hour, or if I had screamed everything that was rattling around in my skull or not. I tried to sleep it off but it merged with my breath and my heartbeat. I went to the office to call or to talk to someone, but the office was closed. Anyway, it didn't matter because who could relate and what would I even say? By now it was too late to have a normal conversation with *anybody* ever again. Now that I knew what was inside of me when I had no distractions, everyone and everything else seemed like a lie on top of the truth that I was indeed crazy. I couldn't believe anyone I knew even loved me at all, when deep down I was a basket case. Or worse, I knew the truth: that deep down they were basket cases, too. What was the point of anything at all? How could I ever enjoy anything ever again?

Then I heard the gongs sound for afternoon meditation.

I didn't want to meditate but I did not want to be left alone, so I headed back to the main hall and took a seat in the back.

As usual, everyone else closed their eyes and went 'inside' – not me.

To keep myself calm and maintain my last shreds of sanity, I decided to nickname everyone: Too Much Beard and No Style and Captain Everything's Wonderful but my skin started crawling. I thought I might have a heart attack. Everyone looked so happy. I wanted to shout at the top of my lungs, *no*, this is not wonderful. What do you think sharks and killer bees are for? To help us understand everything is groovy?

When Luna gracefully rang her bell I almost cried from relief.

By dinner I was a wreck. I piled too much food I knew I wouldn't eat high on to my plate, and no fork. My plan was to punish everyone by eating like a savage. My internal rebellious brat was on overdrive. I wanted to ruin everyone else's peace since I wasn't having any. I marched loudly, 'forgot' to take off my shoes in the mess hall, and took cuts. I thought, they don't call the Pacific North-West the suicide capital of the universe for nothing. Maybe I am unused to this much rain.

I blew off evening meditation entirely.

That night I did not sleep. The rain had paused but my mind was out of control, now with thoughts of chemical warfare and the Pope and Sheryl Crow for no good reason. It was too late for me to make arrangements to get home tonight, but I vowed to leave when the sun came up. I closed my eyes and tried to lie on my side. Snorey bulldozed away, and Hoardie snacked on the loudest granola ever created. I knew I was going crazy, but at least I was not alone.

Day four: The next morning, the office was closed, so I decided to skip breakfast and soak in the natural lithium hot springs, thinking it would do me some good as I still refused to wash my hair or shave my legs or even shower, for that matter.

I trudged over to an enclosed area with viny flowering plants and four concealed, tiled tubs representing the four directions and the four seasons, and checked the schedule to make sure it was the Women Only Day. Mercifully it was.

I opened the gate and chose Autumn, because its temperature suited me the best, but mainly because it was too crowed in the other tubs. Being nude with strangers was not exactly what I had in mind, but my bathing suit seemed wildly out of place next to everyone else who had already stripped down to nothing and hung their clothes on wooden pegs along a redwood overhang.

I tried not to think about it, and lowered myself into the slippery brown-and-blue-tiled tub. Little bubbles formed on every little hair on my legs. Boy, did I need a good waxing. The hair was long and black and coarse. The water made everything super-reflective and up-close-looking. I squeezed a large lump of my leg underwater and thought of car hoods in hail-storms, realising I found me even more disgusting when magnified, especially the dirt in the thick, yellowing, big toenails with black tufts of hair on the little nubby ones. I thought, no wonder all men leave me.

I looked over at the other women: sagging breasts, loose flesh over ageing bones, cellulite, overly bushy pubic hair. Or the skinny ones with dairy-free skin, adorable freckles, boyish hips and patchy, coifed pubes. I wondered if I was alone in my self-loathing. We were all grotesque to my skewed vision.

Just then, two pale feet slipped past me and slunk down into the water. It was Luna. I blushed. I was suddenly embarrassed that I was sharing a naked soak with a teacher, but more than that, I felt ashamed that I had been so careless with my negativity and had the distinct impression Luna could read my every thought.

I went underwater, held my breath, tried to shake her loose. The sound of the humming generator was in my ears, along with my heartbeat and bubbles as they rushed past me to escape. When I surfaced, Luna had let her head drift back on the rounded cement edge of the tub and was now gazing up at the sky, fingers barely touching the water. She seemed to be just listening to the outside sounds, to the birds, the lapping of water, the wet vacuum sound as some women exited the tub, and the sound of wet feet smacking against cement as they moved towards their clothes.

She looked vulnerable and relaxed in a modest way. I envied her tranquillity, her seeming enjoyment of merely being human in some hot water. I mimicked her, pressed my back against the tile, leaned my head back, felt the pulling weight of the water in my hair, the difference between the smacking cold against my exposed flesh and the heat of my steeping skin. I smelled flowers and earth and noticed dragonflies and small, shimmery leaves in nearby trees. Suddenly I felt very beautiful. Suddenly it all seemed so obvious that we were all very beautiful, it was only my mind that was ugly, and for a moment everything was still.

I thought, oh, *this* is what retreat is about, moments of sweetness. I decided to stick out the day and leave the next day. Or maybe the day after that. I thought, eleven days is nothing.

By lunch, however, the rain had returned and my peace had vanished. I was restless.

By dinner, my mind's madness was out of control.

Day five: As I sat for morning meditation, I tried to get back to the feeling in the tub, but the sentence *I am going to die* returned with the consistency of tides. When I was on the verge of hysteria, I got up. My plan was to go to the restroom and gather my wits, but once outside the meditation hall, I just took off running.

Up the path through the woods, past the cabins, past the parking lot, past the welcome kiosk to a nearby yert which looked more like an abandoned circus tent. It was freezing and it smelled like plastic and dirt. I lay flat on my belly, trying not to be absorbed into The Mother. I shook from my core.

Miraculously, a few minutes later, the small wooden door with the stained-glass moon opened and Luna entered. 'What's the matter, dear?'

In between heaving sobs and snot launches I managed, 'I want to die, no one loves me, I have nowhere to go. I have nothing, and I'm afraid. *I don't want to die.*'

Luna knelt beside me now, put a consoling arm around me and rocked me. She brushed my hair with her hand. In her most musical lilt, she told me gently, 'You are only telling yourself a story. Those are just thoughts you are having. Whenever there is contraction in the body, it is your imagination fuelling images to go along with thoughts. They are only thoughts. Try to reloxxcks into right now. Be here, right here; right now, in this moment. You're in imagination, dear, now go to the truth.'

An unnameable terror gripped me and began to swell from deep inside me. I was sweating and shaking. 'What happens when we die?' I asked.

'I have no idea,' she remarked unapologetically, 'but I have a question for you; what really dies? Whom are you referring to?'

Then Luna did something that from the outside would appear to be wholly unremarkable; she lifted my chin in her hands and looked me directly in the eye. The only thing is, that's not at all what happened.

A mystical experience by its very definition is something that cannot be explained or understood by anyone other than the person having it. How do I put into words a momentary flash that illumines everything it touches? A revelation that burns so bright it lights up the darkest recesses of your soul and yet leaves nothing for the mind to grasp, only empty space.

She looked at me for only a few moments, but all was obliterated. What I had known previously – that I was America, the dumpee of a very painful break-up, the embodiment of loneliness and despair, the said daughter of a genius – suddenly dissolved.

Through the transmission of her gaze, I saw the whole of consciousness as particles of dust that could not touch the magnitude of who we really are.

'Accept loss forever' is what Luna said next. 'Let sleeping Buddhas be.'

When my father loved me he set up a projector in his studio and we sat on cushions on the floor and watched black and white cartoons from when he was small. When I laughed he would squeeze my hand. When I was sick he made up stories about Eskimos and camels and drew me pictures of an octopus with a cape. He saw the deepest part of me: hurt and confused and scared and tired and ugly and unwashed and naked. Vulnerable. Utterly exposed. Luna saw me like *that*. Jasper left, my father left, but Luna just beamed at me, luminously. She did not want me to suffer. She saw me and she accepted me just as I was, without asking for anything in return, and because of this it didn't matter if Jasper loved me, because I was love itself, and that the only thing I could count on was impermanence.

'Thank you,' I said, not entirely certain my mind understood what I was even grateful for. Exhausted, I just bowed my head to the floor.

Back on earth, wending my way back to my little cabin, I realized something had loosened in me; I had softened. I felt like something had been hatched and set free.

I held my arms open and pressed my chest into the sky. Looking up past the canopy of trees and into the infinite blue, I saw something that took my breath away. A bird falling towards the earth and, dropping rapidly, almost violently, its beak being pulled towards the ground by gravity in a seemingly perilous nosedive, when suddenly, it pulled up and out at the last possible minute.

I dropped to the damp earth and wept.

'Any relation?' said the man in the red polyester vest and the salt-and-pepper hair behind the United counter at the Portland airport.

'Pardon?' I said, over the din of echoey loudspeaker announcements, crying babies, squeaky luggage carts, and rushing feet. I was still in shock from going from total silence to worldly chaos.

'Any relation?' he said again, smiling shyly. I noticed that his two front teeth overlapped and he kind of whistled when he spoke. 'To Boris Throne, I mean, 'cause I see here on your driver's licence your name is America Throne, born in 1969. You're not by any chance . . .?'

'Yes,' I said proudly. 'He was the most amazing man I have ever known. One of my favourite things I ever did with him, was make colour jokes. We would call out the horrifying colour combinations and we would laugh and laugh for hours. For example, I'd say something like, apple green, orange, and brown. And he'd say turquoise, mildew and Washington DC. If we were driving, cars' interiors would have us peeing in our pants. Strip-mall colour schemes would send us over the edge. The very idea of fabric stores flattened us.'

He promptly blushed, dropped his pen, picked it up again and began typing furiously. 'I loved your father! He was my total hero, screw it, still is.'

'We went to a book-signing in Pittsburgh once, Spoonie and me. People waited for hours for him to sign his book.'

'Which one, *Letters to the Editor? A Catastrophe in Rome? The Gift Show?*'

'No the cubist one, *From Russia With Glove*. He was so amazing, so patient. He waited until every last freak and geek had said his piece. He was kind to every last one. Do you know how rare that is? My mom is probably going to put out another coffee-table book of all his stuff. She runs the Estate. She's amazing too. She's really the glue of the whole operation.' Some people in line behind me began to get annoyed now.

'I waited in line once,' said the counter guy. 'I was so naïve, I showed your dad some of my stuff, I was working with wax at the time, and he told me he thought I should do something with animals instead, so I chose the airlines.' He laughed at his own joke.

I slid my luggage under the metal counter. 'Seriously, if you get a chance you should try to go to Frankfurt. Don't they give you discounts? They are doing this whole retrospective on him you might really like. Or you can see Spoonie's band when he comes to town. They're called Free Dumb. They are kind of like the best painting you ever saw in your life, but with music.'

He coyly looked up from his station. 'I saw him play once. At the Viper Room. They played with the Butt Pirates of the Caribbean and Redeemer.' He dropped his pen again. 'I'm sorry, I'm just really nervous. I don't know if you can tell, but I'm a really big fan. Can I give you a hug? I loved your dad so much.'

I leaned across the counter and held out my arms. I felt the sweaty, airless fabric embrace of all the lonely nights my father's existence got this man through, and I understood something about myself and the beauty and satisfaction of *total* adoration.

He pulled away and wiped his eyes with the back of a luggage tag. 'I'm gonna bump you up to first class.'

TWENTY-NINE

Meat Me in St Louis

'Why can't we give ourselves one more chance? Why can't we
give love, give love, give love...'
— Freddie Mercury and David Bowie

'Mustard,' said Spoonie. Codeword.

'Huh?' I said when I picked up the phone at 10.19 the next
morning from the warmth of my own bed. I was groggy and still
recovering from the fact that Sadie and Swane had had sex in my
bed while I was away. 'Wait, *mustard*?' I said, bolting upright. My
hand instinctively reached for my head. 'Is it Mom?'

'No,' he said, 'no one is dead or dying, I mean, except all of us
every minute, heh-heh, no, I mean, I don't really think it's really any
big deal, but...'

'Then why did you say mustard?'

'Well, when I ran it past Lila she thought it counted.'

'Wait, you told her about mustard?'

'I'm here for you, America.'

'Oh, hi, Lila, I didn't know you were on the phone.' I rolled my
eyes, bit the inside of my cheek. 'So what's going on?'

'On a scale of honey mustard to horseradish Dijon...' Spoonie
mused. 'I mean, it's definitely not Dijon. It's more like Gulden's or
French's in terms of seriousness.'

'I'm not so sure. You're not a woman. It didn't happen to you.'

261

'What didn't happen to who?' I said frantically.

'Well, it didn't happen to you either,' Spoonie said calmly to Lila, ignoring me entirely.

'Even so, I'm a woman and I think from this perspective I should know better. Plus, remember that stalker I had?'

'That's true.'

'Er, um, hello! Remember me?'

Then in unison, they said, 'I think we should meet in person.'

'For French's?'

'Yeah,' they said in unison.

'Can you meet us at Nirvanarama in half an hour?' asked Lila.

'Why can't you just . . .'

'America,' said Spoonie seriously.

I flinched. 'OK, OK. I'll see you both in half an hour.'

I thought, this is *so* my life, find peace and truth and come home to more crap. My mind raced. Was it Grandma? Had my mother squandered away the last of our fortune? Did Lila need an abortion? Calmly, I told myself, my mind is a river and these are just thoughts gently floating downstream.

Outside, birds were chirping away. I could hear an Edie Brickell song in the distance, 'I know I'll be all right as soon as I let go.'

Calmly I found my car keys. Calmly I locked my door and calmly I drove.

I circled the block around a hundred times before eventually settling on a spot several blocks away from Nirvanarama, a trendy high-tech health-food restaurant complete with healing tonics and elixirs along with TV monitors and newsracks spewing out the latest global catastrophes in several languages, including sign. I looked around the restaurant but Spoonie and Lila weren't there, so I asked to be seated at a table to wait. I was nestled in a corner between three confirmed lifelong bachelors and a mother-son combo.

The boy to my right looked like a small, more evil version of Jasper. The mother kept holding food up to his mouth saying, 'Do you like this?' He'd shake his head and scream noooooo! 'OK, how about this?' And he'd scream no again, like she was pouring acid on his skin, which I thought wouldn't have been such a bad idea considering his pitch.

Finally she managed to get some egg in his mouth, but some of it fell on to the toast below and he began to shriek at top volume, 'The eggs are tickling the bread!' He was so adorable, I debated the idea of stuffing him in my purse.

On the television, a young boy in Baghdad was being interviewed about having to go to work to ensure the rest of his family's survival. His father had been killed. He was all of eight. He wanted to grow up and be a blacksmith because he wanted his sister to have a good wedding and his mother to have a new dress.

Then Spoonie and Lila sat down opposite me. They both wore serious expressions and outfits to match – black turtle necks, wool caps and jeans. They looked like adorable foreign spies.

'We have something to show you.' They looked at each other and then back at me. Lila reached into her purse and slid a five-by-seven card into my hand. It was an invitation to Jasper's upcoming art show. It read: 'Bugs and Fishes: New Works by Jasper Husch and Maya Richter'. At the bottom, under the date and time, Jasper had handwritten in perfect block caps: 'I can't remember America's address, so please give this to her but you're all invited! Loveyou-missyouhopetoseeyouthere, love J. P.S. Thanks for the nice message!' I started giggling. 'What an asshole.'

Spoonie punched Lila in the arm. 'See? French's at most, just like I told you.'

'Turn it over, said Lila.

I did. The picture on the back was a picture of two people sitting across from one another in thrones opposite a great chasm. In one chair a naked man with a giant snake-like erection, sat with his back to the girl on the other side of the great divide. The girl with long brown hair sat facing him and held a glowing moon in her lap. She was naked also, but her skin was a map.

'It's me!'

'We know!' said Lila.

I wondered if I had killed Jasper in a previous life, and now he was making it up to me in small, deadly increments. I wondered when the pain would stop, and who or what would be strong enough to put an end to it. I held my breath.

'It's called *Adam and Even Now*. Did you see that?' said Lila. 'I'd be like, what the fuck, right? I think that is totally horseradish Dijon, right?' I could only nod. Lila punched Spoonie in the arm. 'See?'

'What do you want us to do?' asked Spoonie.

'We thought you should hear it from us,' said Lila eyes as big as pancakes. She looked at me with such concern I knew she was family now, and that she really cared about me too.

'Mer? Are you OK?' Spoonie asked.

I didn't say anything, just wiped my eyes on the sleeve of my faded jean jacket, removed an orange and yellow elastic band from my wrist, and piled my hair on top of my head like a wedding cake.

I didn't call Jasper to say I was coming. I mean, he hadn't called me to warn me about any of the bombs he dropped. I didn't know what I would say or do, I only had the sense that I had lost something and that I had to get it back. That I had to get it back from Jasper. I suddenly understood the adrenalin of tripwires and sharpened stakes under leafy forest floors and the aliveness of planning a kill. I frightened myself, as I sped along the 5, foot pressed to the metal, driving on the gas fumes of old wounds.

I wondered what our meeting would be like. We hadn't seen each other or even spoken in almost nine months. I had several fantasy scenarios: 1) I would see him and slap him across the face, turn to go, and he'd come running after me and beg forgiveness. 2) I would see him, slap him across the face and he'd cower in terror and then I'd turn to go and he'd come running after me. 3) I'd see him and slap him across the face, turn to go, he'd come running after me and we'd make love and live happily ever after. There were others, one where I kick Jasper into infertility, one where Jasper spontaneously combusted at the mere sight of me, and one random one where I kicked a pregnant passer-by in the stomach. I sped up.

I am seven again. I hear my father having sex with a lady from my school. I know because I recognize her shoes. I am nine and I bring my father to 'show and tell', but he doesn't pay any attention to me, only flirts with the headmistress and tickles all the kids that no one talks to. I am fifteen, and twenty-one, and every age where my father ever left and my inconsolable mother couldn't mend my heartbreak. Fuck artists. They should all be put down, executioner-style. They are disowned fragments of God that need to fly home before they cause any more destruction.

This is what I'm thinking as I rounded the corner and pulled onto his street with the sickeningly perfect low trees in neat wooden boxes at 3.20 in the afternoon. My hands were sweating.

I found a parking space right out front.

I got out of the car, stood outside the Victorian house I almost didn't recognize because he had painted it. Red and green. I thought, stop and go, story of my life.

I could hear a television on next door. Across the street a cat lazed in a window. From where I stood the house looked friendly. The five big steps leading up to the little landing were cleaner-looking than I remembered. The ocean air made everything sparkle more, like in a lucid dream. He had new shades in the front window and had painted 'Jah Love' on the glass front door.

It saddened me that he thought he was spiritual. I took a deep breath, climbed the stairs and rang the bell. No one answered, so I rang it again. Nothing. I peeked through the window to get some sense as to whether or not he saw me and was hiding or when he might be coming home. I knocked on the door rather loudly. 'Jasper?' I called. This made crazy Mel's parrot, Gambler, start to go berserk upstairs. I knocked again. Gambler squawked, who is it, who is it, over and over. I knocked again, this time so loud the glass shook in its frame. Nothing. Now I was *really* mad.

I looked upstairs at his neighbour's window. A car slowed as it went by. A lady with a stroller passed by. The parrot continued to squawk. Crazing fucking bird.

I sat down on the stoop and buried my head between my legs, and began to cry. I thought, what is the point of anything? I dug my nail into the skin around my ankle until it stung and turned red. Then I thought of the lock box beneath the stairs in the alley, past the trash cans out back, and I wondered if Jasper could be so stupid.

As I turned the key to the back door and went inside, my face felt tingly around my ears. I was light-headed as I set foot in the kitchen.

I ran a finger over the blockwood counter, past tea tins and pots with copper bottoms still on the stove, trying to place the feeling in my gut. The house felt different, lived in. I lifted a lid, mung beans in one, brown rice in the other – his usual hippy mush. I brushed away a hanging ivy strand with yellowing leaves and opened the fridge: yeast-free raisin bread, soy milk, hummus, feta cheese, rye krisps and diet soda. 'Diet soda? Oh, my God, he lives with someone!' I shrieked, not caring who heard me. Diet soda? Cancer-causing diet soda in his vegetarian-tree-hugging-nuclear-disarmament-peace-on-earth-om-shanti-people-come-together-not-to-remain-together-but-to-grow-and-move-on fridge? I couldn't believe my eyes. I closed the door and staggered back. His cats came over and circled my ankles. They meowed, so I put some food in their bowls and headed for the bathroom.

As I rummaged through her things and smelled her fucking grapefruit and honeysuckle body wash, I spotted a photo tucked in the corner of the mirror of a smiling Jasper with a smiling Debi Mazar look alike. I moved to the living room.

The room was essentially a long rectangle with high ceilings separated by panelled double doors. I moved towards his work-space, past his 'technology' – his TV and VCR and stereo system – and past his elaborate alphabetized CD collection. Past Nick Drake, Elliott Smith, Belle and Sebastian, The Pixies, Pavement, Frank Zappa. I thought, my God, I never realized how depressed this poor guy was. Past his Star Wars collection (now out of their boxes on a high, home-made shelf), past his draughtsman's table and open shelves covered with every conceivable art supply, until I found myself before twelve white plaster 'balloons'. They were weighted down with a metal base that had the title of the piece on a small brass plaque. On each of the balloons small canvases of

Jasper's new works were embedded in the plaster faces:

Jesus, barefoot in New York, with a crown of thorns made of Barbie-doll legs.

A ghoulish clown with hollowed-out eyes and a massive erection poking pointedly through the fabric of his colourful striped attire.

Another, a technicolor picture of a nude woman with a smoking cigar sticking out of her vagina, dropping ashes on a caricature of Bill Gates holding a beehive on a stick, like a hobo.

Still another with swans and pelicans in a tarry swamp struggling to get free.

One after the other, brilliantly rendered but awful to behold. Twisted. Sick. Lonely.

In the corner, Jasper had painted one with a deadly traffic accident. Twisted metal and bodies strewn across a darkened highway. Once I had seen such an accident on my way to visiting Jasper. I was just coming for a short stay, but arrived changed forever. I thought now of the heavy-set woman I had seen that day, face down and lifeless, in white shorts, alongside a man I presumed to be her husband, in casual attire. They looked like they might have been vacationing. I had cried as I passed them and prayed for those who would receive the news. All this was depicted inside a giant bloody vagina, lips spread apart, like theatre curtains.

Finally, I stare at the one of me and Jasper, at the two people in uncomfortable chairs across a great chasm, and I'm not angry any more. His work had been under my nose all along, only I never saw it; his silence, my answer.

I moved to the bedroom now, the unmade bed with the new white duvet, the crumpled clothes on the floor, the misshapen blue and white swirled vibrator by the side of the bed. I felt the thick Egyptian cotton of the blanket cover, then I lay down on the bed, pulling the covers up and around me. The nubs of my tennis shoes got a little stuck between the top sheet and the blanket.

I scan the room, the bed, the gardenia smell of her on the sheets, the scented candles, the tantric sex books, the massage oils, the ceiling, the hanging lamp, the way that one speaker wire sticks out too much from behind the cabinet, the yellow walls with their solitariness, that one dangling blind, and not a trace of me.

I pull the blanket up over my nose now, study the horizontal stripes of the stitching up close: white on white, lines that go nowhere, and I know it's really over.

Outside, I can hear the twinkling of wind chimes cling-clanging away. That's something, I think.

Stopped at a traffic light underneath the 101 on my way back onto the five, I watched as a skinny white guy with a dirty face approached the car with a wadded-up brown paper bag and a bottle of Windex while eating a slim jim like a popsicle. I shook my head no, but as I rolled down my window and handed him a fist-full of change he said, 'Name's Clark.' Then he clicked his heels like Dorothy from old Oz and saluted me, holding his little plastic wrapped-beef wand to his eyebrow. That's when I noticed he was wearing a home-made nametag that said Louis.

'Adios, Sanny Franny!' I said as I crossed the bridge.

As the sun came up over the Silicon Valley I thought, yes, I have seen dead bodies and fires on this highway. Not to mention the slaughterhouses. Did you know the word laughter is smack in the middle of slaughterhouse? This occurs to me on the long drive back for the very last time. And even though nothing was very funny, I had to laugh.

THIRTY

Bolifar Carfish Inn

'America, America God shed his grace on thee and crown
thy good with brotherhood from sea to shining sea.'

'When I was young, younger than before, I never saw the
truth hanging from the door. Now I'm older, I see it face to
face. Now I'm older, gotta get out and clean the place.'
— Nick Drake

As my mother and I sorted through various closets, drawers and
boxes in my father's office, I noticed how pretty she looked. The
grey in her eyebrows and at her temples made her look vulnerable.
(Of course she would say her roots need to be redyed.) I noticed
things like the black witch's hairs on her chin (the ones I've started
to notice on myself), and how her pores ran in cascading patterns,
like eyelet lace. I smiled at how her crow's feet were set so deep
they look like bird footprints in wet sand. And how her laugh
lines were there even when she wasn't smiling. I thought about
how much pleasure my mother got from being with me and
Spoonie and how my father was the only one who could really
make her laugh.

It was going to be her birthday soon, and I wanted to make her
a cake. In fact, sitting there looking at her like that, I decided I
wanted to bake her five cakes. I wanted to be her own personal cake

269

chef. Maybe even specialize in it and open up a shop. Or maybe just cupcakes.

I imagine the conversation, me telling her I don't want to take money from her any more and how I want to be a cake chef, and she'll say you mean pastry chef, and I'll say no I don't, I really mean maybe just cupcakes, in fact, and she'll say just keep the money and use it for school and I will, and someday when I have my own money, not that she'll need it, I'll give her mine because I love her more than anything in the world. Only she is lost in thought, folding one of my father's shirts and putting it in the box, along with his easel and the enamel plate with the dried paint on it, and several drawings Spoonie and I did when we were small.

In permanent black ink she labels the box 'For Keeps'.

The day my father died was sunny. I remember that because I was in the gallery and he was talking to, well flirting with, a young woman in a short, cream-coloured skirt. She had seen his work being hung for the show that evening, and had wandered in off the street to talk to him. My father asked me to run and get him a piece of cheesecake and I didn't want to go because I knew he wanted to be alone to flirt in private. I was mad at him because my mother was in the back room. I snuck back in through the back, mainly so I could hide the cheesecake in the back of the fridge. Suddenly there was commotion, and my mother and I ran to the front of the gallery. He was already dead by the time we got there, slumped in the pretty woman's lap. The girl had said, 'He touched his hand to his forehead and just collapsed. I tried to catch him . . .' That's when my mother pushed her out of the way, and held my father in her arms, saying, 'Don't go, my baby, don't go. Not yet.' She just kept rocking him and stroking his hair, saying, 'Don't leave me here; come back, don't leave me behind.' She had tried to catch him, she really had. Then the ambulance came. Sound dropped away. I couldn't breathe. I couldn't do anything but stand there, frozen. The doctors would later say brain aneurysm. I imagined a lump of all the things he wished he'd said, travelling from his heart all the way to his head.

★ ★ ★

In the cemetery, standing under an elm, my brother's shoe lace came undone. My mother wouldn't look at me. I squeezed her ice-cold hand and watched her lips tremble. Then the men in cheap grey suits lowered the mahogany box with the sky-blue satin interior into the ground. He would have hated the colour and design. Then we sprinkled dirt and gardenia petals on the lid and the men with shovels began to pile the soft, moist dirt back into the hole. And he was gone forever.

Digging deep into musty boxes, I find a photo of me at age five. I am carrying a little blanket and I have on big plastic rings and a crocheted bikini. My father is holding my hand but his face is cropped off, all you can see is me and red Speedo-type bathing-suit bottoms and pale, hairy knocked knees.

Then I found an envelope of slides. Old paintings. I held them up to the light. *If all else fails choose D, none of the above*, a painting of pure sky, and *Barely Mammal*, a Ku Klux Klan guy holding a gun to the head of a black Raggedy Andy doll, and a favourite called *Gargoyle*, which is just a gargoyle looking after some pigeons with a fountain and a roller-skating street scene in the distance.

Tucked in a book of my father's, I find a photo of him and my mother and Spoonie and me. We looked so happy it seems unreal that he wasn't here with us now. I also found a little wooden toy I bought for my father in a toy store in Germany. It came with music paper to make your own songs. You could punch out the holes on a long, rectangular piece of paper by sight, and then play what you made on the little crank piano. My father made drawings on all the pages and then we played them. I remember one was of a snot monster, for Spoonie, and when he played it for us it actually sounded scary. All of the pieces were framed afterwards and promptly sold.

My very favourite one was called *Bolifar Carfish Inn*. It had a tiny cabin with little, dancing, insect inn keepers, and a real wood-burning fireplace. In the little pond, the fish were tiny people.

That's when I realized what I missed most about Jasper and my father and their paintings: time. It's the time they took to put into them, the time they took to make, the time they took away from me. The time they *chose* over me. I was jealous of their paintings because they had their time, their total attention, because it is what I did not have enough of with my own father, time. I was jealous of their paintings, and now I wasn't.

'How about Cups and Dishes,' said Camille, beaking my reverie. 'What?'

'Cups and Dishes. Instead of Bugs and Fishes. Spoonie and Lila came up with it. It's only for family. I told them Lila can say it too when Lila and Spoonie get married this summer, but not before. Are you coming to the concert tonight? Spoonie is performing with Despairagus and Suzanne Summers' Thighs.'

'They're getting married?'

'Oops, I wasn't supposed to tell you.'

'God, nobody tells me anything!'

'Oh, well, I'll go wake them up so you can congratulate them.' She yawned. 'You're up early.'

I thought, isn't that so like life, just when you think you can't get any happier, you can and you do. The heart keeps bursting open wider and wider, until it explodes. Then I saw it.

Shining up at me from the bottom of deepest deep of the soft old cardboard box. There, hanging on a maroon ribbon. I slipped it over my head and held it in my hand. I noticed the weight of it against my breast. The ribbon feels warm against the nape of my neck. It's the charm my father gave me. I picture him perfectly now, standing in that airport, waiting for it to be finished, so long ago. I recall his wild, white hair in points like a meringue, like flapping bird wings, smelling like Winstons and dandruff shampoo, his hands, the tips of his fingers curling upwards like the wings of a hawk, like Buddha's fingers, and I hear his deep, resonating voice. He is laughing.

I read it slowly. It says, I love you, America The Beautiful.

Later at the show, Spoonie played an Auden poem he set to music. I thought about how happy I was for him and Lila and about how much Spoonie looks like my father. Especially the way the light hits his cheekbones.

'Beloved,' he sang, 'we are always in the wrong
handling so clumsily our stupid lives,
Suffering too little or too long
Too careful even in our selfish love
The decorative manias we obey
Die in grimaces round us every day
Yet through their tohu-bohu comes a voice
Which utters an absurd command:
Rejoice!'

As I watched Spoonie strut across the stage, I wondered if my
father was proud of him too.

Sadie and Swane looked over at me then and smiled. They had
big white flowers behind their ears and were toasting each other
with blue drinks with pink umbrellas. (It *is* their fourth-month
anniversary after all.)

Later, Spoonie invited a handsome man from Rows Five
Through Seven to join him onstage. He was wearing a painter's
smock and a skirt and played didgeridoo, saw and stand-up bass in
a cover version of *Amazing Grace*. It was the coffee guy.

While Spoonie and Lila made their engagement official in the
little club with the pretty phosphorescent insects on the wall, he sat
down next to me. He removed two mugs from a blue backpack,
opened up a silver thermos with the mudflap girl, and I smelled the
cinnamon and ginger.

'Unleaded' he said as he poured a cup for me, chai with milk and
a little too much sugar. 'You seem different.'

'Do I?' I said, taking another sip. 'How?'

'Well, I don't know yet. More open maybe?'

'Yet, huh?' I blushed, grateful it was dark. Just then he took out
a red plastic cylinder with a yellow top, unscrewed the top and
blew bubbles in my direction. Then he dipped the wand back into
the clear soap, slid the container toward me, and handed it to me.
He started to get up to walk away.

'Wait,' I said. 'That is so sweet.'

'Yeah, well, I'm rot-your-teeth-sweet.'

That night, safely back in my bed, I had a dream that I was a long-distance runner. It is always better than flying to me because it is to feel what it's like to have stamina and endurance, to see something through to the very end. In the dream I am pacing myself perfectly, breathing, and feeling perfectly in-sync with my body and the scenery I pass. Past aspens with shimmery leaves and parked cars and dogs and people, I run past picket fences and Jym watching TV, past Charlie licking stamps, past Spoonie and Lila dressed like penguins in top hats and tails – don't ask me why – past my mother talking on the telephone, while feeding birds dried crusts of bread. Past Sadie and Tulie rolling around on green, green grass, past Jasper fast asleep in a hammock. And past my father who stands on an endless green lawn, watering the great yard, in a pink dress, with his white hair in pigtails, waving goodbye.

THIRTY-ONE
Welcome Pointlessness (Balloons)

'You will find me down by the river getting high on my mortality. I'll be holding hands with my nameless beauty or whoever wants to stand next to me.'
— Sinead Lohan

The next day I went to visit Otto at the coffee place downtown and that is how it came to pass that I am scrunched in my seat, watching a guy show up early for our date, wondering whether or not I should get out of my car and go through with all this. What do I need a guy for when I finally get that the trick to life is getting out of your own way, and letting the pure hit of reality break your heart? Because it will. No matter how well behaved you are, no matter if you pay your bills on time or not, or if you ever know what you do for a living. I don't need a man, I see that now not even a man who 'come vit rose'. I don't need anybody or anything; it's just nice to have someone to talk to. Really talk to. Someone to notice the stuff with. I guess all I really want to tell myself is that life goes on. It just does. So I unscrunch a little in spite of myself. Yeah, but why get out of the car? Why bother if I'm whole and lit from within, and all? Because, just as I'm thinking all this, I see Tom Hanks drive by with his wife Rita.

They are in a beat-up black '82 bronco and I realize I've graduated. I'm no longer Meg Ryan living out the fantasy on screen

275

romance anymore, I'm Tom's real-life wife Rita, and she smiles and waves at me for no reason at all. That's why I get out of my car. That's why I go to the cross-walk and push the cold metal button with the little dancing man.

And that's why, when it says 'walk', I do.

In my own time, in my own way, clutching the little good-luck coin at my heart.

Everything is in slow motion now. To my left and right cars wait for the light to turn green. Beside me, cars pass, full of people coming from somewhere or going to somewhere. People with cell phones making business deals, people heading into town or towards the water or the hills. To love their spouses or murder their mothers or take their dogs to the park. Smiling people, frowning people, angry people, short, fat people, people with bouffant hair and eyeglasses and fear and regret and loneliness and buried dreams and desires and gardening abilities and a knack for making money or losing car keys.

'Fear of intimacy issues' zips by in a red Porsche.

People, people everywhere. The light is green for go, then yellow for slow down and check it all out, then red, for stop. Colours. The colours my father loved, red and gold and green, like the flag of Africa, jah, love, man. Like the flag of Budapest. Green like hills, *aloha*. Yellow like hair, red like hearts. Red like roses.

I feel the heat of the engines as I walk past, and I feel like I'm on a runway.

I'm a model.

A model citizen. Ghandi carrying a message of peace, Jesus being walked to the fateful hill. Buddha watching spears turn into flowers when they meet my skin. So soft. Chrissie Hynde doesn't let anyone shake her hand. What a lovely thought, that only those close to her get to know how soft her skin is. Once I saw a deer stand perfectly still in the middle of the road. Right in the middle of the city.

Otto sees me now and my face goes all sweaty. I read somewhere that in certain Indian cultures you are allowed to be a part of the festivities as soon as you show your first smile that, based on the smile, you are given a career, a home, a mate. He smiles like that.

As I step onto the curb I looked up in time to see a white balloon float up and past me, making its escape into the wild blue. I turn my head and look back at Otto now. I cross that street.

Otto stands up to greet me and, as he does, he hits his knee on the underside of the table. I lurch forward, trying to catch the rose as it tumbles off. My little good-luck charm taps my breastbone. A gust of wind comes up. The orangey-pink petals scatter. I lean in to help. He hands me the stem and kneels down to collect the fallen blossoms. People in the café stare or move their chairs back, some try to help.

Otto keeps scooping, chasing the soft flower animals as they scatter for cover under nearby tables or customers' shoes or into the sunlight on the sparkly grey sidewalk. Otto walks back with careful steps. He opens his palms and reveals a small handful. Then he holds his cupped hands close to my nose, so I can smell the luminous petals. The lines in his palm look like a mountain range on a small relief map.

'It's from my garden,' he says, as soft as Tulie's ears.

I feel the weight in my legs like little roots digging their fine threads deep into the earth. I lean in a little more, smelling the musk of his skin mixed with the heavy fragrance of the bloom. When I lift my head up I see he has tears in his eyes. He blinks once and lets his hand fall to his sides. The rest of the petals drop to the ground and blow away on the wind, dancing along the sidewalk as they go.

For a moment we both stand absolutely still and look into each other's eyes. His are blue. He smiles. I smile too. I think about storybooks and fairytales and epic movies about epic love.

'Hi,' he says, finally, his voice cracking.

Once there was a girl who lived ever after, sometimes happily, is what I'm thinking, but what I say back is, 'Hello.'

Acknowledgements

This author gratefully acknowledges the following for their inestimable contributions:

In London, my always enthusiastic, endlessly supportive beacon of an editor Doug Young, the keen-eyed copy editors and typesetters who made this book pop, and, in the publicity department Emma Capwell and Rebecca Purtell for helping others see me the way I see myself.

In New York, the best literary agent in the solar system, Jimmy Vines.

In Florida, for her freelance ass-kicking line edit, Heather R. Price.

In Los Angles, my unofficial editors (under the loving guidance of my inspirationfestguruempress soul-sister Claudette Sutherland): Gina Lake, Trista Delamere, Emily Schlaeger, Cynthia True, Tulis McCall, and Janel Maloney. Along with special guest appearances by Karen and Henry Scott, Claire Stansfield, Gail Zappa, Diva Zappa, Brendan Smith, Giti Khalsa, Jason Ross, Joe Sehee, Stephen Lisk, Roddy Mancuso, Peter Stuart, Tory Mel, and Ahmet Zappa.

For putting up with my many mood swings and for making this book possible on a minute to minute basis: My family, Utie, Beeshu, Lisa, Pat McMahon, and Olive.

My friends, David and Lindsey Strasberg, Kate Luyben, Simbiat Hall, Melissa Bushell, Frankie Miles and Sammy, Sandipops, Bridget Gless, Lynn McCracken, Emily, Lukas, Simon, Niki and Berthold Haas, Mollye, Kevin and Miranda Stein, David Baer and the Schermerhorn clan, Peter Turman, Laura Milligan, Greg Behrendt, Greg Miller and Beth Lapides, Patton Oswalt, Joy Goring, Doug Benson, Brian Posehn, Gary Mann, Robin and Bianca Finck, Lief and Lone Tilden, Jo Cobbett and Mickael Skelton, Lazlo and Adam Small, Alice Warshaw,

Jeff Garlin, Michael O'Brien, Willie Mercer, Tracy Pepper, Gabrielle Roth, Lynn Franks, Rob and Marisol Thomas, matchbox twenty, Tom, Jane and Brian Doucette.

My healers Maria Bartolotta, Robert Coffman, Michelle Matisse and Victoria Mestetsky.

A special thank you to my writing angels, Cameron Crowe, Amy Heckerling, John, Roy London, June Bauer, Kristin Harm, John Wells, and Rob Cohen.

Da business, Pearl Wexler at Paul Kohner, Andrea Moss and Michael Lippman, and everyone who helped me gather lyric copyrights! Mariel Sloatman, M.J. Duchovny, Brent, and Francis Okwu.

Why Cook, Kinko's Studio City, Crunch Gym, and Eccobana in SF for pear-vanilla candles.

In Portland, Catherine Ingram for whom there are literally no words.

God.

Myself.

FZ.

Music.

And most of all, my beloved real-life Otto, Paul Doucette.